ARIETTA

Kevin McGann

ARIETTA

Hometown Publishers

Hometown Publishers
www.hometownpublishers.com

© Copyright 2021
Kevin McGann

First Published by Hometown Publishers September 2021.

ISBN: 978-1-7777725-2-9 (Paperback)
ISBN: 978-1-7777725-3-6 (E-book)

Library and Archives Canada (LAC) national library collection.

Cover Design by Kevin McGann.

Dedication

To Mathew, Jessica,

Daphne, and Brendan

To my parents,

Maria and Charles

Acknowledgements

All the wonderful people and establishments

in St. John and St. Thomas, USVI,

and Manhattan, New York City.

Chapter 1

When do you say enough is enough? Leave everything you own, think, and know behind? When do you sacrifice it all, take that chance, and find the strength and courage to find you? Arietta had struggled with these questions far too long; she knew what she had to do, but deep down she knew the truth: she was scared, scared of taking that step into the unknown. She looked out of her executive third floor office down at the people below; she could have had a suite on the top floor, but she liked being close to the street and watching the people.

The sun was starting to set in the Manhattan sky and people were off work and heading to enjoy their Friday night. A group of girls dressed in small skirts and dresses laughed as they entered the martini bar across the street. A group of men with their ties off and holding their jackets entered a pub on the corner. She wondered if these groups of young people would meet later on, maybe one group would venture into the other's establishment or perhaps they would be leaving and bump into each other on the street or maybe later at a club. Waiting at the lights was an older attractive man wearing a suit and holding a bouquet of flowers. He was soon met by a stunning blonde wearing a tight-fitting red dress that looked as if it had been made just for her body. They passionately kissed then crossed the street into an expensive restaurant. Wedding anniversary or birthday? she thought. As they entered, she noticed a woman to their right walking past them towards the subway carrying bags, one was from a grocery store and the other from a child's clothing store, and she wondered if she was heading home to cook dinner for her husband and her family or maybe she was a single mother.

Arietta looked up from the street and caught her reflection in the window. She was an attractive forty-year-old woman with long auburn hair, stunning emerald, green eyes, a beautiful smile, and a flawless creamy complexion, but all she saw was unhappiness. She thought about how many times she had looked in a mirror and asked herself, "Is this my destiny? Is this me? Is this all there is?"

"Arie," a voice called from behind.

She was too busy thinking.

"Arietta," said the voice in a louder tone, snapping her from her thoughts.

She turned around to face Graham, Senior VP, and standing behind him his right-hand man and VP of Marketing and Sales, Vincent.

"Yes, I know the meeting is in three weeks and this merger is important to you both…But we know how mergers sometimes end up." She took her eyes off Graham, glanced up at Vincent, then back at Graham.

"Not again," replied Graham and looked behind him.

"That was a long time ago. We were both young and both realized we had made a mistake," said Vincent cautiously.

"At least the merger was a success," replied Arietta with a smirk and looked down at the ground as if contemplating what to say next but only thinking of what Vincent had just said.

Graham sat back in his seat and gave Vincent a look of hopelessness; Arietta had been fighting this merger tooth and nail, he was unsure why, but without her support it would never happen.

Arietta moved over to the window and looked out once more. A couple in their forties, casually dressed, holding hands, were walking, and talking, and she noticed he was making her laugh. The girl stopped walking, ran her fingers through his hair, and kissed him softly on the lips. The girl pulled away and Arietta could read her lips and his same response back. A thousand thoughts and emotions ran through Arietta's mind; she was fighting hard to hold back the tears.

"Arie, we need this mer—"

"I'm going away for a while," she said to her reflection.

"What?" Graham asked somewhat puzzled and unsure about what she had said.

She turned around and faced them and said in a voice that they had never heard before. "I am going away; I need some time."

"To think about the merger?" they both asked.

She smiled at them, grabbed her bag, and quickly walked out of her office and onto the street. She slowly took a deep breath of air; she felt like she had been drowning and had just been pulled up to the surface.

As she walked, she looked at people coming towards her and wondered what their stories were. She passed a sports bar and glanced inside; she could see people talking and laughing. Then stopped outside a chic restaurant and looked through the window, how lovely it looked with its beautiful white tablecloths, romantic lighting, and air of intimacy. She wondered how many women would be wined and dined by the man they loved and how he would make her smile, feel beautiful, feel special. She thought about those same women getting ready, putting on that special lingerie and dress, knowing that after dinner, they would go back to her place and over a glass of wine, dancing to soft music, he would gently kiss her, unzip her dress, and how she would let it fall to the floor. Then he would stand back and admire her lingerie, her body, her beauty, her. She smiled at the thought then caught her reflection in the window and her smile disappeared. She turned and continued down the street. She stopped at a high-end clothing store and bought several summer dresses. Then bikinis and suntan lotion at the Beach Shop. She passed the lingerie store and walked for almost a block before turning around and going in. She was set. She hailed a taxi, went to her condominium, and packed. Her cell phone rang, it was Graham, and she let it go into voicemail. It rang again, and she ignored it. She needed to leave now, or she felt she never would. With luggage in hand, she walked out of her condominium onto the sidewalk and waited while the doorman waved down a taxi. Her phone rang and she turned it off.

She was up at six the next morning, had a light breakfast, showered, and put on one of her new dresses. She took the hotel shuttle to the airport and walked up to the airline counter. "What is the next available flight you have that I can get a seat on?"

The lady behind the counter looked down at her computer, then up. "In twenty minutes to Anchorage, Alaska."

"Alaska? I don't want to go to Alaska."

"Okay," replied the lady, somewhat confused. "Where would you like to go?"

Arietta thought for a moment. "Somewhere hot, with clear blue water, sandy beaches…where I can escape…but there has to be people…and children…but very romantic…somewhere…where I can find me."

The lady smiled at her. "I know just the place." She looked down at her terminal and her fingers darted over the keyboard. "St. Thomas, US Virgin Islands, leaves in forty-five minutes." She looked up at Arietta. "There is a beautiful resort on St. John, it's the St. John's Resort, and it's exactly what you are looking for."

Arietta gave a smile and handed her a platinum credit card and identification.

The lady gave them back along with her boarding pass and asked her to wait a minute while she went to her bag, grabbed her phone, and did a search. She wrote down a number and passed it to Arietta. "Here is the number for the resort. Ask for a room on the beach."

"Thank you," replied Arietta.

Arietta went through security, found the departure gate, sat down, and turned on her phone: eight voice mails, fifteen texts, mostly from Graham. She realized she would have to let him know, but rather than call she left a text that read, 'Going away for two weeks, you are in charge, not answering your calls or texts.' Then she called the St. John's Resort, made her reservation, and hung up. Then it suddenly hit her, her journey had begun.

The turquoise water reminded him of her beautiful eyes and the speckled sandy shores of the light sprinkling of freckles on her nose and cheeks. He thought about her long blonde hair and remembered when they went out, how she used to wear it loose and past her shoulders, and in the morning when she went to teach, she would put it in a French braid or up in a bun; either way, she always looked beautiful. He thought about how they first met, their first date, and their first kiss as if it were yesterday. He remembered how they talked about having children, growing old and being grandparents. They were the best of friends and had a perfect life; then one day it all changed, and she left, never to return. That was the same day he stopped believing in love, in happiness, in God, in himself. He had desperately struggled to pick up the pieces of his shattered life and put them back together but everything around him, every place he went, everyone he met, reminded him of her; so instead, he found companionship in the bottom of a bottle and endless days and nights lying on the sofa, contemplating ending it all. That was almost seven years ago, and things had gotten better but the hurt, the sadness, the bitterness, the loneliness were still very real, and this journey was making him think of her all over again. His head started to ache, so he closed his eyes and tried to forget about her, and eventually drifted off to sleep. He was abruptly awoken by a voice over the speaker.

"Ladies and gentlemen, this is your pilot speaking. We are starting our descent into St. Thomas; we ask that you please put on your seatbelts…it's a beautiful sunny summer morning in the US Virgin Islands with temperatures currently in the eighties…we hope you enjoy your stay, thank you for…"

James tuned out the pilot's voice and looked out the window as the plane landed and pulled to a stop. He watched the ground crew busily removing the suitcases and placing them on the tarmac and wondered if they were happy. The sun was shining brightly, and it was warm, but the breeze was refreshing as he walked off the plane and down the stairs. He put his foot on the tarmac and whispered, "I am here." He picked up his luggage and walked inside toward a man standing by a sign for the St. John's Resort. "Good morning," said James.

"Good morning, sir, are you staying with us?" asked the man with a wide grin.

"I am," replied James, as he looked away from the man's smile and down at his clipboard.

"What is your name, please?"

"James Davenport."

"Here you are," replied the man as he looked over the list and ticked off James's name. "My name is Lewis," he said as he went to the desk and pulled out some tags. "You can leave your bags here," he motioned as he placed them on the luggage, "and they will be in your room when you arrive…here is your pass for our private ferry. The minibus is just out there," he said as he pointed to a white bus outside. "I am waiting for two other couples then we will be on our way, about fifteen minutes or so." He walked James over to the bar, asked him what he would like to drink, and handed him a Painkiller and said, "Welcome to the US Virgin Islands."

"Thank you, Lewis," replied James as he lifted his glass and took a sip of his drink. He went outside toward the bus, a band was playing steel drums, so he quietly sat and listened, until it was time to board.

They arrived at the dock and Lewis informed him that the ferry leaves on the hour. "So, you can sit here and wait thirty minutes for the next one or go for a walk around Charlotte Amalie," suggested Lewis. James decided to go for a walk.

James left the dock and crossed over Veteran's Drive. He strolled up a side street and into the Market Square; it was vibrant. The vendors were busily pushing jewelry, clothing, local trinkets, and produce while the cruise ship tourists were busy trying to haggle for a lower price. He moved away from the Square and into a small alleyway where the locals were offering Tarot, palm, and psychic readings; James politely refused. He looked over at an attractive girl dressed in traditional gypsy attire, leaning against a wall; she pulled up a chair and sat down, never taking her eyes off him.

"You will never find her if you don't let her go," she said in a low and alluring voice.

He felt her eyes go through him. "Who, me?" asked James nervously. He looked behind him, there was no one else there, and looked back at her, her eyes immediately met his.

"You will never find her if you don't let her go," she repeated. She stood up, walked over to James and was inches away from him, she stared deeply into his eyes, his very soul. Her eyes rolled, and James could see the whites of them. She started to fall, and James caught her.

A middle-aged woman came out of the doorway yelling, "Lily!" and ran over to her daughter. "Please, can you carry her inside?" asked her mother frantically.

James picked Lily up in his arms and followed her mother into a dark room and placed her on the sofa. The girl was out. James looked over at her mother. "Is she okay?"

"She will be," said her mother as she sat and calmed herself down. "She gets these thoughts, images, feelings from people, and it puts her into a trance, a spell; she can't break out of it until she collapses from exhaustion."

James looked over at the girl then back at her mother. "Does this happen often?"

"Not for a very long time…and it's only certain people." She hesitated. "What did she say to you?"

"It didn't make sense."

The woman stood up. "Everything she says makes sense." She walked over and grabbed his hand. "She has seen more than you know."

James felt uncomfortable, no, scared; he needed to leave. Then he paused for a moment and let rationale take over and realized this was all an act, a scam. With his free hand he reached into his pocket, removed the woman's hand, and placed a twenty-dollar bill in it.

The mother looked at the money and stood back. "You don't believe?"

"Not in anything…not anymore."

"Why not, my James in shining armor?" asked the girl on the sofa in a sleepy voice, her eyes still closed.

James suddenly turned and looked at her and a feeling of utter fear came over him, his face went pale. He had to get out of there. He stumbled to the door, went outside and quickly walked down the alley onto the main street and started to jog. He eventually stopped, lifted his head, and took a deep, long breath.

"Would you like a seat at the bar or on the patio? The patio has a beautiful view of the harbor and a cool breeze," asked the tall, muscular waiter in a thick accent as he looked at James and the beads of sweat on his forehead.

James looked to his right and realized he had stopped at the entrance to the 'Haven Bar and Restaurant.' "Patio would be fine," replied James out of breath. He followed the waiter to a table, sat down, and ordered a beer.

The waiter came back and poured the beer into a glass. "Is this your first visit to the islands?" he asked.

"Yes," replied James, still a little shaken. "Are you an islander?"

"Yeah, I was born here, I go to the University of Miami, football scholarship, I'm back here for the summer to make some extra money," he explained. "My name is Demetrius, but people call me D-Mon. If you need anything let me know."

"Thanks, D-Mon," replied James.

"Enjoy, and welcome to the islands," he said in a loud voice with a big smile.

James laughed at his antics and watched him go to another table, then looked out at the harbor. D-Mon was right, the view was incredible.

As he sat sipping on his beer, he thought about what had just happened. He knew those types of places were fake and they told people what they wanted to hear. The pretty girl, the meaningless words, the staring, the fainting, the mother, and the foreboding 'only happens to certain people,' scam, had to be! He paused, thought some more, then whispered, "My James in shining armor." That was tough to rationalize. And what did the girl mean by, 'you will never find her if you don't let her go'?

Several hours later, Arietta walked off the plane, down the stairs, and onto the tarmac. She whispered, "I am here." She walked inside, met Lewis, and signed in. They walked to the bar, and she asked for a Cruzan Confusion. She went outside, sipped on her drink, and listened to the steel drums for a while before boarding the minibus.

The road from Cyril E. King Airport was narrow and winding. There were beautiful red ginger flowers on both sides of the road and the hills were a bright green; she opened the window and could smell their sweet fragrance. In the distance, she could see Charlotte Amalie with its colorful rooftops. There was a cruise ship in the harbor, and around the ship she could see a scattering of small boats and yachts. "How beautiful," she said.

The minibus arrived. Arietta got off and walked toward the ferry.

James's concentration was interrupted by a door slamming closed. He looked across the street and noticed a woman with long, auburn hair wearing a stunning, mint-green dress moving slowly from a white minibus to the dock.

"Another beer?" asked D-Mon.

James looked at his watch, ten minutes. "No thanks, I have to go." He paid D-Mon, finished his beer, and crossed the street.

Chapter 2

Arietta boarded the ferry. The main deck was almost full, so she went upstairs and walked to the middle and sat to the left. A few seats in front of her was an older couple, and one seat ahead to her right was a woman with a young girl wearing a pretty straw hat. Arietta looked up at the sky and loved the feeling of the bright sun and cool breeze on her face. She closed her eyes and enjoyed the moment.

James showed his pass, boarded the ferry, and went upstairs. He said hello to the older couple, then the woman and the girl in the hat. The girl pointed out the pirate ship in the harbor which James acknowledged with a pleasant smile and a nod. The woman in the dress was meditating, sleeping or something, so he let her be. He went two rows past the woman and the girl and sat down. As the ferry left the dock, the captain informed them that the Tiki Bar was open upstairs, bathrooms were on the lower deck, and the ride would take forty-five minutes. Caribbean music played from the speakers at the bar and most of the passengers on the lower level moved upstairs and surrounded the music. James remained in his seat and looked out at the water and thought about how much she would love it here.

"Hi, there," said a young voice.

It startled James. Kneeling on the seat in front of him was the young girl with the straw hat. "Hello," he replied.

"My name is Caleigh. What's your name?" she asked in a curious way.

"My name is James." He looked just over the girl's shoulder and noticed the woman was on the phone.

The girl followed James's eyes and turned to look at her mother, and then back at James. "She's talking to my doctor."

Arietta could hear them talking and glanced to her right. She could see the girl but not the person she was talking to.

"I've been in remission for quite a while now, and my mom is asking him about the sun or something, I don't want to keep wearing a hat." She removed it, showing her short black hair. "Do you like it? It's starting to grow back?"

"Your hair looks very pretty," replied James. "How long are you going to let it grow?"

"Well, it used to be down my back to here," she motioned with her hand to the middle of her back, "so I think that long."

"Caleigh," said her mother, standing over her. She looked at James. "I'm sorry, she likes to socialize." She looked over at Caleigh. "Let's leave the man alone."

"His name is James and he's nice." She looked at James. "This is my mom; her name is Cheryl."

Cheryl had deep-blue eyes and shoulder-length raven hair. She was wearing a short, navy-blue dress that caressed her body and showed off her round breasts, slim waist, and shapely legs. She turned to James and extended her hand. "Cheryl."

James stood and shook her hand. "James, nice to meet you." James sat down and offered her a seat, which she accepted.

"So, what did he say, mom?" asked Caleigh as she leaned over the back of the seat.

"No hat!" she replied.

"Yaaaaay," yelled Caleigh in a happy voice and pretended to throw her hat overboard.

Cheryl and James laughed.

Caleigh looked over at the people standing at the bar. "I'm thirsty. Can we get a drink?"

"Of course," replied her mother as she stood.

"Can you watch our seats, James?" asked Caleigh. "We'll be back sooner than you can say, hat overboard," and laughed hysterically at her own joke.

James smiled as he nodded his head.

Caleigh ran to the bar, and Cheryl turned towards James. "I hope we aren't bothering you; we can sit back in our seats?"

"No, not at all," replied James.

"I'm dying for a beer. Do you want one?"

"Sure," replied James.

"We'll be back," said Cheryl smiling and went after her daughter.

Arietta had been listening to the conversation and realized they had left. She was interested to see who the young girl and her mother had been talking with. She went to stand to go to the bar when the young girl sat next to her.

"My name is Caleigh. What's your name?"

She smiled at the young girl. "Hello, Caleigh, my name is Arietta."

The young girl's eyes widened. "I love that name. It's so pretty."

"Thank you, so is yours."

"Caleigh, I have your drink," said Cheryl, standing next to her. "Are you coming to sit with us?"

Caleigh took the drink from her mom. "I'm going to sit with my friend Arietta."

Cheryl looked over at Arietta. "I'm sorry, she's a social butterfly. I'm Cheryl."

"Nice to meet you, I'm Arietta," she replied. "She's fine, besides, we girls have lots to talk about," she said, looking at Caleigh.

"Caleigh, I'm going to sit with James, come over when you're done."

Arietta watched Cheryl sit, and for the first time she saw the man behind the voice, James.

James and Cheryl sipped their beers, and he listened as she talked about Caleigh and her battle to beat cancer; Arietta and Caleigh talked about fashion, hairstyles, music, and boys.

The boat was ready to dock. Caleigh stood up to go sit next to her mom. "I hope we see each other around the resort?"

"You can count on it," replied Arietta.

"James, thank you, it's so nice to have a man to talk with. Most of my friends are single moms like me, so it's mostly woman talk," said Cheryl.

"Anytime," said James smiling and noticed Caleigh coming over. "I heard you were talking girl stuff," he said to her.

"We were, it was so much fun," she replied, sitting in the seat in front of him.

Cheryl stood up, whispered "thanks again," and sat next to her daughter.

Arietta looked over at Caleigh and her mom and gave them a smile. At the same time, James looked over at Arietta, and for a brief moment their eyes met. Arietta quickly turned and faced forward.

The ferry docked at the St. John's Resort and the passengers disembarked.

Chapter 3

Arietta walked off the dock and followed the path. To her right was a beautiful pool surrounded by chaises, umbrellas, and a scattering of cabanas. She walked into the elegant lobby, signed in, and followed the directions to her beach front room. She opened the door and went inside. The room had a king-size bed covered with a pure white duvet and several big, fluffy pillows. There was a thirty-two-inch flat-screen television, refrigerator, chest of drawers, armchair, and a desk with a chair. The bathroom was marble and had an oversized tub. She put down her bag, opened the patio doors and went outside. She was steps away from the white sandy beach and the transparent blue water. It was lined with palm trees, chaises, and umbrellas. Beyond the shoreline, there were boats docked in the harbor, past them the blue sea and a collection of small islands. The breeze blew on her face. She closed her eyes and took in a long, deep breath. She opened them and looked around the patio; it had two chaises, a table with two chairs, and a couple of steps that led down to the beach. She smiled, went back inside, and left the patio door open to let the gentle breeze blow the white curtains. She unpacked her clothes, placed them in the drawers and closet, and then took a shower. She stood and looked at her new bikinis; first day, she thought and decided on the black one: it was conservative, cute, yet sexy. She grabbed a towel, went onto the patio, and sprayed on suntan lotion, then picked her spot on the beach and walked over to claim it. She moved the chaise into the sun and put it in a semi-upright position so that she could look around, then put down her towel and lay on her back.

There were couples and groups scattered along the beach, talking and drinking, and young children building sandcastles. In the water there were families and couples swimming, and a group of teenagers kayaking and windsurfing. And off in the distance, she could hear calypso music playing. She liked the distraction of the lively activity and continued to observe and listen. After a while, she decided to go in the water to cool off. As she swam away from the shore, she looked down and could see small tropical fish darting back and forth. She floated on her back, enjoying the warm sun on her face and body. She hadn't felt this relaxed in a very long time. She went back to her spot, ordered lunch and a drink, and kept to herself. As the afternoon came to an end, she got up and went to her room. She looked over the resort's daily events and noticed there was a 'Welcome Reception' for guests from seven until ten.

James opened the door to his beach front room. He walked in, sat on his bed, and put his head between his hands; he wondered if he'd made the right decision to come. He thought about Caleigh, Lily, and her. He opened the patio door, then took off his shirt and pants and lay down on the bed. The pillows were soft, and the bed was comfortable. The breeze felt good on his body. He looked at the clock, closed his eyes, and drifted to sleep.

James heard a voice and walked out to the patio. It was dusk, and he wondered how long he had slept. The voice was low and called for him by name; he followed it. He walked along the shoreline to a secluded part of the beach. In the distance, there was a distorted image sitting on a large towel. As he got closer, the voice became louder.

"James," she said.

"Who is it?" replied James.

"Come here," she said, motioning him to sit next to her on the towel.

"Lily is that you?" he asked. "Who are you?"

"Don't worry about that," she replied. "I'm here because I'm worried about you."

"Me? Why?" he asked, trying to focus on the image.

"You used to be so carefree, happy and loving," she said. "You've changed."

He was confused. "How do you know me?"

"I know you," her voice said sadly. "You need to find yourself again…that man who was happy…who loved to smile and made others happy."

He reached out to touch the apparition, and it started to dissolve.

"My James in shining armor," she said in a fading voice then disappeared.

James sat up on his bed in a cold sweat and fear in his eyes. He looked outside, it was still daytime, and then at the clock: it confirmed he had only been sleeping for twenty minutes. He put his head back on the pillow and whispered, "It was just a dream," and stared at the ceiling, wondering if he was losing his mind. After several minutes he suddenly sat up and said, "I have to get out of this room." He put on his bathing suit, a buttoned shirt, and went to the pool. He picked a table close to the water, ordered lunch, and quietly ate his sandwich. He went in and out of the pool, watched the children swimming, people interacting, and listened to the calypso band; it was calming. A few hours later he dried himself off and went back to his room.

Chapter 4

After an hour of getting ready, Arietta looked at herself in the mirror. She had curled her hair and let it hang just past her shoulders away from her face. The sun today had given her a nice color, so she went light on the makeup. The powder-blue dress clung to her shapely body, complementing her hair and eyes. She liked what she saw. She put on some lipstick and walked away from the mirror. Moments later she returned and looked at herself. What am I doing? she thought. Ignoring it won't make it go away. She looked down at the sink and thought about how many times tear drops of mascara had fallen in her sink at home. She felt her eyes start to water and caught herself. "No more," she said. "No more!" She looked up in the mirror. "I will deal with them when I'm ready…I will deal with it all when I'm ready!" she said out loud. She grabbed her handbag and walked out the door.

It was a warm evening, and the slight breeze felt nice on her skin as she entered the Island Waves Bar and Grill. There were buffet tables off to the right, a bar to the left, and reggae music playing softly over the speakers. A waiter approached her and asked if she wanted a glass of champagne. She quickly thought back to all those suffocating work-related receptions and their trays of champagne, and politely refused and went to the bar and ordered a beer. The place was busy with singles, couples, and families. As she continued to survey the area, she noticed several single men looking in her direction. She quickly passed over their stares. Out of the corner of her eye she noticed someone coming towards her.

"Arietta, I was hoping I would see you."

She looked down at Caleigh. "You look very pretty tonight," complimented Arietta.

"Thank you," she replied, twirling to show off her cute dress. "I even made up my hair," she said happily.

"I love it," she said as she leaned over to her and whispered, "You're the prettiest girl here."

"Thank you," she replied and gave her a hug. Caleigh grabbed her hand and led her to a table where her mom was sitting with an older couple.

They said hello as the older couple excused themselves to go talk to their friends. Arietta sat down next to Cheryl and Caleigh stood in the middle.

"What time is it, mom?" she asked.

"Seven fifteen," she replied.

"He's not here. He's not coming."

Cheryl and Arietta looked at one another, then Caleigh. Intrigued, they both asked, "Who's not?"

"James."

"James," replied Cheryl and started to tease her. "Has he stood you up?"

Caleigh gave her mother a displeasing frown. "I knew I should have gone over and talked to him at the pool and asked if he was coming."

"Why didn't you?" asked Arietta.

She went silent and looked over at her mom then back at Arietta. "He looked sad."

"Maybe you could have cheered him up," suggested Arietta.

She glanced over at her mom again, and Cheryl answered, "Caleigh was going to, but I told her maybe later; he looked like he needed some alone time."

Some children ran by. Caleigh kissed her mom on the cheek and left, pretending to follow them.

They watched her run away then Cheryl turned to Arietta. "He had that look, it's hard to explain, you know, the one where people are physically there but their mind isn't, they seem distant, as if something is pulling them. Does that make sense?"

Arietta nodded. She knew that feeling, oh, too well.

"Caleigh just thinks he's great," continued Cheryl. "He's a really nice guy, very down to earth and genuine." She looked around the place. "Not like some of the ones here," she whispered. "I have been hit on twice already. Don't get me wrong, they're nice enough and polite, but really,

I'm here on vacation with my daughter…One even mentioned the resort has evening babysitting. Can you imagine?"

"Really?" asked Arietta. "What single guy would even know that, never mind mention it!"

"I know," she replied, and they laughed. "Us girls need to stick together," she concluded. They agreed, cheered one another, and had a drink.

Cheryl looked over at the children running around then at Arietta. "Heaven forbid one of these guys would invite Caleigh along." She took a sip of her drink. "Just once I would like to meet someone who would sweep me off my feet and have Caleigh on his shoulders."

"That's a nice way of putting it," said Arietta with a kind smile.

"Arietta, do you believe in romance, love, being swept off your feet and never landing?"

Arietta thought for a moment and quietly replied, "I don't know."

They were both thinking about the question when their thoughts were cut short by two men who had just gotten enough courage to leave the bar and come to their table to introduce themselves.

James was lying on the chaise, looking up at the stars. In the distance he could hear people talking, laughing, and music. The phone rang. He walked inside and picked it up.

"James, please?" asked a young voice.

"This is James."

"James, where are you? Why aren't you at the reception?"

Suddenly he recognized the voice. "Hi, Caleigh."

"Say you're ready and on your way, please."

"Actually, I was going to take it easy tonight—"

"Please, please come. My mom is here and my play friends from today."

"Well, I—"

"My mom made a joke in front of Arietta that you stood me up!"

James smiled. "Well, we can't let them believe that…I'll be there in ten minutes."

"Yaaay," a cheerful voice said on the other end. "I will be waiting for you." She hung up the phone and went back to the entrance to wait for James.

James got ready. He really wasn't up to going out tonight but now, for some reason, he was glad he was. He walked to the bar and in the distance saw Caleigh waiting for him. He stopped and pulled off a red ginger flower.

"James," she said, running over to him. She stopped and twirled her dress.

"You look very pretty. I love your dress and your hair."

"You noticed," she said and gestured a pose, showing off her black hair. She saw he had one hand behind his back and tried to look around. "What do you have there?"

"The second prettiest thing here," he said, giving her the flower.

"I love it, I will keep it forever," she said with the happiest of smiles.

"Shall we?" asked James.

"We shall," she replied and put her arm through his. They walked in and she pointed out the buffet, the bar, and the kids playing over on the beach, then walked to the back where her mom and Arietta were talking with the two men. "Good evening, Mother, Arietta," she said in a theatrical voice. "Stood up, I think not…I even got a beautiful flower," she said, showing it off and emphasizing her point by putting it to her nose and smelling it. She gestured to them to see if they had received one. "Maybe next time," she said, looking down her nose at the two men sitting there. "James and I will be leaving you now and sitting over there." They turned around and walked toward an empty table. On the way she looked up at James, and they laughed aloud. Behind her, she could hear her mom and Arietta laughing, too. The two men were confused.

James pulled out a seat for her; she glanced over at her mother's table, acknowledged the women, smiled, and sat down. James sat next to her. The waiter came over, and they ordered their drinks.

James looked at her and smiled as she admired her flower. "What did you do today?" he asked.

"We went to our room, it's right by the pool, it's right over there," she said, pointing in its direction. "We unpacked then we went to the Market

Deli and picked up lunch, and we ate it on the beach, then I went to the Kids Club, met some friends, and signed up for some activities. Then we went for a walk around the resort, so I know where everything is, and then we went for a swim in the pool."

"That sounds like a fun day."

"It was…we saw you in the pool."

"You did? I didn't see you."

"I was playing in the shallow end with my mom and some kids. You were in the deep end."

"Oh, I see. You can't swim in the deep end?"

"I can…but my mom said it looked like you wanted to be on your own. I thought you looked sad and was going to come over and make you happy." She looked up at James. "Were you sad?"

James looked at her. "I guess sometimes adults get sad, too."

"So, my mom was right saying that you wanted to be on your own," she confirmed with an unhappy look.

James looked at her. "Caleigh, anytime you see me, you come over and say hello."

Her face lit up. "You mean it?"

"Only if you promise you will?"

"Pinkie promise," she replied, and they crossed pinkie fingers and shook on it.

The waiter dropped off the chocolate milk and beer, and they sat and talked about the resort for a while.

"I'm hungry."

"So am I," replied James.

They went over to the kid's buffet and grabbed pizza, hamburgers, chicken fingers, and fries.

"You don't want any grown-up food?" she asked.

"You are kidding, yuck…besides, I thought it would be more fun to share all this."

"Definitely," she replied, "but we need to make sure we save room for dessert."

"You mean dessertsss," he replied, emphasizing the plural.

"Dessertsss," she confirmed and gave out a laugh.

Before long, a boy with food sat down with them, then a girl, then a brother and sister. Caleigh introduced her new friends to James. The kids ate and talked about their day while James ate, smiled, laughed, and listened.

Cheryl watched Caleigh walk away with James and look back at her and give her a smile as James pulled out her seat. Cheryl smiled back. The two guys sitting in front of Cheryl were in their late twenties and leaving tomorrow and looking for a one-night stand; they were pleasant enough but not interesting. Throughout the conversation, Cheryl's attention kept drifting over to her daughter and James; they were laughing and talking, not like here, these guys were dull. She watched them go to the buffet table, sharing food, and then being joined by other children; they were having so much fun. She decided she wanted to join them and stood up to excuse herself.

Arietta watched James pull out the chair for Caleigh. Caleigh looked over and smiled at her, and she smiled back. She watched her looking at her flower and talking to James; how attentive he was to her. He was always cheerful and had such a lovely smile. She watched them eating pizza, chicken fingers and burgers, the other children joining them, and how playful and happy they all were as they ate and talked. She wanted to be a part of their fun and junk-food feast and stood up to excuse herself.

Inadvertently, Cheryl and Arietta had both stood up at the same time and looked awkwardly at each other and at the two men.

"I have to go see to my daughter," said Cheryl. "She's over there with a friend, and I want to make sure she is eating something and is okay…" She looked over at Arietta.

"By friend, she means my boyfriend, he's watching her, they are on…" Arietta was searching for something.

"A pretend date," finished Cheryl.

"Yes, a pretend date…and right now it looks like more children have joined them, and he seems to have his hands full, so I, we, better go help him out."

The two men looked over at James sitting with the children and thought poor guy. "We understand," replied one of them. They stood up, said goodbye, and watched Cheryl and Arietta walk away, then one of them glanced over at the bar. "Look at those four!" he said, and they quickly finished their drinks and went to the bar.

Arietta and Cheryl held in their laughter until they were closer to their destination.

James heard them laugh and looked up, noticing Arietta and Cheryl heading his way. Arietta was wearing a powder-blue dress and Cheryl's was peach with a floral print; they both looked stunning.

"Can we join you?" asked Cheryl, containing her laughter.

"This is my mom and my friend Arietta," said Caleigh, introducing them to her friends.

James stood up and pulled out a chair for each of them.

"I'm so hungry I could eat an elephant," said Arietta which made the kids laugh.

"Or a hippopotamus," said one.

"A rhinoceros," added another, which made the kids laugh louder.

James looked around at the table and noticed there wasn't much food left. "Oh, oh, girls and boys, looks like we're out of food!" He gave them a mischievous look. "Looks like we need another junk food trip." The kids quickly jumped out of their seats and ran to the buffet, returning with an assortment of food.

As they ate, the manager stood on the stage and spoke about the resort, its facilities, its programs, special events and its restaurants. He thanked everyone for choosing the St. John's Resort and to enjoy their stay, and if there was anything anyone needed, make sure to ask him or his attentive staff. He spoke about the reggae band that would be starting in fifteen minutes and about the live entertainment at the resort. As he was talking, James looked over at Arietta and watched her as she ate her pizza; she had beautiful green eyes, perfect skin, and gorgeous auburn hair.

"Dessertsss," whispered a voice in his ear.

He looked over at Caleigh. "Yes, dessertsss but after everyone has finished eating, okay?"

"Okay. Will you come with me?"

He smiled. "Of course."

Cheryl looked away from the manager and at James, wondering what her daughter was asking him.

"Dessert," he mouthed.

"Oh," Cheryl mouthed back.

James smiled at her, and she smiled back. She had a brilliant smile and seductive blue eyes. She turned her attention back to the manager and listened to his closing remarks.

Caleigh noticed everyone had finished eating. "Who wants dessertsss?" she asked, looking around the table at the kids raising their hands. The children looked on as the adults slowly lifted theirs too. They all stood and went to the dessert table. They ate, talked, and laughed until the band started to play then everyone got up and danced. It was getting late, and the children were getting tired. One by one the parents dropped by to pick them up and take them to their beds. Caleigh sat on her mother's lap and quickly fell asleep.

"Time for me to get this one to bed," Cheryl said as she tried to get up.

James stood up and took Caleigh from her, so she could stand up.

"It was easier when she was smaller," she said, as she reached out her arms to take her back.

"Do you want me to carry her to your patio?" he asked.

Cheryl looked relieved. "You don't mind?"

"Not at all, lead the way."

Cheryl reached down, took off her shoes and grabbed her and James's beer. She looked over at Arietta. "Kick off those shoes, grab your drink and follow me." They followed Cheryl to her poolside room. She put the drinks on the table, opened the sliding door, threw in her shoes, and took Caleigh from him. "Won't be a minute," she said.

Arietta had thrown her shoes and handbag on the floor and was sitting on a chair facing the pool, watching the people swimming. James sat next to her and looked up at the stars in the sky.

"It's a beautiful night," she said.

James looked over at her and realized she was now staring at the stars. "It is," he replied, looking up again. "Not a cloud."

"I don't think clouds exist here at night," she said conclusively. "I'm sure the view from the beach is spectacular."

"She's sound asleep," said a voice from behind them as she closed the door. "We should sit at the edge of the pool and put our feet in the water."

"That sounds wonderful," replied Arietta, standing up. "My feet are sore from all that dancing; they could do with a soak."

James took off his shoes and put them next to Arietta's. They finished their drinks then sat at the curved edge of the pool; Cheryl was in the middle and James and Arietta on either side. The pool area was nicely lit up, and the band's music floated over from the bar and added to the tropical ambience.

"This feels amazing," said Arietta as she looked at her feet in the water.

Cheryl and James agreed.

"I love this place," said Cheryl as she looked around. "It's beautiful…relaxing."

"The beach, the water, the food, the music, the room: it's perfect," added Arietta.

"And the men," said Cheryl teasingly to Arietta.

"What!" said Arietta as she light-heartedly pushed Cheryl's arm. "They came over to see you, what was the one's name, the one talking to you about his boat?"

"Skip," she replied.

"But you can call me Skippy," they both said, laughing out loud.

Cheryl and Arietta told James the conversation from start to finish and how they both stood up to leave at the same time; they couldn't stop laughing as they told it.

"I am so glad we came over and sat with you and the children," said Arietta. "It was so much fun, and I was dying to have some pizza."

"What about the desserts?" Cheryl asked. "They were unbelievable."

"You mean dessertsss," corrected James, imitating Caleigh.

They all laughed.

"I loved dancing with them," said Cheryl. "Caleigh was so happy." She looked at Arietta and James. "She thinks you two are the best."

"She's a lovely girl," complimented Arietta.

"Thank you," replied Cheryl. "She is great, she's my angel…and that little angel will be a little devil tomorrow morning as she tries to get me up! So, I think I'm going to call it a night and get some sleep," she said.

"It's been a long day," said Arietta as she stood up too.

James stood and followed them to the patio to put on his shoes. He watched Arietta put on hers and pick up her bag. They said goodnight to Cheryl and walked onto the path towards their rooms.

"You have a beachfront?" he asked.

"I do," she replied, looking at him. "The view is amazing and I'm steps from the beach and the water. I can't wait to hear the lapping of the waves tonight."

"I was sitting on my patio earlier looking out, it was incredible, and it's so tranquil."

"Makes you forget about life for a while," she commented.

"It does," said James.

They walked in silence until Arietta stopped. "This is mine."

"I'm next one over," said James, pointing to the next building.

"Well, it was nice meeting you, neighbor," she said playfully. "I'm sure we'll bump into each other."

"I'm sure we will," he replied with a smile and watched her walk to her door.

She turned, smiled, and said, "Goodnight."

"Goodnight," he replied and went to his room. He stripped down to his boxer shorts, opened the patio door and sat outside on the chaise. Forget about life for a while, he thought. Definitely, but not her.

Arietta closed the door behind her and took off her dress. She removed her bra, kept on her panties, put on an oversized T-shirt, and went outside to lie down on the chaise. Forget about life for a while, she thought. Definitely, because it's the one I'm never going back to, all I need is the courage. She listened to the waves as they gently kissed the shoreline and smiled, then thought about him.

Cheryl undressed, put on her pajamas, washed the makeup off her face, and brushed her teeth. She slid into bed next to her daughter, thinking about their day, their night, and him. She grinned and fell asleep.

Chapter 5

James woke up, got ready, and walked out onto the patio. The sun was shining, and the air was warm. There were yachts and motorboats off in the distance, kayakers and sailboarders in the harbor, and children playing on the beach. He walked down the steps onto the path towards Arietta's patio and was almost there, when…

"No, I don't want to talk about it now, I need some time alone." Silence. "You haven't noticed how distant I've been, how unhappy I am." Silence. "This is not about you, it's about me." Long silence. "No, I don't want you to find me…I don't want to see you, never mind talk to you." Longer silence. "Please, give me some time and stop pressuring me…leave me alone…don't call back…I'm hanging up."

It went quiet and then James could hear her crying. He knew if he kept on walking, she would see him, and she may know he heard her.

"James, James." It was the brother and sister from last night, Joseph and Susan; they had spotted him from the beach.

He heard the chair move on Arietta's patio and realized she was standing up to look. He stood still for a few moments, then started walking slowly towards her patio. "Hi, kids," he shouted loudly and waved at them.

"Good morning," said Arietta. She was still wearing her oversized shirt and was resting her arms on the patio deck. She had tissues in her hand and her eyes were red.

"Good morning," he replied. He watched her wipe her eyes. "You okay?"

"I'm fine, just some problems at home, nothing I can't handle."

"Okay," he said changing the subject. "I was just going to get some breakfast. Do you want to come?"

"I'm not ready," she said in a confused way. "I would need to get ready."

"I can wait."

"You can?" she asked with a smile starting to show. "I'll be about twenty minutes."

"James, James," said Joseph and Susan. They stopped right in front of him. "Come see our sandcastle."

He looked at Arietta. "I'll be waiting on the beach."

"Okay," she said and took off into her room.

He looked at the kids. "Let's go see your castle." He followed them down to the shoreline, and they stopped in front of it. "This is fantastic," he said. He helped them build a moat, fill it with water, and put some shells around it. Then Susan got some drink umbrellas and placed them on the rooftops.

"Perfect," said Joseph.

"Here comes Arietta," said Susan.

James looked up. She was wearing white shorts and a green tank top; her hair was in a French braid; she looked beautiful.

"Wow, this castle is amazing!" she said and listened as Susan and Joseph described it to her. "What are you going to call it?"

The kids talked quietly with one another and decided on a name. "St. John's Castle," replied Joseph.

Susan walked over to Arietta. "And you will be the queen." She pulled James up. "And you will be the king...Joseph will be the prince and I will be the princess."

"Well, thank you, young, fair princess," said Arietta, bowing her head.

Susan curtsied back. "You're welcome, malady."

"The King and I are off to our royal breakfast feast and will leave the castle under your care," continued Arietta.

"You can count on me," said Joseph, standing noble pounding his chest. They all laughed.

They said their goodbyes and the children went back to their castle while Arietta and James walked to the Terrace Restaurant. They went to the buffet, picked out their food, and sat back at their table, where they had a wonderful panoramic view of the island and the pool area.

"Sorry about before," said Arietta.

"Nothing to be sorry about," replied James. "You seem better."

"I am, thanks for asking me to breakfast."

"You're welcome," he said pleasantly. "How was the rest of your night?"

"It was wonderful," she replied and talked about the soothing, rhythmic sounds of the waves and how they made her drift off to sleep. He complimented her on her hair, and she talked about how this is one of her favorite ways of wearing it. "When I'm feeling casual and comfortable…and being lazy," she added with a laugh. "How did you sleep?"

"Good," he said, which was close enough to the truth.

They finished breakfast and went for a walk. They talked about the resort, the island, the food, the beach, and the pool. They chatted about the people they had met, about the kids and about the staff. Intentionally, they never spoke about themselves or asked each other personal questions; their lives were too complicated. They stopped and grabbed an iced coffee from the Market Deli then went to the pool bar and sat at a table facing the harbor. Three men in their early seventies sat at a table next to them.

"Everything is taken care of, Gio," said one of them.

"I know, I know," Gio replied. "I just want everything to be perfect for her. We should have had one of the women help us."

"You couldn't have planned it any more perfectly, she will love it," confirmed the other one. "Besides, you want it to be a surprise."

"You wait here while we get the manager to go over the details with him again," he said as they both left him. Gio looked over at James.

James acknowledged him with a "Hello."

"Hello, young sir, miss," he replied and walked over to them. "Mind if I have a seat?"

"Please do," said James. He looked nervous and flustered, so they waited for him to talk.

"I…well, we…my wife and I are renewing our vows Tuesday."

"That is so wonderful and exciting!" said Arietta.

"Wonderful, yes, exciting, yes, nervous and worried, yes," said Gio anxiously.

"Why?" asked Arietta.

"At eighteen my wife and I eloped and got married. We left Italy and came to live in the USA, New York City. We had brought shame and disgrace to our family, our church, our way of life…you see, my darling, my wife and I were from different sides of the tracks, to coin an American phrase, so we ran," and with his two fingers on the table showed them running. "In the USA we lived with family who, how shall I put it, were more modern, and believed in love having no boundaries. My two friends and their wives also eloped and joined us a year later."

"Wow, that's a fascinating story!" said Arietta astonished and somewhat confused. "But I don't understand, it was such a long time ago; why are you nervous and worried?" She looked over at James, who was confused too.

"Ah, I missed out the most important part." He sat more comfortably in his seat, and Arietta and James, intrigued, moved slightly forward in theirs. "When we were married, there was only my wife and I, my two friends and my wife's two friends, and it was a civic ceremony; no mass, no reception, no dance, no cake and no honeymoon." He took a deep breath. "I know she always wanted a nice big wedding, Catholic mass, a celebratory reception with dinner and dancing, and to dance to our song. So, we agreed that on our fiftieth wedding anniversary we would go to a fine resort, bring our family and friends, and celebrate our big day, at no expense!"

"What's the problem?" asked Arietta.

Gio hesitated. "Me, my friends, and the manager are men, and most of us old. There is a young girl helping us organize but…"

"She is unfamiliar with your Catholic background, your traditions and your music?" Arietta asked.

"Yes, that's it, unfamiliar. I have told my old friends that we need a woman who has some knowledge of this to help us, but they think I'm being difficult."

Gio caught James's look and noticed him making a notion with his eyes to Arietta, finally catching on. He turned to Arietta. "My lovely girl are your parents from Europe?"

"Yes, they came here separately and met in the US," she said and hesitated, "Actually…to New York City."

"I bet you've heard them talk about their life back home, where they were born and so on?" he quizzed.

"I did, many times."

"Did they have a big wedding?"

"No, small, but they…" She stopped and realized where he was going.

"They had a magical renewing of their vows?" he asked and smiled.

"They did," she replied. "On their fortieth." She thought back to that day and how happy they were.

He gave her a moment. "And who organized and planned it all?"

"Me," she replied. She looked at Gio's earnest face, then over at James who nodded encouragingly, then turned back to Gio. "How can I help?"

Gio, surprising them both, jumped out of his seat, kissed Arietta on the cheek and did a little jig. He turned to James. "You will have your girlfriend back soon," and helped Arietta off her seat, grabbed her coffee, and walked with her towards the hotel; on the way they met his friends and the manager.

James chuckled as he heard the men cheering on finding out Arietta was going to help. He drank his coffee and looked out to sea, watching the boats. Someone whispered in his ear,

"Sorry to leave you alone." Arietta had run back to him. "I'll see you later," she said. "This is so exciting!"

He watched her run off and was happy for her.

Arietta had overseen dozens of work-related dinner receptions, dinner parties, staff parties, birthday parties, and events catering to the needs of their diverse clientele but helping to plan a reception and make an unforgettable memory for complete strangers was going to be so different and so much more fun. She caught up with the group of men and said, "Let's get started."

Chapter 6

Cheryl waved to Caleigh as she headed up the dock. She sprayed on some suntan lotion, threw it back in her beach bag, put her chaise in a semi-upright position, fixed her towel, and lay down on her back. The waiter came by, and she ordered a Bay Breeze. To the right she noticed James in the distance looking for a spot on the beach and called him over.

"Use this one," she said, motioning to the chaise next to hers and removing Caleigh's towel. "She's learning to kayak where the water is shallow; she's on the dock," she explained as she pointed to her daughter.

James, looking up at the dock, waved to Caleigh; she waved back. He put his towel on the chaise, unbuttoned his shirt, and placed it on top of his flip flops. "This is beautiful."

"I know," said Cheryl. "It's so picturesque!"

"What have you guys been up to today?" he asked.

"Like I predicted, that little devil dragged me out of bed early. We went for breakfast at the Terrace Restaurant, which was delightful…let's see…oh, then we came back, Caleigh showered, and we changed…I dropped her off at the Kids Club. They went on a nature walk and learned about plants and animals, while I went for a swim and hung around the pool, had lunch on my patio; she had hers at the camp. I picked her up, and we went for a swim in the pool, then we came here."

"Busy," said James.

"Sure was. Now it's time for a little relaxation," she replied. The waiter came by and dropped off her drink. "Another one of these for James, please," she said to the waiter as she pointed to her drink.

"Yes, miss," he replied and left.

"What have you been up to?" she asked.

James told her about building the sandcastle, meeting Arietta, having breakfast, and walking around the resort. He then told her about Gio.

"Get out of here," she said and tapped James on the arm. "I was in the pool when I saw her walking and talking with three old men and the manager and going into the hotel with them. I thought what the heck is going on." She laughed out loud. "You know, I thought maybe one of them had grabbed her butt or said something inappropriate." She laughed louder, and James laughed with her. The laughter subsided, and she asked, "Does she know how to do that stuff?"

"I have no idea," replied James.

Cheryl laughed. "You mean you suggested to Gio that she help him, and you didn't know if she could?"

"I guess so."

They both laughed again.

"But she did offer and seemed excited to help, so I'm guessing she has some skill at it," added James.

"Come to think of it, she did seem very excited and enthusiastic when she was talking with them and so did they," she said as she watched the waiter give James his drink.

"Cheers," he said and touched her glass and took a sip.

"Oh, Caleigh meant to tell you something last night and I guess with all the excitement she forgot, so quietly remind me to remind her if I forget."

"Okay," he replied.

They both looked over and watched Caleigh. There was one instructor on the dock, helping her get into the kayak and another in the water, holding it. She got in safely and in no time was paddling around.

"I want to go see her. Want to come in for a swim?" she asked.

"Sure," he replied and stood up.

She walked slightly in front of him and was wearing a turquoise bikini. Her bum looked firm, shapely, and sexy, and her wiggle was hypnotic.

They swam close to where Caleigh was and watched her. She was happy to see them and waved, almost tipping over. Then she paddled off to be with the group.

"You have a really wonderful girl," said James.

"She's very special, I love her more than anything," replied Cheryl. She looked at James's broad shoulders but quickly shifted her eyes when he turned to look at her.

"If you don't mind me asking, where is her father?"

"You mean her biological dad," replied Cheryl. "Well, I shouldn't really say it that way; we were in love at the time."

"You don't have to—"

"It's fine and it happened such a long time ago…I was working my way through college and was taking courses to be a medical assistant at a doctor's office, which is what I do today. At that time, I was working in a bar, and they had live bands and solo acts playing there, so I started talking to this guy who sang and played guitar on his own on Thursday nights. He was cute, and we were both single, so we went on some dates, and we hit it off. He used to write me songs, sing them to me, and play them at the bar; he was very charming. We were together for a few years. One day he was asked to be the lead singer in a rock band, so he joined. Eventually he started coming home later, smelling of perfume, late calls on his cell; it didn't take me long to realize he was cheating on me. He left me and went to live with his band; of course, she was living there too…shortly after that I found out I was pregnant. At first, I wasn't going to tell him, but I thought at least he should know. You must understand, I didn't want him back or anything to do with him; it just didn't feel right him not knowing. So, I went to where he was living, and there he was, on the couch, drugged out. He didn't even know who I was, so I walked out and left, without saying a word. I didn't know it at the time, but apparently he had started doing drugs just before he left me, and it got much worse after he moved out." She paused for a moment and dunked her hair in the water, then continued. "A few weeks later I heard they had all moved to Los Angeles to try and make it big. He ended up in rehab a few times, and from what I understand, the last time he never left."

"What does Caleigh know?" asked James.

"I tell her the beginning of the story about us being in love, the songs, and the fun times. I showed her pictures of him, and eventually gave them to her." She stopped and looked in the distance at her daughter. "Then I told her he had an adult sickness and that he died before she was born."

James was silent for a moment. "What did you do after he left?"

She looked back at James. "I moved back in with my parents, worked at the same bar, and finished college. My parents helped me raise Caleigh until I got my assistant job and could support myself." She went silent for a moment. "That was eleven years ago…time flies," she said, looking over at Caleigh, "but it was all worth it."

"You've done a wonderful job raising her," James said sincerely as he looked over at Caleigh.

"Thank you," she replied. "I think so." She swam around to the back of him and put her hands on his shoulders, raised herself up, and pushed him underwater.

Underwater James turned around, grabbed her waist, lifted her up and threw her with a big splash.

"I'm going to get you for that," she said and went after him. James deliberately swam slowly away, and she caught up to him and jumped on his back. James could feel her breasts press against him. He went down in the water and swam several feet behind her and surfaced. She was looking around for him. He splashed her to get her attention. "There you are," she said and swam over to him. "I need a drink," she said as she splashed him and quickly swam to the shore.

They got out of the water, lay on their chaises, and had a drink.

"Has there been anyone else?" asked James.

"I went on a few dates but dating guys my age and having a daughter is tough. Most guys either don't want that responsibility or think you're easy because you got pregnant young, so I kind of stopped dating…and when Caleigh was diagnosed, she needed all my attention and time, so it worked out well."

James waited for a while and had some of his drink. He looked out at kids kayaking and asked her, "how did you pay for Caleigh's treatment?"

"It wasn't easy. I had some medical coverage, so I used that, received some money from charities and people doing fundraising in the community…working at the doctor's office helped because they knew my situation, and the doctor I work for also worked at the same hospital Caleigh went to, so he would speak to the doctors there…but mostly it was my parents; they mortgaged their house to help me. I pay them back as much as I can each month, and we talked about me moving in with them and saving my rent money, but we all like having our own space. Besides, Caleigh likes visiting them, and they like visiting us." She sipped her drink. "We got this vacation through the 'Make-A-Wish Foundation,' you've heard of that?"

"I have," he said. "I thought most children want to go to Disney?"

Cheryl laughed. "You can choose your own place as long as the cost is similar, and most kids pick Disney. Not Caleigh, she wanted a place where real pirates used to come, a place with history, sun, sea, and a beach. Plus, she heard me comment about how beautiful this place looked and thought I deserved a vacation, too. She said we were both getting what we wanted. So, I saved up and made up the difference in the price and here we are."

It started getting late and Cheryl noticed the kids were arriving back at the dock, and the parents were gathering there, waiting to pick them up.

"I need to get her," she said.

"I should get going," replied James. "It was nice talking with you."

"You too, maybe one day I will hear how you're still single," she said with a curious smile.

"Maybe," he said nervously.

"I'll see you around," she said, walking toward the dock.

"Cheryl," he called.

She turned around. "Yes?"

"If you're free tonight and want some company for dinner, would you like to go together, you know, as friends?" he asked cautiously.

"That would be nice, come by around six," she replied smiling, and turned to walk away, her smile fading fast.

"Cheryl," he called again, waiting for her to turn around. "It's up to you, if you want to come alone that's fine, I know you may want a night out, but if you want to bring Caleigh along, that's no problem."

Cheryl walked back to him. "Are you sure?"

"Definitely," he said reassuringly.

She wanted to hug him right then and there but thought better of it. "Okay, we will be waiting," she said, smiling as she watched him walk away. "James."

He turned around.

"Thank you."

"I'll see you ladies around six."

She turned and walked happily to the dock.

Arietta walked out of the pool and dried herself off. The dip was refreshing and just what she needed. She put on her wrap and started for her room; she noticed James in the distance and quickened her pace to catch up with him.

"James," she called.

He turned, saw her, and waited. "How is it going?"

"Really good, I met with Gio and his friends, the manager, and Janice who is the girl that works here and is coordinating it. We talked for a couple of hours and went through exactly what he is looking for. There is some fine-tuning but it's mostly adding things and arranging things to be done in a certain way…it's going to be incredible."

"Sounds like you are going to give them a perfect day," said James.

"I hope so," she said excitedly. "Tomorrow morning, I have to go over to St. Thomas and meet some people, do you want to come and keep me company?"

"Okay, what time?"

"I'll meet you at nine on my patio," she replied. "Janice and I are meeting with the chef tonight at the restaurant around six to talk about the menu."

"I'm going there with Cheryl and Caleigh for dinner at six."

"Maybe I will join you after I'm done."

"You should," he replied. "That would be nice."

"What did you do today?" she asked. "I checked the pool and beach, and I couldn't find you."

James told her.

"I must have just kept missing you…Well, here we are, back where we met," she said, stopping at her patio. "Hopefully see you later at the restaurant."

"I hope so."

She went inside and checked her phone: six voicemails and twelve texts; she chose to ignore them. She needed more time.

Chapter 7

James arrived at the patio at six and knocked on the glass door. The door opened, and Caleigh came out.

"You like my beautiful pink dress?" she asked. "I picked it out especially for you because I know you like pink."

"You look so pretty," said James, "and I do love pink."

James looked up at Cheryl walking out. She was wearing a white tight dress that brought out her cinnamon suntan and blue eyes. She looked stunning and extremely sexy. "Wow, Cheryl, you look amazing."

"Thank you, James," she said and realized she was blushing. "You look very handsome."

"You do," added Caleigh. "I really like your blue shirt."

Cheryl closed the patio door, and they walked to the Terrace Restaurant and were given a table that had a spectacular view of the harbor. Inside, a pianist was playing soft dinner music that drifted gently out to the patio. The waiter handed them menus and a wine list.

"Some wine?" asked James.

"That would be nice," replied Cheryl.

"Red or white?" he asked.

"A nicely chilled white," she replied.

"And you, young lady?"

"James, a nicely chilled chocolate milk," replied Caleigh, teasing her mom.

James ordered a bottle of French white wine and a glass of chocolate milk. They talked about the boats and yachts in the harbor. The waiter brought the chocolate milk, then opened and poured the wine and placed the bottle back in the ice bucket.

"Cheers," they all said and took a sip of their drinks.

"This tastes so good," said Cheryl, "and chilled to perfection." She looked at James and gave him a nice smile.

"James, what color are your eyes?" asked Caleigh.

"Come look at them and tell me?" he asked and maneuvered his chair so she could stand in front of him.

"Blue," she confirmed.

"So, they are blue," he said.

"But yesterday I could have sworn they were green. I even told my mom." She looked over at her mom who nodded yes.

"They probably were," he said.

"That's impossible!" she stated.

"My eyes sometimes appear green or blue, usually depending on what I wear; today I'm wearing blue, so they look blue, yesterday…"

"You had green on," said Caleigh.

"I did."

"That's neat. So, what color do you call them?"

"I guess, hazel," he replied.

Caleigh went back to her seat and said, "James, you are full of surprises."

The way she said it made Cheryl and James laugh.

The appetizers came, and they shared fried calamari, shrimp cocktail, and conch fritters. For the main meal, Caleigh had a burger and fries, Cheryl, seafood pasta, and James, lobster, and scallops in a garlic sauce. Cheryl and James tried each other's food, drank the bottle of wine, and ordered another.

James and Cheryl passed on dessert, but Caleigh ordered a chocolate sundae. They drank their wine and watched the sun setting.

"It's even more beautiful at sunset," said Cheryl.

"It is," said a voice behind them.

"Arietta," shouted Caleigh and jumped out of her seat to give her a hug. "I haven't seen you all day."

"I've been here and there…"

"And everywhere," finished Caleigh.

"Yes…I heard you went kayaking today."

"Yeah, it was so much fun," said Caleigh and went back to her dessert.

"How's the menu coming along?" asked James.

"It's going to be unbelievable," she said, as she sat down and watched James pour her a glass of wine. She picked up the glass and had a sip. "Umm, delicious." She looked at them and began to explain. "The chef is incredible and can make anything, so nothing is out of his area of expertise, which means everything is a go," she said excitedly.

James was taken in by her enthusiasm and how happy and excited she was. "Sounds like Gio and his wife are in for a very special occasion."

"Rio!" replied Arietta.

"Rio?" questioned Cheryl.

"That's her name, Rio," said Arietta.

"Rio and Gio," said James.

"How cute is that?" said Cheryl.

"I know, his name is actually Giovanni, but no one has called him that for a very long time," Arietta said. "Rio and Gio! It works perfectly with the event!" She took another sip of wine. "I have to go and get a shower and change. I'll see you later." She stood up.

James filled up her glass and passed it to her. "Here, take it with you, nothing like a relaxing wine after a busy day."

She smiled and took the wine. What a nice sentiment, she thought. "Thank you, I will definitely enjoy it," she said and left.

They watched the sun disappear and the lights come on one by one, on the boats and yachts in the harbor, and around the pool.

Cheryl moved her seat close to James. "It's breath-taking," she whispered.

She was so close he could smell her sweet perfume.

The next table over, the couple stood up and slow danced. "You should dance, mom," said Caleigh, "like them." She pointed to the couple.

Cheryl and James looked over at them and each other. "We can't be upstaged," he said.

"Or disappoint my daughter," she added.

They stood away from the table and slow danced by the ledge. It had been an awfully long time since a man had held her, and she savored every moment. The music stopped, and they sat down.

"Thank you," he said.

Cheryl smiled. "You're welcome."

"Can I go swimming now?" asked Caleigh.

"Of course," replied Cheryl. "You've been so well behaved tonight. How can I say no?"

James picked up the bottle of wine and filled up their glasses. They left the restaurant and went to Cheryl's patio. James pointed to a table by the shallow end and walked over to it. Cheryl went inside to help Caleigh find her bathing suit, then sat with James, and watched Caleigh jump in.

Caleigh swam over to the edge, got out, and walked quickly to James. "I almost forgot again, it's my birthday on Friday and I'm having a party. I'm turning twelve. Can you come?"

"I wouldn't miss it for the world," he said.

"Yaayyy," she shouted and dramatically jumped in the pool.

"That's what she wanted to tell you last night," said Cheryl.

"How nice. You're having her party here?" James asked.

Cheryl went quiet, and James felt something was wrong. "Is everything okay?"

"It's a couple of things," replied Cheryl and looked at him nervously. "She wants to have her party here, and I talked with the girl who organizes the events and because her birthday is so close, she told me she has very limited time and resources to help me; she also told me it would be less expensive if I book the activities directly. Caleigh's last few birthday parties have been in the hospital, so this year she wants something special, a pirate theme with costumes and face painting, and the list goes on and on. Not only do I not have the time to plan that, especially with her being around me all the time; I wouldn't know where to begin."

"Okay, that's not too difficult to work out. What's the second thing?" he said, leaning over towards her.

"I'm embarrassed to say it." She looked anxiously at the pool and Caleigh splashing around.

"Just come out and say it," said James. "I'm sure it's nothing that can't be worked out."

She looked at James. "Everything here has a price and it's not cheap. As you know, I had to make up the difference for this vacation, so I was only able to put aside five hundred for her party and I don't think it's close to enough. I feel embarrassed talking about it," she said and glanced away.

"You shouldn't be," said James comforting her.

"I have always taken care of us and been self-sufficient. I have tried to put Caleigh off by suggesting that she have her party when we get home, but she has her heart set on having it here."

"Cheryl," said James. She wouldn't look at him. "Cheryl." This time she did. "First, let me plan her party."

"You?" she said doubtfully.

"Well, I have a feeling I know someone who will help me, if not, take it over from me," he said with a grin.

"Arietta?" asked Cheryl.

James nodded.

"You think she would? She would be perfect."

James looked taken aback.

"Not that you wouldn't," she said with a laugh.

James laughed with her. "I agree, she would be perfect, and I'm sure I can help out with this one." He thought for a moment. "Let me pay for the party."

"No, I couldn't let you do that. It would feel like I was taking advantage of you, of our friendship, and I would feel awkward being around you, knowing that you paid."

"Okay, well, you think about it."

"I will but I don't think I will change my mind. I will make do with what money I have."

James looked at her. "I was thinking about something you told me about earlier, 'Make-A-Wish.'"

"Yes," she said curiously.

"They collect money from people, donations, and then use that money to help kids go on vacations and such," he said.

"Yes."

He drank some of his wine and stood up. "I'll be back in a few minutes," he said and left. On the way to his room, he met Arietta and told her to come with him, and she followed him to his room. James found his cheques and filled one out.

"What's going on?" asked Arietta.

James sat down with her and explained Caleigh's birthday, and Cheryl's two problems and how they were going to help her. "If you want to, that is?"

"Of course," she said eagerly. "What do I have to do?" She listened as James explained.

They left his room and headed to the pool. Before they arrived there, Arietta ducked into the bar and found a spot where she could see them and ordered a drink. She watched James as he sat down next to Cheryl.

"What are you up to?" asked Cheryl.

"I am making a donation," he replied. "Now, I could mail it to 'Make-A-Wish,' tell them who it's for and have them contact you and forward it onto you but that would take some time, or…" He playfully sat back and looked at her.

"Or?" she asked. "Or what?"

"I could skip all that red tape and give my donation directly to Caleigh's guardian," he said. He showed her part of the cheque. "It says, 'Caleigh's Birthday Party Donation' right here at the bottom next to memo." He folded it in half and smiled.

"I can't," she said. "It still feels like it's you paying."

He called the waiter over. "If I needed to mail something, can I do it from the hotel?"

"Yes, sir, we use Federal Express," he explained.

"Thank you," he said. He offered her the cheque and Cheryl reached over to take it. "Promise me you won't unfold it just yet?"

"Promise," she said and smiled. "Thank you for your donation."

Arietta saw her take the cheque; that was her cue. She went to their table, put her drink down, and sat. "Oh, that shower felt great, and the wine made it that much more delightful."

"Guess what?" asked James.

"What?" Arietta asked.

"I'm going to plan Caleigh's birthday party on Friday," said James.

"You!" she said. "Do you know the first thing about planning a child's party?"

"No," replied James.

"Do you know anything about planning anything?"

"That would be another, no," he said.

She looked over at Cheryl.

"I don't have the time and he offered," she said, shrugging. "I figured I better take any help I can get."

James looked at Arietta. "If you think you can do a better job and have the time, then you can take it over," he suggested, "and I can just help you out."

She looked over at Cheryl, who with her eyes was begging her to say yes. "Okay, I'll do it but as far as I," she looked over at James comically, "I mean we, are concerned, it's important to us that Caleigh believes only you planned this party for her. That's the only condition, okay?"

"Okay," replied Cheryl. She looked like she was about to cry. "Thank you, thank you, thank you." She reached over and hugged Arietta, then pulled back. "But I don't want it to take up too much of your time."

"Honestly, a few hours at the most," she said reassuringly, "and I will keep you updated." She looked over at James. "So, how can you help?"

"First, I can be the treasurer and accountant, just to make sure you stay on budget," he said, trying to act serious.

"Fine," she said, laughing at him and turned to Cheryl. "How much were you looking at spending?" She watched Cheryl lift up the cheque.

James interrupted. "Cheryl received a nice donation from a charity to cover the party." He reached over and took the cheque. "I believe I will take that," he said, grinning. "I am the treasurer." He showed Arietta the amount.

"Nice," said Arietta. "Sure that will be more than enough." She stood up and looked at Cheryl. "Let me go get a pad and pencil, and we can write down the particulars," and left for the hotel front desk.

Cheryl was staring down James who had a grin on his face. "You think you're pretty clever." James was ignoring her and waving at Caleigh and the kids in the pool. Cheryl stood up and walked over to him. She leaned over and with her hand moved his face towards hers. "You planned that out, didn't you, while we were sitting here. You had it all planned out, just like that." He gave her this look as if he didn't know what she was talking about. She stood up, reached over, kissed him on the cheek, and whispered, "thank you, you've made my biggest fear and worry disappear.

You're a kind and thoughtful friend." She hugged him and went back to her seat.

Arietta came back. They wrote down the details and within twenty minutes they were done. "Is there a second thing?" asked Arietta, looking at James.

"What?" James asked with a confused look on his face.

"Well, you said first, I can be treasurer and accountant. I was wondering if there was a second thing you can do to help me plan this?" she asked and looked over at Cheryl and winked.

"I can be your right-hand man, your go-to guy," said James.

"Okay," replied Arietta. "I will let you be my assistant." She turned to Cheryl, and they both laughed.

James gave Arietta the 'I'm not amused look' which made them laugh all the more.

Caleigh got out of the pool; she was tired and ready for bed. Her mother dried her off, and they both said goodnight. Caleigh went into the room. Cheryl stopped and thanked them both again and went inside. Arietta and James walked down towards the bar.

"Still early, want a drink?" asked Arietta.

"Sure," said James.

They went in, ordered drinks, and decided to sit at the bar. Arietta was looking at him, waiting for him to look back, which he did.

"What?" he asked.

"That was a really wonderful thing you did," she said.

"Thank you."

"Why did you do that?"

"She needed help, so I'm helping out," summed up James.

"That's it," said Arietta. "That simple."

"Well, yes and no. Yes, in that she needed a friend's help, and no, because she's had a lot to deal with financially, physically, and mentally." James told Arietta about Caleigh's father, the pregnancy, the treatments, and the financial burden on her family. "I just wanted to help out and make her life a little easier, less stressful, and let her enjoy her daughter's birthday and their vacation."

"I didn't know she went through all that, that's a lot for a single mom," she said sadly. "Yet she's come through it all okay. She has a great outlook, she's fun and has a wonderful daughter…and she is unbelievably beautiful."

"She does have a great personality," replied James, pretending to ignore Arietta's last point.

"You're something else," she said and playfully pushed him, causing James to almost fall off his seat. She grabbed his arm and laughed while she helped him up. "I'm sorry," she said, still laughing.

He laughed and straightened himself in the chair. "Are you okay with the event planning? You have two now. You know you are supposed to be on vacation and relaxing."

"It's all good, for Rio and Gio I just have to meet a couple of people tomorrow and confirm some things, and then I'm done. Janice is responsible for making sure it all runs smoothly. Caleigh's party will be a walk in the park, three hours tops, and again Janice will be responsible for making sure everything runs like clockwork." She stopped for a second. "Besides, it's so much fun, and I get to meet people, make people happy and give them great memories."

"You could have said no, but you didn't."

"I guess…but you gave me a gentle push in both situations. I'm not a hundred percent sure I would have otherwise." She looked at him. "But I'm really glad you did."

"But you made the decision. This is all you, so don't sell yourself short. You're doing something really amazing and special for these people."

"Thank you, I guess I never thought about it like that," she said, giving him a smile.

"I get the feeling you have some experience overseeing events."

"Oh yeah…dinner receptions, special events, parties…you name it, I've overseen it…" She took a long drink.

James decided it was best to change the subject and watched her as she drank; she was wearing a short skirt, tank top, and had her hair in a ponytail. "You look very pretty tonight."

She looked at him shyly. "Thank you," she said, as she fidgeted with her hair. "I didn't spend much time on the hairdo."

He moved her hands away from her hair. "You look perfect," he said, admiring her, then took a sip of his drink.

She watched him for a few moments and smiled.

They talked about the restaurant, the food, and the sunset, then finished their drinks, and headed to their rooms.

"Third time today," she said as she stood in front of her patio doors. "I will see you at nine."

"Nine," he reconfirmed and said, "Goodnight."

"Goodnight," she said and went inside and walked into the bathroom to wash her face. She looked at herself in the mirror and knew that this vacation and helping to plan these events were a helpful distraction from dealing with the inevitable choices she knew she needed to make, but they were also giving her time to think, and most importantly, to be herself.

James went into the room, lay on his bed, and looked up at the ceiling. He was confused about these feelings he was having; he hadn't had them for an exceptionally long time, and felt extremely guilty, but most of all, he felt like he was betraying her.

Chapter 8

On the ferry, Arietta explained that the parish priest from St. John was working on St. Thomas today, so she had to meet him there. They arrived at Charlotte Amalie at eleven and walked to the Saints Paul and Peter Catholic Cathedral. Standing outside was a group of twenty children with several plastic buckets, asking people walking by for donations. Behind them there were signs they had made that read, 'Help Us Repair Our Lady of Mt. Carmel.' Arietta approached a woman named Mary, who was the children's teacher, and asked her where she could find Father Bartholomew. Mary looked behind her and pointed to him walking out of the cathedral. Arietta walked over to him while James stayed behind. Arietta spoke with the priest for a few minutes, and then realized James wasn't with her and walked over to him.

"He wants to talk inside where it's a little quieter and more private," she said. "Are you coming?"

James shook his head. "I don't think so."

"Why not?"

"Think I will just hang around out here," he said cautiously. "I haven't been inside a church for a very long time."

She looked at him oddly and said, "Okay." Then went back over to the priest and spoke with him.

The priest walked over to James. "Good morning," he said.

"Good morning, Father," he replied kindly.

"Arietta says you haven't been inside a church for quite some time?" he asked.

"Yes."

"We are a church of God, all religions are welcome, even those that have none," he said in a reassuring voice.

"I know, Father. I'm actually Catholic, just not a practicing one anymore," answered James.

"Oh, I see," he said and looked at James for a moment. "Something has turned you away?"

James was extremely uncomfortable with his direct question. "Guess you could say that." He hesitated for a moment. "I lost my faith many years ago."

"I understand," said the priest. "Many people in life have events or circumstances placed on them that make them question their faith, some will even go so far as to blame God." He thought for a moment. "They often forget all the great and glorious things that God has given them and this wonderful life and world to enjoy them in."

James was silent.

"I see much conflict in your eyes," said the priest, looking at him. "If you ever want to talk, please contact me," he said and squeezed James's shoulder. "Don't worry, you don't have to come into my church. We can meet at the bar across the road; I enjoy a nice cold beer once in a while," he leaned forward, "and to be honest with you, it gives me an excuse to get out," he said with a wide grin.

James smiled back and politely said, "Thank you."

The priest walked away to meet Arietta and talked with her as they walked to the cathedral doors. She stopped and briefly looked back at James, then went inside.

The teacher was standing close to James. "How is the fundraising coming along?" he asked.

"It's okay, a little slow. We only started last week, and I'm sure it will pick up," she said optimistically.

James read the sign again. "You're repairing a statue in the cathedral?"

"What?" she asked and looked at James pointing toward the sign. "Oh, no," she replied. "That's the name of our church on St. John. Our roof needs to be replaced…it has had several leaks and we have made band-aid repairs, but the contractor says it needs to be replaced or it will just continue to get worse. We don't get much tourist traffic on Cruz Bay, so we came over here." She looked around. "But here isn't much better, it's mostly locals walking by, and they can only give a little or not at all."

James looked around and had a thought. "When we arrived here, there were several cruise ships docked in the harbor. There was only one here the other day and the Market Square was busy."

"I would imagine it will be hectic there today," replied Mary and suddenly had an idea. She went into the cathedral and minutes later came out with the children's choir gowns. She looked over at them. "Children, come take a gown and put it on please." They did as she instructed. "Children, we are going for a walk," she said. The children grabbed the buckets, and James picked up the signs, and they followed her in a line down Kronprinsens Gade to the Market Square. Mary organized the children in rows, and gave the younger siblings, who were not in the choir, the buckets, and the task of collecting the money. She asked James to place the signs on either side of the choir. Slowly the cruise ship passengers started to stop and look at them. Mary gave the sign, and the children started to sing. The tourists listened to them, and in no time the buckets were filling up. The children seeing the donations, sang with all their hearts.

Thirty minutes later, Father Bartholomew and Arietta walked out of the church. The priest looked around in alarm, searching for Mary and the children. One of the parishioners told him they had walked over to the Square. As they got closer, he could hear their angelic voices, and as he turned the corner, he saw the money being put in the buckets and was overcome with joy. Mary waved him to come and take over, which he did.

James and Arietta listened for several minutes, put some money in a bucket, and walked toward the main street. In the background, the children stopped for a break, and the crowd applauded. On the way, Arietta asked James what had happened, and he explained it to her.

"That was nice of you to help out," said Arietta.

"It was nothing," said James.

"I guess sometimes you have to walk off your front doorstep and take that chance and see what's out there," said Arietta.

"I guess so," replied James.

They walked down the street, and James came to a familiar alleyway.

"Let's go down here and have a quick look in the stores," suggested Arietta.

There was no way James was going down there again. "There is another entrance further on that's closer and has more stores," he said hastily. He picked up his pace and passed by the alley. Safe, he thought.

"What's the hurry?" asked Arietta.

He looked at her. "No hurry," he said and turned to look up the street.

"Yeah, what's the hurry?" Lily asked. She had darted from her seat, came around the corner, and stopped right in front of him. She had that same stare.

"Who is this?" asked Arietta.

"This is Lily."

"What is she doing? Why is she staring at you like that?"

James glanced at Arietta. "It's not good," he replied, scared.

"You don't want to walk down the alley and see me, my James in shining armor…you can't hide; I knew you were here and would be walking by," she said without losing her stare. "Why do you keep on breaking her heart? Why did you give up your faith? You can make her happy by being happy. But you would rather feel guilty and cower on your bed and feel sorry for yourself."

"Hold on," said Arietta.

Lily ignored her, and James motioned with his hand to Arietta it was okay.

Lily continued. "But she has told you already," she said and moved close to his ear and whispered, "in your dreams." She pulled away. "Remember, you will never find her if you don't let her go." She placed something in his hand.

"Lily," said a loud voice from behind, it was D-Mon. Her trance was broken, and she went limp. James caught her. D-Mon came over and took her in his arms. "I will take her home," he said to James, noticing he looked very pale and turned to Arietta. "I'm working at the bar, go upstairs onto the patio, and I will be there soon," and left with Lily.

Arietta also noticed James didn't look good. "You okay?" No response. "James!" she said in a louder voice, and he looked at her. "You okay?"

"Yeah…yeah…I'm good." He walked with Arietta to the Haven Bar, and they sat upstairs on the patio.

She waited for a few minutes and noticed the color coming back to his face. "What the heck was that all about, James?"

"I don't know," replied James.

"That's Lily," said a voice approaching; it was D-Mon.

"Who is Lily?" asked Arietta.

"A shot of rum to calm the nerves and a bottle of beer," he said and placed them in front of James. He looked at Arietta. "Not who, what." He looked at her for a moment. "Can I get you something to drink?"

"Beer," she replied.

He came back moments later and poured the beer into a glass and placed it on the table along with the bottle and took a seat.

James drank his shot and was silent as D-Mon talked.

"Lily is a psychic and has special powers...sometimes she can see people's past, present, future or all three...When people, mostly tourists, come to see her, she can easily control it, she tells them something that she would never know, then offers them some words of encouragement. It's always something positive and meaningful, so people walk away feeling happy and content...Ninety-nine percent of the time she is just like you and me." He stopped and looked at James. "But sometimes she isn't, and she goes into this trance, and it takes over her."

"And?" asked Arietta.

"And that means that she has a powerful connection with someone, someone like James or maybe someone else in his life." He reflected for a minute. "Could be a lost soul, a soul in limbo, a release, a coming to terms...could be one of many things."

Arietta looked at James and thought about his reaction back at the church and what the priest had said to her. "How do you know what it is? What you have to do?"

"That's up to James to figure out," said D-Mon and looked at him. "That was not your first encounter with Lily?"

James shook his head. "No."

"You met her before?" asked Arietta.

"It was the day I arrived, Saturday."

"Do you know what she is saying? Does it make any sense?" she asked.

James shook his head again. "No."

D-Mon gave James a doubtful look.

James reached down to grab his beer and realized he was still holding the trinket that Lily had given him and placed it on the table. It was a necklace made out of string with beads all decorated in different colors. James felt like he was going crazy.

"What is that?" asked Arietta.

"That was for you," D-Mon said and sat back in his seat and looked at them both. "She has been working on that since Saturday night; she painted each one by hand and kept repeating the twenty-four children's names and their colors…Sarah is pink, Andrew is blue, Michael is blue and—"

"Lauren is yellow, Christopher is red, Emma is purple polka dots, Olivia is—"

"You know what this means?" asked D-Mon.

They both stared at him.

James suddenly realized that he had spoken the names and colors aloud and fumbled for the answer. "Yes, it's a poem written by twenty-four children. That's also what it's called, 'Twenty-Four Children.'"

"Does it mean anything to you?" asked Arietta.

"Only that I know the poem," he replied and sipped his beer.

D-Mon stood up and looked at James. "Well, I hope she helps you find whatever she thinks you have lost or are looking for."

James looked up at him. "D-Mon, how do you know her?" he asked.

"She's my sister," he replied and started to leave.

James went quiet.

"You're D-Mon?" asked Arietta.

"Yes."

"I called. I'm supposed to meet with you today to talk about the music," explained Arietta. "You're the DJ tomorrow night at the reception at the St. John's Resort?"

"Oh, yes! Yes, I am."

"Do you have some time now?"

"I do," he said, and sat back down again.

"Janice said that you are an excellent DJ and have all types of music?"

"I DJ here and back at my college on Saturday nights in Miami; I have been doing it for years," he explained, "and over those years I have acquired quite a collection of music."

"Well, the couple is in their seventies, and they have given me a list of specific songs and an overall idea of the music they want. There will also be younger people there, too." She handed him the list. "I'm hoping you can get a feel for what they want and fill in the gaps."

He took his time and looked over the list. "Not a problem."

"Great," she said. "If you have any questions, you can contact Janice. She knows how to contact me."

James put the necklace in his pocket and looked out at the harbor at the pirate ship. "D-Mon, do you know when that pirate ship sails?"

"Usually sunset cruises," he replied.

"Do you know who runs it and if they do private events?" James inquired.

"My uncle does, and they do."

James looked at Arietta, and they both smiled and turned to D-Mon. Twenty minutes later they left him, and for the next hour they stopped in at the local stores and met with the people that D-Mon had highly recommended; some were for purchases, others were for bookings. After they finished, they took the ferry back.

"I just need to update Janice on my conversations with Father Bartholomew and D-Mon, and my part of the planning for Rio and Gio is done."

James smiled at her. "You're really enjoying it, the planning?"

"I really am," she replied happily. She looked at Charlotte Amalie fading in the distance and turned to James. "Are you, all right?"

"I'm fine," he said, forcing a smile, then changing the subject. "Do you want to cool off in the pool?"

"Definitely!" she replied. "I have to drop by the front reception first, so I will meet you there."

James watched as Arietta removed her wrap and revealed a purple floral bikini. She had a slim build, with perfect breasts, and a toned waist. She waved to him, jumped in, and swam over.

Arietta had noticed James looking at her and smiled to herself. "I bumped into Cheryl and Caleigh; they are changing and going to join us," she said.

Caleigh could be heard first and then seen as she jumped into the water. She swam over to them to say hello, then went to play with her friends. Cheryl was shortly behind her, wearing a navy-blue bikini. Arietta watched her as she walked down the steps and into the pool and thought she had a perfect figure. She wondered if James thought the same and looked over at him; he had his back to her and was clowning around with the kids.

"This is exactly what I needed," said Cheryl as she swam up to Arietta.

"Same here," replied Arietta. They swam over to the side, and Arietta told Cheryl about D-Mon and how he had given them the names of people to contact for Caleigh's party and what they had done. "So, everything is booked, and the items are being delivered on Thursday, so all I have to do is meet with Janice and iron out the final details," she explained, "and that's it, the planning is done."

"I'm so excited," said Cheryl. "Thank you," and gave her a hug.

They talked about tonight and agreed to meet for dinner.

Chapter 9

James had just finished getting ready when he heard a knock on the patio door. He pulled the curtains to one side and saw Arietta standing there and opened the door. "Come in."

"I thought I would return the favor," she said, handing him a glass of wine.

"Thank you."

"Cheers."

"Cheers," he said, as they touched glasses and had a drink. He watched her as she walked around the room. She was wearing a short blue floral dress that fit her perfectly in all the right places, her hair was straight and passed her shoulders, and her tanned face showed off her brilliant green eyes. Her perfume was light, sensual, and captivating. "You look absolutely breath-taking."

She turned and smiled at him. "Thank you," she replied. "I love these rooms," she said, sitting in the armchair. "They are gorgeous."

James sat on the edge of the bed and nodded in agreement. "And when the curtains are open and you look out, the view is spectacular."

"Every night I leave my patio doors open so I can hear the waves and feel the breeze, it's so incredible." She looked at James drinking his wine. "You look very handsome tonight."

"Thank you," he replied shyly.

"Let's go outside," she said and went onto the patio. She leaned on the ledge and looked out at the water. "It's another beautiful evening."

"It is," said James as he stood next to her.

"When I got back to my room today, slid underneath my door was an invitation to Rio and Gio's renewal ceremony; it was for me and a guest, which they are assuming would be you since Gio is under the impression that we are together." She turned around and looked at James. "I would like to know if you would go with me? Now, before you answer, let me explain my reasons to you." She paused and took a deep breath. "First, I don't want to go there on my own, sit on my own, eat on my own and be pulled out of my chair to dance out of sympathy. Second, I would really like you to see what I did to make their day special. Third, I want you to be a part of it and selfishly let me know what you think. Finally, I really would enjoy your company, and we would just be going as friends. Unfortunately, I can't guarantee that others won't be thinking otherwise." She let out a nervous laugh., took a sip of her wine, and continued. "I know you and I have been incredibly careful not to ask each other any personal questions about our lives, and I think it's because we are either not ready to answer those questions or don't want to ask them. I don't know what the situation is with you, and your life, and not going inside the cathedral today. It's none of my business, but they are renewing their vows in a church and if you say yes, you would have to be saying yes to it all; I don't just want you to show up to the reception…I know I may be asking a lot of you, maybe more than I should, but I really want you to come with me…and you being a part of what I have done would make it that much more special…If I am asking too much, I understand and apologize, but I'm hoping whatever your doubts are, if you can let them go just for one day, and take me?" She took a nervous sip of her wine. "You don't have to answer me right now because I want to give you some time to think about it, but I would like an answer before the end of the night." She stopped and looked out to the sea.

"Thank you for asking," he said and gently squeezed her hand. "Let me think about it and I will let you know."

She liked the soft touch of his hand and let herself enjoy it for a few moments before she changed the subject. "Let's go meet the girls and get some dinner."

As they walked to the Island Waves Bar, James thought about what Arietta had said and about her question. It was true the last time he walked out of the church, he vowed he would never walk back in, but Arietta was such a kind person, and she had done so much work on helping this couple plan their ultimate day that he felt awful not accepting her offer straight away; deep down he wanted to go and see what she had done and share the moment with her…but what about that man she was talking to on the phone? From what he could gather, it sounded like he wanted to fix things, and he didn't want to get in the middle of that…Then again, she did clarify going as friends. He looked over at her and how beautiful and sexy she was. He was confused.

"You're quiet. Are you okay?"

"I'm fine," he said and decided to think about it later. "I wonder how many people D-Mon knows on the island and is related to?" asked James.

"I think everyone who we spoke to was his relative."

"I think you're right," said James and they both laughed.

"But he is a great person to know, especially when it comes to event planning. It makes my job that much easier having a contact like that," she confessed.

They sat with Cheryl and Caleigh at a table overlooking the beach and the harbor. The wind blew ever so gently, and they could hear the symphonic waves caressing the beach. Inside the restaurant they could hear a large crowd of people talking and laughing and having a good time. They ordered their food and ate dinner. Caleigh talked about her day at the camp and what she and her friends did. Cheryl talked about her day at the beach and told them that tomorrow they were going to go to Charlotte Amalie to have a mother and daughter day. Their plan was to do some shopping, buy Caleigh's birthday present, go sightseeing, and have dinner. The girls talked about the Market Square and the stores. After dessert Cheryl told Arietta and James that she and Caleigh had a long day tomorrow and had to be up early in the morning and needed to head off to bed and excused themselves. A few minutes later Arietta noticed Caleigh had left her cardigan, so James ran after them and met Cheryl walking towards him.

"Caleigh's cardigan," said James.

"I was coming back to get it, thank you," she replied and took it from him. "Can you walk me back to my room?"

"Of course," said James and walked her to her patio.

She stopped and looked at him with her hypnotic blue eyes. "I thanked Arietta today and I just wanted to thank you for helping with Caleigh's party. It means the world to me, and I know it will to Caleigh, too." She hugged him and kissed him softly on the cheek. "Thank you," and was about to turn away and stopped. "I missed talking with you today, and with me being off the island tomorrow, I was hoping we can spend some time together when I get back, maybe Wednesday?"

"I would like that," he replied.

"Wednesday it is," she confirmed and said, "goodnight."

James walked back and sat down next to Arietta. "Cheryl was on her way back to get it," he said.

"Arietta, Arietta," called a voice. They both turned and looked at Gio walking out of the restaurant. "Come, come," he said and pulled her out of her chair. "Your boyfriend too," and proceeded to pull James up. "Come with me." They followed him into the restaurant. "These are my family and friends," he said and pointed to an exceptionally large group of men sitting around several tables taking up most of the restaurant. He turned to the group and quietened them down. "This is the angel that I have been talking about." The other, older gentlemen who had met Arietta the day before came over and kissed her on both cheeks while the other men said hello. "And this is her boyfriend, James." He looked at both of them. "Please sit down with me and join me for some wine." Two chairs were pulled next to Gio; they sat, and wine was poured. He looked at Arietta. "I heard you have taken care of everything magnificently," he said. "I know Rio is in for the best day of her life." He leaned down and whispered to them both, "She is not here tonight. It's bad luck for me to see the bride before the wedding. So she is with the women at the other restaurant, and I must admit I have never seen her so happy." He stopped and thought, then looked at Arietta and realized. "You need to go and join them."

"I...I don't know, I'm not sure. I wouldn't want to intrude," she replied.

Gio gave her a frown. "Intrude, how could you intrude? You are my saving grace, you are family." He looked at James. "Take her to my wife and come back." Arietta and James looked at each other. "Go, go," he said, handing Arietta her wine. "You two will still have the end of the night together."

They both stood up, and James walked Arietta to the Terrace Restaurant. They spotted a large group of women in the corner, who were much louder than Gio's group, and walked over.

A woman in her fifties approached them. "Can I help you?"

Arietta was silent.

James spoke. "She is looking for Rio."

"Rio, why?" she asked cautiously.

"This is Arietta and—" Before he could explain about Gio and what he had said, he was cut off.

"Arietta!" she said and looked over at the table. "Rio! It's Arietta!"

All the women shouted, "Arietta!"

Arietta was pulled towards the women as James was being pushed out of the restaurant and told to join the men. Arietta turned and briefly caught James being physically shown the door by three very old women and laughed at the sight. After the three women threw him out, they turned and broke into a loud laugh as the oldest one gestured to the other two that she had grabbed his bum.

Rio gave Arietta a big hug and a kiss on each cheek and made a spot next to her. She put her hand over her mouth and calmed herself down. "I don't know what to expect, and I don't want to know so don't tell me. I want to live and breathe every moment as it happens."

"I promise I won't," replied Arietta. "Besides, Gio made me sign a non-disclosure contract."

Rio laughed at Arietta's joke. "It wouldn't surprise me," she said, looking at Arietta. "Gio is right; you are an angel, and a beautiful one at that." She squeezed her hand. "Come and meet everyone."

James walked back into the bar as Gio shouted, "He made it back in one piece!" All the men laughed. James wasn't too sure what it was he meant. Gio motioned him to sit next to him while one of his sons occupied Arietta's vacant chair. Gio passed him a wine and looked around, shouting, "Salute!" All the men responded with a "Salute!" and drank their wine until it was empty. The waiters ran around and refilled their glasses. Gio looked at James. James didn't notice everyone had gone quiet and was listening. "We had a bet whether or not you would make it back in one piece. You know, those women can be very unforgiving and treacherous to a man who crashes into their sanctuary," said Gio as all the men laughed. He grinned and patted him on the back and looked at them. "But I knew you would be safe."

"How?" asked James.

"You were dropping off an angel," he said and laughed aloud. All the men laughed with him.

Gio looked over at his son, Rocco, who was finishing writing numbers and names in a small black book and had an exceptionally large stack of fifty and hundred-dollar bills. He gestured to Gio he was done.

Gio stood up. "All bets are in, so now let's get the results." He looked at James and motioned him to stand up. As he did, Gio sat down, and Rocco stood up.

"James, we have a few questions for you to answer regarding your recent trip to the sanctuary," said Rocco, trying to contain his laughter. "Okay?"

"Okay," said James, unsure about what they were going to ask him.

"First question, describe the lady that approached you?" asked Rocco.

James looked at Rocco, then Gio, who gestured to him to answer. He looked at the men and described the lady.

"That's Sophia!" shouted out a few of the men.

Others shouted, "No, it's Annabelle!"

Rocco asked James, "Did you catch her name?"

"I did," he replied.

"If you please," he said and gestured with his hand to reveal the answer.

For effect, James reached down and slowly picked up his wine and took a drink. All the men waited patiently as James slowly placed it down. Gio shook his head and laughed. He loved it. "It was…Annabelle!"

The winners stood up and cheered while the losers were quiet.

"Second question," said Rocco. "Did they ask you to leave, or did they throw you out?"

James smiled. "They threw me out." Again, there were cheers from the winners. James took a sip of his wine, and Gio gave him a wink.

"Third question, how many women threw you out, one, two, three, or four?"

James continued to play along. "Not four," he said to the frowns of a few. "Not one," to the frowns of a few more. The men who had picked two or three were waiting. "Three!" he confirmed.

Again, the winners cheered.

"Question four, did anyone of the three grab you, shall we say, inappropriately?"

"Yes," replied James.

"Oohhh," taunted the crowd.

Rocco was trying to talk and hold back his laughter. "Question five, where?"

James laughed and spoke. "My bum."

At which all the men fell around the place, laughing.

Gio handed James his wine, which he drank a mouthful.

It took Rocco a few minutes to gain his composure. "Last question, and this is for the big money…Do you know the name of the perpetrator?"

The men laughed louder.

"I do," replied James.

"Please," said Rocco laughing. "Please, tell us her name."

James looked around at all the men. "Well, she had a very strong hand and a very good grip." He began to laugh along with the men. "She went by the name," he took a sip of his wine, "Nana!"

All the men laughed hysterically. James joined in as he sat down.

Gio was laughing so hard he was having a tough time trying to stand up; eventually he did and patted James on the back. He waited for the laughter to stop and spoke. "I would like to thank James for being such a good sport." The men clapped their hands in agreement. Gio lifted up his glass and looked at James. "To James. Salute!" Everyone stood, raised their glasses towards James and replied, "Salute!" and drank them empty.

James sat down and noticed Rocco putting his book away and the envelope in his pocket. "No pay-outs?" asked James.

"No, all the money goes to the bride and groom. The fun is in the guessing and being right, and teasing those who were wrong," replied Rocco and patted James on the back.

"Let me give you something," said James, reaching for some money.

Rocco stopped him. "That's unnecessary." He touched where the envelope was. "You made this happen, and not only that, you played along and made it fun." He looked over at his father. "Making my father laugh as you did is priceless, thank you." He gave James a kind smile and excused himself.

James talked with many of Gio's friends and family, and as the night came to a close, Gio approached him.

"So, it's a big day for me tomorrow, and I need to get a good night's rest. I will see you at the church tomorrow," he said, noticing James was hesitant. "You're not coming?"

James felt awkward. "It's just that I haven't been to church in a very long time," he replied.

"Really, you're not a Catholic or religious?" Gio asked.

"I'm a Catholic…well, I used to be."

"Hmm," said Gio. "Used to be." He looked at James and pulled him off to the side to a quiet corner. "Can I ask you what happened?"

James looked unsure.

"As God is my witness." He realized what he said. "I mean…well, you know what I mean." They both laughed. "I don't want to pressure you, but sometimes talking to someone…well, I don't want to say stranger because I don't look at you as that but let's say someone who will not pass judgement, can be sometimes helpful."

James smiled at his honest face and spent the next twenty minutes explaining his reasons.

"Oh, I see," said Gio. "I understand now." He thought for a moment. "I am not going to give you this lengthy speech or lecture about me, my wife, my family and how religion is a big part of that, but I will say this: if you can turn your back on your faith and blame God when things are bad, perhaps you should embrace your faith and be thankful to God when things are good," he said and gestured behind James.

James turned around and saw Arietta walking towards them. He looked back at Gio and smiled. Gio smiled back and kissed him on both his cheeks. "You are a good man…and I am an old one and must go to bed." They both stood up to meet Arietta. "We had a wonderful night," said Gio.

"As did we," replied Arietta.

"Well, I will leave you two and say goodbye. Enjoy the rest of your evening." He kissed Arietta on each cheek and went off to say goodnight to the others.

James and Arietta said goodnight and left the restaurant.

"Feel like soaking your feet in the pool?" suggested James.

"That would be wonderful," she replied.

They walked to a table and kicked off their shoes and sat on the edge of the pool. They talked for an hour about their nights. They laughed about James getting thrown out by the three old women and laughed louder when they talked about Nana squeezing his bum; James told her about the six questions. Arietta talked about Rio and how nice she was, and all the women and who was married to whom. Eventually, they stood up and headed back to their rooms. They stopped in front of Arietta's patio doors and looked at each other.

"Arietta, it would be my honor and a privilege to go with you to the ceremony tomorrow, and yes, I mean all of it."

"Oh, James!" she said. "Thank you, thank you, thank you." She put her arms around him and squeezed him tightly.

James put his arms around her slim waist, feeling her breasts press up against him. He could hear her breath on his ear and smell her sweet skin and fragrant hair; he had those feelings again, the ones he hadn't felt in a very long time.

She didn't let go and positioned her face in front of his and kissed him on the cheek. "Thank you, this means so much to me." She removed her arms and went over and opened the door.

"Arietta," said James. "Thank you for asking me." He walked over and kissed her on the cheek. "I want you to know that going with you means so much to me."

"Thank you," she said, smiling, "goodnight," and entered her room. She was ecstatic.

James left and went into his room. Be thankful to God when things are good, he thought and lay down on his bed. He soon fell asleep.

It was the distorted vision again. She was in the sea up to her waist and she was calling and waving to him; he went into the water after her. As he got closer, she swam further away and further out. He followed her.

"You will never catch me," she said.

"Who are you?" he asked, trying desperately to reach her. "Why won't you stay?"

"I can't stay; you know that." She swam further out. "You need to move on, believe again, fall in love, and be happy…you must."

"I did believe, I loved, and I was happy."

"I know," she said and disappeared under the water.

James looked around, but she was gone. He was in the middle of the sea, and the island was so far away. He started swimming for the shore, but the wind started blowing and the waves got bigger and bigger. A big funnel appeared, and he tried to swim out of it, but it was too strong, and he was hopelessly getting pulled down, down.

James woke up, soaked in sweat. He sat up and ran his hand through his wet hair. He was scared and confused about her, and about the feelings he had been experiencing recently. He felt guilty and ashamed, and he felt like he was…lost…lost at sea and getting pulled down into the deep unknown.

Chapter 10

James knocked on her door and Arietta opened it and invited him in. "I'll just be a second," she said and went into the bathroom to put on her red lipstick. "Okay, I'm ready," she said as she walked over to him. She was wearing a beautiful, emerald-green summer dress which complimented her eyes and figure, her hair was down and slightly curled around her shoulders, and with her tan there was little need for makeup.

"Wow, you look beautiful," said James.

"Thank you," said Arietta. "You look extremely handsome; that light blue shirt really brings out your eyes."

"I'm glad it's casual attire," he said. "I don't think I would survive wearing a suit and tie."

"Well, the nice thing about being in the Caribbean, casual is their formal," she confirmed. "Shall we go?"

They walked towards the resort's main entrance, and Arietta told James that she spoke with Janice this morning and, "everything was a go, fingers crossed, it will be perfect."

"I'm sure it will be," reassured James.

At the main entrance, the guests were being shuttled to the church in minibuses. One just left so Arietta and James waited ten minutes for the next one and boarded with several other guests. They sat down, and James gave Arietta the window seat so she could look out. The bus was air-conditioned and comfortable and took them through winding streets towards Cruz Bay; on the way Arietta pointed out the harbor, the boats out in the sea, and St Thomas in the distance. Ten minutes later the bus came to a stop in front of Our Lady of Mount Carmel Church, and everyone stepped off. They walked inside where the ladies were ushered to their seats by Rio and Gio's nephews. Arietta and James looked around the church and talked about the stained-glass windows and how each portrayed a different image of the Stations of the Cross. They discussed the magnificent altar and the incredible mezzanine. The organist played softly as the pews filled up, and just before three, Gio and his best men came from the right side and stood in front of the altar. The music stopped.

"He looks very handsome in his suit," whispered Arietta. "They all do."

Moments later the organist started playing the Wedding March. Everyone turned and looked to the back of the church. Rio's girlfriends, both wearing dusty rose tea-length dresses walked down the aisle, shortly followed by Rio, who was wearing the same style dress but in white and holding a bouquet of white orchids. She had both her sons escorting her and was smiling at everyone she passed as she slowly made her way to the altar. Her sons kissed her on either cheek, left, then their father took her hand. They turned to the priest, and the mass began. During the ceremony, Mary and the choir of children appeared on the mezzanine and sang several hymns. Their voices were angelic; it was a wonderful feeling. Arietta went up for communion; James did not and remained in his seat. He did kneel alongside her as she prayed, but she wasn't sure whether he actually did or not. The ceremony ended with the priest introducing Rio and Gio Dimarco, and everyone cheered and clapped. The couple walked down the aisle and acknowledged everyone they passed with big, beautiful smiles. Outside, the church bells rang, and pictures were taken. They then got into a horse-drawn carriage and waved to everyone as they left.

The shuttles started to take the people back to the resort. On the way, Arietta explained to James that Rio and Gio were going to tour around the area for about thirty minutes to enjoy the moment and spend some time together and take in the scenery, but it also allowed her time to shuttle the guests back to the resort and be there before Rio and Gio arrived. They walked off the bus, and a hotel employee pointed them in the direction of the path leading to the cocktail reception and told them to follow the signs that read, "Aperitivo." They followed the signs, chatting about how beautiful the ceremony was. They made their final turn, and in front of them on the manicured lawn was a massive canvas tent. James's eyes widened in awe as they walked inside; the opposite side of the tent was open to the white sandy beach, the crystal blue water, and a magnificent view of the harbor and surrounding hillsides. Inside, there were several bars, and next to them were tables with fruit, cheese, crackers, vegetables, dips, olives, nuts, and shrimp; and walking amongst the guests were servers with trays of hors d'oeuvres. The round dining tables were covered in light blue linen and situated both inside and outside the tent. There were speakers all around playing soft, easy-listening music; high enough so you could hear it but low enough so you could talk.

"You planned the church?" James asked.

Arietta nodded.

"Rio and Gio's carriage ride?"

She nodded again, excitedly.

"And what part did you plan here?" he asked and inquisitively looked around. "Not the tent."

"No," she replied. "But they did want to keep it completely closed off, but I suggested they open this side up and put tables and chairs both inside and outside so people could either sit in the shade or out in the sun; either way everyone could enjoy the stunning view."

James smiled at her. "Multiple bars?"

"Me," she replied.

"Multiple tables of food?" he asked.

"Me, again," she said, "and I suggested light and refreshing finger foods. The hors d'oeuvres were Rio and Gio's idea. They wanted servers walking around to make sure guests were offered and served food, which I think is a very nice touch."

"Wow!" he said and put his arm around her and gave her a squeeze. "You have really done an amazing job."

She was so happy he was there. "It's not over yet," she said teasingly.

"What else?" he asked.

She walked away towards the bar and turned her head to him. "You will have to wait and see." She gave him a beautiful smile. "Are you coming?"

He followed her, and they ordered a rum and Coke, made a small plate of food, and sat at a table outside. The soft breeze caressed their faces as they talked and took in the view.

Twenty minutes later a voice came over the speakers, asking everyone outside to come inside for a moment. They stood up and went in. It was

Rocco on the microphone. "Ladies and gentlemen, please get ready to cheer, yell, scream and clap as loud as you can for Rio and Gio, fifty years to the day." Everyone erupted with loud cheers and clapping as the staff pulled away the tent door flaps, and Rio and Gio walked in. They moved through the large crowd, saying hello, shaking hands and kissing cheeks.

"They look so happy," said James.

"They do," agreed Arietta.

He whispered in her ear, "What you have done here today is a very big part of that."

"Thank you," she said, proudly smiling. "It looks like they are going to be busy for a while with family and friends."

"Then, may I escort you back to your seat," he said and opened up his arm.

"You may," she said and put her arm through his as they walked back to their table.

Throughout the afternoon they talked to the people they had met the night before but kept within close proximity of one another, neither of them knowing whether it was because they didn't want to be left on their own or be separated from one another. They never got the chance to talk to Rio and Gio, and several minutes after they had left, Rocco informed the guests that they had fifteen minutes to finish their drinks and head to the Grand Ballroom.

Arietta and James followed the paths and instructions of the staff to the ballroom. They looked at the seating chart and found their number and their table, then looked for their names on the place cards and took their seats; they were the first ones there. The table was beautifully draped in white linen, and the center pieces were bouquets of red ginger flowers and baby's breath. On each side plate was a rectangular box containing two truffles and scribed on the outside:

Resting against the wine glasses was a card bearing the same insignia and a thank you message and blessing from them both. Everyone had a personal menu in Italian residing in the middle of their place setting, also with the insignia. He looked at his name card; the insignia was there too. As James looked around the ballroom, he suddenly realized that this insignia was sporadically decorated throughout the room. Even the white wedding cake had it scribed over the three layers; it complimented the red ginger flowers, the white table linens and gave the ballroom a warm, romantic, tropical feel. What a great idea, he thought.

Once the tables filled, the servers came around and poured red or white wine.

"Ladies and gentlemen, the bridal party," announced Joey, Rio and Gio's younger son. Everyone clapped as the two couples walked in the room and took their seats at the head table. "Now, please stand and give a warm, loud welcome to Rio and Gio." The guests stood, clapped, and cheered, as they entered the room and sat at the head table. Then Joey asked the priest to come up and say a blessing before the meal.

The servers first brought out the antipasti, after the primo piatto, then sorbetto, then the secondo piatto with contorno, and finally, dolce. During the meal D-Mon played a mixture of classical music and dinner music, and the servers made sure your wine glass was never empty. After the final plates were cleared, the servers reappeared with bottles of Prosecco and started to fill everyone's flutes, leaving the half-empty bottles on the table.

Joey spoke. "Please stand and raise your glasses and join me in a toast to my parents, your family, your friends, Rio and Gio."

"To Rio and Gio," everyone replied and drank.

Joey continued. "Usually at this time, it is typical that several people stand up and give speeches; this is not so at a traditional Italian wedding." Several guests shouted out, "Evviva gli sposi!" which was met with a big laugh. Joey tried to contain his laughter. "Yes! Long live the newlyweds!"

Gio stood and helped up Rio. "Maybe not new, but young at heart!" replied Gio and gave his lovely bride a long kiss and embrace, which was met with loud cheers.

Joey continued. "Rio and Gio have told me not to talk too much because, and I quote, 'they want to get this party started!'" This was met with loud applause. "But before we do, they have asked for a little more patience and a few moments of your time so that they can say a few words." He turned to his parents, "Momma, Papa, please" and turned to the guests. "Rio and Gio." The crowd applauded.

"Thank you, Joey," said Gio. "As Joey has so eloquently mentioned, we do want to get this party started, but first Rio and I would like to say a few words…words of thanks…so please hold your applause to the end. We would like to thank the resort for putting on such a wonderful celebration. I know the rest of the evening will be as unforgettable as the beginning. We would like to thank Janice who helped coordinate the event and make it run like clockwork, and we would like to thank the staff, the servers, the cooks, and the DJ. But, most of all, we would like to thank you, our family, and friends, for being here and helping us celebrate this magical, wonderful, and memorable day." He put his arm around Rio, and they both said into the microphone, "thank you." The guests stood and clapped. Gio raised his arms to quieten them down. "There is one special person I would like to thank and for you all to recognize; she is very humble and asked that I didn't, but we would not sleep well tonight if we didn't acknowledge her now." Gio went back a couple of days and told his story, starting from his anxiety, to meeting her and up to today. "The shuttling of the guests, the full Catholic ceremony, the church, the horse-drawn carriage, the tent, the setup of the tables, the food tables and bars, the truffles and thank-you cards, Italian signs, the Italian menu, the traditional Italian meal, and Prosecco…Everything was perfect."

"Perfect, we are living a dream," added Rio. "Look at this," said Rio, pointing to the wedding cake, then pointed right at the Rio and Gio insignia on it. "This is all her idea…She told me it meant that Rio and Gio are together, inseparable, and are one. How appropriate, special, and beautiful is that?"

"Arietta, my angel, please stand and be acknowledged," said Gio.

Arietta stood up, and the guests applauded loudly.

"Come up here, my dear," said Rio. "Come up."

Arietta walked up to them, and they both gave her a long hug.

"You have given us one of best day of our lives, and me, my dream wedding," said Rio, as she started to cry.

"There, there, dear," comforted Gio as he wiped her eyes dry and looked at her. "I love you."

"I love you," she replied, and they kissed.

The crowd gave out a big, "aahhh."

Gio looked around at the crowd and then the DJ. "Let's get this party started, D-Mon!"

"We will, but before we do," replied D-Mon, "it's customary for the bride and groom to have the first dance, so Rio and Gio, please go to the middle of the dance floor, and ladies and gentlemen, please form a big circle around them."

Arietta took off behind the head table and headed back to James. She grabbed his hand, and they both joined the circle.

D-Mon waited, and satisfied everyone was in place, played their song.

Rio and Gio danced gracefully across the floor to Dean Martin's, 'That's Amore.' Everyone in the circle sang along to the chorus. The song ended, the crowd applauded, and Rio and Gio cried tears of joy. Their friends and family walked over and hugged them.

"I am DJ D-Mon, if you have any requests, please let me know, in the meantime…Rio and Gio! Let's get this party started!" and cranked a dance tune.

D-Mon played a mixture of hits from the fifties through to the eighties, and some current Top 40. He did all the wedding favorites like the Chicken Dance and one of the biggest hits of the night: the Macarena.

Arietta and James danced all night; they did dance with others but mostly with one another. Throughout the night, whether they were dancing, at their table, or at the bar, guests approached Arietta and complimented and congratulated her on a magnificent day and incredible night. James lost track of the number of kisses she received on the cheek.

An hour before Rio and Gio were scheduled to leave, the wedding cake was placed on a table. Rio and Gio cut the first two pieces and placed them on plates. The staff then cut up the remainder and put them on plates and placed them on the table for the guests to enjoy. Along with the cake, there was also a choice of cappuccino, espresso, coffee, or tea.

Arietta and James were sitting at their table, taking a rest from dancing when Rio and Gio came over and gave them each a slice of their wedding cake. They thanked Arietta again and told her how perfect the day had been. As Rio was talking to Arietta, Gio turned to James. "I'm glad you came."

"I received some good advice from a very wise man," he replied, complimenting Gio.

"That's very kind of you," said Gio. "I just opened the door, you walked in."

James looked at Gio and noticed something in his grin. "You knew I would come."

"If I were a betting man, I would have bet yes." Winking, he patted James on the back. "By the way, thank you for playing along last night; I have never laughed so hard." He leaned over, "Watch out for Nana!" he warned, then laughed out loud.

James laughed too.

Rio stood up next to Gio and they each kissed Arietta and James on the cheek, followed by a hug, then left to talk with other guests.

The night was winding down, and D-Mon told everyone to get on the dance floor for Rio and Gio's final song of the night. He played 'New York, New York' by Frank Sinatra, and the place went crazy. People were arm in arm and kicking up their legs. Towards the end of the song, Rio and Gio started to walk to the exit. Along the way, a staff member gave Rio her bouquet, and they waited for the song to end.

D-Mon asked that everyone clear the floor with the exception of the single women. Rio turned around and threw her bouquet over her head, then grabbed Gio's hand and walked slowly to the exit and listened. They heard Arietta's name being called aloud as she stood on the dance floor, holding the bouquet of orchids. Rio and Gio looked at one another and smiled, then quickly left.

James walked over and escorted Arietta off the dance floor and to their seats.

"I can't believe I caught it," she said.

"Well, taking out those four girls in front of you probably helped," joked James.

"Ha, ha, very funny," she said.

"To the catcher of the bouquet, cheers!"

"Cheers," she replied.

Throughout the night they sat, talked, and danced. The last song was announced, and it was a slow one. They got up and held each other remarkably close. When the song ended, they returned to their table to collect their belongings and wedding favors. A server approached and gave them a bottle of Prosecco, a corkscrew, and a flute each. "Compliments of Rio and Gio," he said. "They said you can't refuse." They smiled at one another, took the items, and said thank you to the server as they left the ballroom. Outside they walked past the pool and onto the beach. They took off their shoes and walked down the shoreline and away from the resort. Arietta stopped and looked up at all the stars.

"Wait right there," said James, put down the items on the sand, and took off. He came back with two chaises and set them up, then took off again and came back with a small table and placed it in between them. He picked up the items and placed them on the table. "If you want to watch the stars, we should be comfortable," he said and with a gesture of his hand, he offered her a chaise.

She curtsied. "Thank you, kind sir," she replied, as she took his hand and let him help her lay on one.

James sat and opened the Prosecco, pouring them each a glass. He passed one to her, then lay down on his chaise. They sipped on their drinks and pointed out the constellations.

Arietta turned to him. "This has been such a great night, a great day."

"It has," he replied. "You did an amazing job; you should be very proud."

"Thank you," she said and thought for a moment. "I am." She reached out her hand and touched his arm. "Thank you for being there for me and being a part of it."

"Thank you for asking me. I'm really glad I went."

She realized her hand was still resting on his arm and removed it. "I was a little nervous," she confessed.

"Really? I never noticed, and I'm sure no one else did either. You were very calm and collected…Very professional."

She smiled at him. "You say the kindest things." She looked up at the stars and talked about how beautiful they were. She commented on the gentle sounds of the waves and how relaxed it made her feel and the soft breeze, "so calming, comforting, and tranquil."

James agreed.

For a while they lay there in silence and let the Prosecco and the island seduce their senses. The bottle was empty, it was getting late, and Arietta was tired. They stood and picked up their items and walked to her patio. She opened the door and went inside and placed them on the floor and came back out. "I had a lovely time," she said and kissed him softly on the lips. "Thank you." She turned around and went inside, leaving the door open.

Chapter 11

Arietta woke up and looked at the time. "Ten," she said. She quickly dressed and went to the Market Deli to pick up something for herself and thought she would get something for James, too. She was looking at the selection when she felt someone standing closely behind her and turned around. "James!"

"Morning," he said. "What looks good?"

"The bacon, egg and cheese on a bagel," she replied. "I was going to pick up something for you and drop it off."

"I was thinking the exact same thing," he replied. "Maybe we can go somewhere and enjoy it together."

"I would like that," she said and ordered the bagels and coffees. They went to the pool area, sat at a table, and talked about yesterday. They finished their food and decided to meet in thirty minutes to go for a swim in the sea. They headed back to their rooms and were laughing about something when they noticed someone sitting on Arietta's porch. Arietta stopped laughing.

"Hi, Arie," said the voice.

Arietta was agitated. "What are you doing here?"

"I asked you to come home so we could talk, but since you weren't going to come and see me, I decided to come see you."

"You shouldn't have come. You shouldn't be here," she replied and nervously looked at James.

"I'm Graham," he said, standing; he walked over and shook James's hand.

"James," he replied.

Graham looked at him for a moment. "You look familiar to me," he said. "Have we ever met?"

"I don't believe so," replied James.

"Have you been on television?" Graham asked.

James let out a small laugh. "No."

"Guess you remind me of someone," he said and sat down again.

James looked over at Arietta. "I should leave you two alone." He looked over at Graham. "Nice meeting you."

"You too," he replied, still trying to figure out where he had seen his face before.

"I'll see you later," he said to Arietta and walked towards his room.

Arietta watched him walk for a bit, then turned to Graham in an angry voice. "I will be back to deal with you."

Graham made an exaggerated scared face as she left, but deep down he was.

"James," called Arietta.

He was just opening his door and turned to her. "You okay?" he asked.

"Yes," she replied with half a smile. "I'm not going to be able to make that swim and probably won't be around this afternoon or this evening either. I need to deal with Graham."

"That's fine," he said. "I understand."

She sadly walked away from him.

James went inside, changed, and left by the front door to take the long way to the beach just in case they were still on the porch. As he walked past the bar, he heard a voice calling his name in the distance. He looked around and eventually spotted Father Bartholomew waving his arm and walking towards him.

"James, I'm glad I saw you," he said. "I was hoping we could talk for a few minutes?"

"Of course," replied James.

"It's a very warm day today," he said, looking at the sun and wiping his forehead with a handkerchief.

"How about we get a shaded table and have that cold beer?" suggested James.

"That would be lovely," he replied. They both sat down and ordered. The beers arrived, and the priest took a big sip. "Ahh! That tastes smashing," he said and looked around. "This is a beautiful place."

"It is," agreed James.

Father Bartholomew looked at James. "I just wanted to thank you for coming to the church yesterday; it was nice to see you there."

"I wasn't sure I could go through with it at first," replied James.

The priest looked inquisitively at him. "May I ask what changed your mind?"

James told the priest what he told Gio and what Gio had told him about being thankful.

"I see," said the priest. "It all makes sense now." He sat back and looked at James. "Small steps sometimes are the best ones."

"I believe so," agreed James.

He looked thoughtfully at James and said, "I do confessions on Saturday or by appointment if you like," then gave him a smile.

James smiled back at the priest. "You're referring to me not taking communion," indicated James.

The priest's smile got wider, and they both laughed.

"Maybe," said James.

"I will take that," said the priest and drank some of his beer. "I also want to thank you for helping Mary out with the children and moving them to the Market Square; we raised almost a thousand dollars that day. We are going back there this weekend." He leaned toward James. "Me, Mary's and the children's spirits are soaring as high as the clouds." He then reached into his pocket and pulled out a thick envelope and whispered, "This is between you and me."

James nodded.

"Rio and Gio gave me all the money they received yesterday from their guests at the reception and the money they raised the night before, almost twelve thousand dollars," said the priest with a look of disbelief. "Gio owns a construction company in New York and is going to send several of his top men to oversee the new roof."

"That is great news," said James.

"It is," replied the priest. "It is…sometimes the Lord moves in mysterious ways." He patted James on the shoulder and drank his beer. "I must go now and start to make arrangements for ordering the materials." He shook James's hand, thanked him again and walked away, then turned around and cautioned him, "James, watch out for Nana!" he said, bursting into laughter.

Gio, James thought as he shook his head, laughing.

The priest walked down the path, and James could still hear him laughing.

James went to the beach, noticing Caleigh and Cheryl; he joined them.

Arietta walked back to her porch. "Why are you here?"

"You can't run here and stick your head in the sand," he stated. "We need to talk."

"I told you we would talk when I was ready." She walked towards him. "Get off my porch and get off this resort."

He stood up. "I will leave your porch but not this island."

"You better not be staying here," she said furiously.

"Relax, I'm staying a few resorts away…you know…to give you your space," he said, trying to make a joke. But she wasn't laughing; instead, he saw something in her face that he hadn't seen before.

Arietta couldn't take it anymore. She had tried her best to hold them back, but couldn't, and started to cry.

"Arie, I'm sorry. I…I…didn't want to upset you like this."

"Just go," she said. "Just leave me alone." She went into her room, locking the door behind her.

Graham had never seen her like this and was worried. He left and went back to his resort.

Arietta lay on her bed and cried for an exceptionally long time. She was scared. She knew what she had to do but wasn't sure whether or not she had the strength to go through with it.

A few hours later, Graham called her on the phone and asked for a truce. He suggested they have dinner tonight and go out like they used to, with no business talk.

She was hesitant. "No business," she reconfirmed.

"Promise," he replied. "Everything but."

She agreed to meet him at five at the Terrace Restaurant.

James made a sandcastle with Caleigh and Cheryl and listened as they talked about their mother-and-daughter day.

"We went to the Market Square and we each bought a straw hat," said Caleigh. "They are very cute."

"Then we bought bikinis," said Cheryl.

"We're wearing them," added Caleigh and showed hers off. "Then we went and walked around the shops for a while, and I got some island jewelry."

"We had lunch at a casual restaurant overlooking the harbor, and it was so beautiful," said Cheryl. "The burgers were amazing."

"After lunch we went sightseeing and climbed the ninety-nine steps," said Caleigh with a frown. "There are actually a hundred and three! When we arrived at the top, we went to Blackbeard's Castle, and I had my picture taken in the stockyard…then…" She tried to remember.

"We went to the Emancipation Gardens," said Cheryl.

"Yes, we went to the gardens, they were so pretty. There was a post office there and other government buildings, and they were all so colorful and cute," she said cheerfully.

"We then took a taxi to Frenchtown and had dinner on the patio and watched all the people going by," explained Cheryl, "and the sun faded, and the stars appeared; it was magical."

"Sounds like you guys had an awesome mother-and-daughter day," said James, looking at them.

"It was," said Caleigh, looking at her mom. "We had so much fun."

"Best day ever," her mom replied.

It was getting late, and time to go. Caleigh asked if she could go for a quick swim in the pool, which Cheryl agreed to. They left the beach and watched Caleigh run ahead and jump in.

"Are you doing anything tonight?" asked Cheryl.

"No, no plans," replied James.

"Caleigh has a movie night at the Kids Club, and they are having a sleepover, you know, to give the parents a free night…There is a Sunset Cruise Party, and I was wondering if you would like to join me?"

"That would be wonderful," replied James.

"They have hors d'oeuvres, a buffet and an open bar on board, and I have already bought the tickets, so you can't run off and buy them," she said, playfully poking him in the side.

"You have bought them already?" he asked.

Cheryl realized what she had said and blushed. "Well, we talked about getting together today, and I was really hoping you would come."

"I'm teasing you," he replied and tickled her side, which made her jump a little and give out a small scream.

She nudged him good-humoredly. "Meet me on my patio around five."

Chapter 12

When Arietta arrived at the restaurant, Graham was already there. She walked over to him, pulled out her chair, and sat. The waiter came over, and she ordered a rum and Coke.

"This is a nice place," said Graham.

"It is," she replied.

"What have you been doing here?" he asked.

She told him about the welcome reception, trip to Charlotte Amalie, and Rio and Gio's ceremony and reception, purposely leaving out the part she played.

"Wow! That sounds like a beautiful reception," he said approvingly. "Fifty years? Don't see that these days."

"No," replied Arietta. "Nice to know it still exists."

"Who is James?" he asked curiously.

"A friend," she replied. "We met here."

"He seems like a nice guy."

"He's a really nice guy, very kind and thoughtful," she replied. "He was a lot of fun at the reception."

"Was he married? Kids?" he inquired.

"I don't know but I know he loves children."

"You don't know?"

"We don't talk about that stuff," she said. "We don't talk about the lives we left behind; we are enjoying the present, the here and now."

"But one day your lives catch up to you, and you have to deal with it," he said honestly.

She gave him a disapproving look. "Do you have to ruin it?" she asked.

He realized what he said and wished he could take it back. "I'm sorry."

She couldn't be too upset with him because he was right; his being here was proof of that.

Graham changed the subject. "What does he do?"

Arietta just smiled back.

"Okay, I got it, you don't know, and I'm guessing he doesn't know who you are or what you do either," he said. "Well, I won't say anything, promise."

"Thank you." She reached out and squeezed his hand; one thing she knew was that he had always kept his promises. She let go and looked down at the pool, and on the pathway, walking towards them, was James. Her first instinct was to stand up and call him, but she caught herself just in time.

"You know, I swear I have seen him before; his face is familiar," said Graham as he looked at what had caught her eye, "but I can't put my finger on where."

"Really?" she asked as she looked at him. She knew Graham was exceptionally good with faces.

"Maybe I'm confusing him with someone else," he said, although in his mind he didn't think so. "So, Arietta, how have you been doing?"

She wanted to tell him the whole truth, but she wasn't ready. "I've been doing well. This place is relaxing," she said, looking around and down by the pool. "It's a…" All of a sudden, she saw James and Cheryl walking out from behind the palm tree by Cheryl's patio. She waited to see Caleigh, but she never came out, and realized she wasn't with them. She watched as they headed towards the bar, then passed it, and out towards the dock.

Graham was looking at her and assuming she was thinking of the words to finish her sentence. "It's a…" he said.

Arietta's attention came back to the table, and she turned to Graham. "Oh," she said. "It's a nice escape."

"It sure is," he said. "I can see how one can forget about life for a while here."

"You should bring Violet here," she said.

Graham almost choked on his drink. "What?" unsure he had actually heard those words come out of her mouth.

"Just saying, maybe you should." Although he may not have believed her, she was being quite sincere.

Graham looked at her. In the time she had known Violet, Arietta had never mentioned her; he was caught off guard.

"How is she doing these days?" she asked, interested.

He looked at Arietta and wasn't sure if she was messing with him to get back at him for showing up or being genuine, but something in her eyes told him it was the latter. "You okay?" he asked.

"Never been better," she said and knew she had unintentionally thrown him into a panic. "So, tell me what you two have been up to?"

Graham was happy that she had asked and was genuinely interested, so he let his guard down, and throughout dinner and dessert talked about himself and Violet; he liked that Arietta had joined in by asking him questions and laughing. They left the restaurant, and he walked Arietta to her door. "I must admit, Arie, this place is agreeing with you."

She was happy that he had noticed.

"We need to talk, soon," he said.

"I know," she replied.

"I'm going back to New York tomorrow, it will give you some more time on your own," he said, looking around, then back at her. "I will wait for you to call me."

"Thank you," she said. "I will." She gave him a hug and a kiss on the cheek.

"Arie, I didn't just come here to talk about business; I came because I was worried about you," he said truthfully.

"I know that now," she said, "and it means a lot that you did. I'm glad that we got to spend time together tonight."

"Me too, it was a lot of fun, and it reminded me of the old days," he said as he thought back. "Goodnight, Arie," he said and walked away, then turned around. "Thanks for asking about Violet."

She smiled at him.

"You know I'm in love with her," he confessed.

"I know," she replied. But business is business, she thought and watched him turn and walk away. "Graham." He turned around. "I'll call you tomorrow with a day to meet, promise."

He smiled, gave her a wave, and continued down the path. He stopped by the pool and looked back in the direction of Arietta's room and realized she was different; she was more like the Arietta he once knew.

Arietta went into her room and decided she would go for a dip in the pool. She changed into her bikini and swam for an hour. She thought about James and Cheryl and wondered where they had gone and where Caleigh was. She stopped by the front desk and was informed about the movie night and sleepover at the Kids Club and the adults-only Sunset Cruise Party. She left and walked past the bar; they had a live band playing and it was busy. She thought about getting ready and coming back but decided on an early night instead. She changed into her pajamas, poured a glass of wine, and went outside. She lay on the chaise and looked out at the sea and at the stars in the sky.

James walked down the path and around the bend towards Cheryl's room. He looked up at the palm trees and something caught his eye; he noticed Arietta and Graham at the restaurant. She was smiling and reaching over and holding his hand. He quickly looked away to give them their privacy. He arrived at Cheryl's patio, and she was sitting, waiting.

"Here," she handed him a glass of wine, "we have a few minutes before we have to board." She looked up at him. "You look very handsome."

"Thank you," he said and helped her up from her chair. She was wearing a striking low-cut, black dress. "You look stunning!"

"Thank you," she replied.

"How is Caleigh?"

"She is over the moon. She is so excited about tonight! She had her pajamas on an hour before she had to be there," she said and laughed. "There were over twenty kids, so I'm sure they will have a fun time."

"Most definitely," said James. "As will we."

"I know, this is going to be so much fun, and it's a perfect evening."

They finished their drinks, walked to the dock, and boarded. They ordered a glass of champagne and stayed on the main deck at the front of the boat. There was a good-sized crowd, mostly couples. The music was soft, light, and played gently through the speakers. The last passengers boarded, and the boat left the dock. They decided to get something to eat and went down to the lower deck to pick out some food and ate it quickly, then grabbed another glass of champagne and went back up to the main deck to admire the view. The boat sailed down Pillsbury Sound. They were surrounded by the cays to the north, St. Thomas to the west and St. John to the east; the scene was magnificent.

"This is absolutely gorgeous," cooed Cheryl.

James looked at the setting sun's rays softly caressing her beautiful face and the gentle breeze blowing against her body and pushing her dress, revealing her sexy outline and her hard nipples. She was an alluring and seductive sight to behold. "It is," he replied.

She drank her champagne and looked at him. "James, how come you never talk about yourself?"

"I guess I like my privacy," he replied.

"Okay," she said and was going to leave it at that.

He felt very awkward talking about his past but felt bad because she had been so open with him. "If you want you can ask me."

"Are you sure? I don't want to intrude."

"You're not," he said with a reassuring smile.

She turned and rested her body on the railing. "Have you ever been married?"

"Once, twelve years ago, for five years. I've been on my own for the last seven," he replied.

"Do you have any children?"

"No."

"Why have you stayed single for so long?"

"When my wife left, it was very difficult and painful for me; I guess I never want to feel that pain again. So, I decided to stay on my own," he said. "I guess I stopped believing in lots of things."

"Like what?"

"My wife and I were Catholics, so I gave up on my religion, my faith."

"Really?" She paused for a second. "Do you think you will ever find them again?"

He let out a nervous laugh. "If you had asked me that last week, I would have said no without hesitation, but things have happened this week that have made me question myself and opened me up to do some things I thought I never would."

Her interest was heightened. "Such as?"

"Yesterday I went inside a church for Rio and Gio's ceremony. It's the first time I have stepped foot in one in seven years."

"What made you change your mind?"

He told her about Gio telling him to be thankful for the good things.

"Be thankful for the good things," she repeated and looked off into the distance. "When Caleigh was sick, I almost gave up on my faith. I had asked myself too many times, how God can hurt such a young, innocent little girl?"

"What stopped you?" he asked curiously. "Was it because she started to get better?"

"No, it was actually when Caleigh was at her worst. She was really sick and weak. She looked up at me and whispered, 'Mom, if you don't believe, you won't go to Heaven, and if you don't go to Heaven, I will never see you there.' I held her close and cried. And since that day, every night before she goes to sleep, we both say our prayers." She thought for a moment. "When I think back, she must have heard me blaming Him."

"It all worked out in the end," said James, comforting her.

"Yes, it did," said Cheryl as she looked at James, "and I am thankful for every day I see her." She looked at the sea and wasn't sure whether to ask or not, but he did say it was okay. "Do you ever think you will fall in love again?"

He followed her gaze out to sea. "I don't know."

"What happens if you met the right person? You know, someone who understands what you went through and would never leave you?"

"There's no guarantee to that," he said, challenging her.

"I guess nothing in life is a guarantee," she replied. "But it's kind of sad to live in fear of it and never take that chance."

He went quiet.

She realized she probably had asked him enough questions and changed the subject. "My champagne is empty, another drink?"

"Yeah," he replied, and they walked over to the bar.

"I'm done with champagne; I need a beer," she suggested.

"Beer sounds good," confirmed James.

They ordered a beer and went back to their spot. The sun was starting to melt on the horizon, and it was a spectacular sight. She moved in close to him. She knew they were friends but was hoping he would put his arm around her, which he did. Together they watched the sun disappear and the night appear; the stars materializing one by one.

The soft music was turned off, and a voice spoke. "Ladies and gentlemen, the sun has gone so let the party begin!" Everyone shouted loudly. The DJ cranked the music, and everyone danced on the main deck under the star-filled sky.

Cheryl pulled James up to the dance floor. They danced and drank all night and only stopped to cool off. A couple of hours later, the ship started to head back to the dock, and they stood and watched as St. John grew bigger.

"Thank you for coming," she said. "I had a great time."

"It was a fun night," he replied. "Thanks for inviting me."

"You know, it's only nine thirty!" she said in a festive voice. "The night's still young!"

"What do you want to do?" he asked enthusiastically.

"I can hear live music at the resort beach bar; that's where we are going," she confirmed.

They disembarked and walked to the bar and found a seat. Most of the people from the cruise started wandering in, and in no time, it was packed; the party began again. They danced and drank until the bar closed and were a little drunk as they walked to Cheryl's room.

"Want to come in for a night cap," she asked. "Caleigh is getting dropped off at ten tomorrow, and I want to make the most of my free night."

"I'll come in for one," he said, following her inside.

She poured the drinks and gave one to James. He sat down in the armchair while she sat on the bed. "I almost forgot. I saw Arietta today with some guy I've never seen before. I was taking Caleigh to the Kids Club around five, and I looked up at the restaurant, and she was sitting down next to this guy. Do you know who he is?"

James told her about the conversation he had overheard a few days ago and what had happened earlier on today.

"You think that's her husband or boyfriend?" she asked.

"I don't know, but I'm guessing one or the other."

"From what you heard, it sounds like they are going through a divorce or separation," she stated.

"Sounds that way. Looks like she is the one who is leaving," he suggested. "It seems to me he wants to talk about it."

"That's too bad she is going through that." She took a sip of her drink. "Although she seems to be managing it well, I mean with taking on the planning for the ceremony and birthday party," said Cheryl.

"Maybe she is doing that to keep herself occupied and her mind off of it," suggested James.

"You're probably right," confirmed Cheryl. "Poor girl, I would like her to know she can talk to me, but I wouldn't want her to know we had been talking about her." She thought for a moment. "It's probably best to wait until she brings it up."

"That may be best," agreed James. "I think if she wanted to talk about it, she would."

"Maybe tomorrow I will do something with her and see if she opens up at all."

"That's a good idea," said James.

"It is," she said. "I just need to figure out what we could do?" Cheryl thought for a moment. Then she looked at James. "Would you mind if I changed out of this dress?"

"No, go ahead, get comfortable," he said.

She went to her drawer, pulled something out and went into the bathroom. She came out minutes later, wearing pajama shorts and a tank top. "That's better," she said.

James looked at her breasts and her hard nipples poking through her tank top. Her legs were long and shapely. She was a beautiful and sexy woman.

"Can you hold me for a minute before you go?" she asked, and before he could answer, she lowered the light and sat on his lap.

James put his arm around her as she lay on his chest. They were quiet for a few minutes. She lifted her head up to his and kissed him on the cheek. "I really like you," she whispered, then snuggled back into his chest, and within a few minutes she was sound asleep. James let her sleep for a while, then picked her up and gently placed her on the bed and put the sheets and comforter over her.

Chapter 13

The early night had done Arietta good; she was up at eight and full of energy. She showered and dressed, then thought about calling James. It was only nine, so she decided against it. She went for a long walk along the beach and around the resort, then took the stairs to the Terrace Restaurant and picked a table overlooking the pool. She filled her plate at the breakfast buffet and went back to her seat. As she ate, she noticed she could see Cheryl's patio in between the palm trees. A few people from Rio and Gio's ceremony dropped by to say hello and informed her that Rio and Gio had left for a week-long honeymoon in the British Virgin Islands taking their family and close friends with them. Saying goodbye, the small group left for the beach. Arietta went back to finishing her food when out of the corner of her eye she saw Cheryl walking out in a robe to sit on her patio chair. She was drinking a cup of coffee, and it looked like she was talking to someone inside her room. She then noticed Cheryl turn to speak to the person walking out. Arietta couldn't tell who it was; the palm trees were in the way. She held her breath…It was Caleigh. Arietta let out a sigh of relief, quickly finished her breakfast and went down to see them.

"Good morning."

"Arietta," shouted Caleigh who ran over and gave her a big hug. "I had so much fun last night. I watched a movie with all my friends, and we had a sleepover. I just got back at ten." She looked over at her mom. "She was still in bed sleeping."

Arietta looked at Cheryl who looked a little hungover and tired. "Did you have a good night?"

"It was amazing and so much fun. I haven't laughed and danced like that in a long time. James is such a great guy, and it was so nice of him to go with me. It would have been awkward going on my own, especially with most of the people being couples." She told her about the cruise, the food, the sunset, and the beach bar.

Arietta now wished she had gone to the bar last night. "Wow! That sounds like a lot of fun."

"It was," said Cheryl. "What are your plans today?"

"Nothing special, I have to make a ten-minute phone call but that's about it."

"I thought maybe all three of us could go to the spa and get our nails done and a massage. What do you think?"

"I would love that!" replied Arietta. "What time?"

"I'll call them now," said Cheryl and stood up, noticing Caleigh had a sad face. "What's wrong, Caleigh?"

"I don't really want to go to the spa. I want to do something that's fun," she replied.

Cheryl looked over at Arietta.

"How about we see what James is doing, and maybe you can do something with him?" suggested Arietta.

Caleigh's face lit up, and she headed to the room.

"Where are you going?" asked her mom.

"Really, Mom," she said, giving her mom 'a look.' "To call James," she replied and went inside.

Cheryl looked at Arietta, and they laughed. "She reminds me of myself when I was younger," said Cheryl.

"And she looks so much like you. Boys are going to be banging down your door when she gets older," commented Arietta.

"Don't remind me," she said. "I don't know how my parents put up with me!"

"Mine too," added Arietta.

Caleigh came back with a smile on her face. "My date is coming to get me in an hour; we are going snorkeling," she said and turned to walk back in.

"Where are you going now?" asked her mom.

"To get ready, silly."

Cheryl and Arietta laughed out loud. "Let me call the spa. I'll be back in a minute."

Arietta looked over at the pool. She was a little upset she had missed the cruise and the bar last night.

"Eleven thirty," said Cheryl as she walked towards her.

"Okay, I need to go make that call and will be back around eleven fifteen," she said and went to her room. She called Graham and agreed to meet him on Monday. Graham was surprised but glad; he wanted this meeting sooner rather than later. She then called James and asked him if he wanted to walk with her to Cheryl's and agreed to meet him outside her front door at eleven fifteen.

"Heard the cruise was a lot of fun," she said as she closed the door behind her.

"It was we had a great time," replied James. "I hear you two are off to the spa?"

"Yes, it's going to be wonderful!" she said, and told him about all the treatments they offered as they walked to Cheryl's patio.

"James!" said Caleigh excitedly, jumping up and running to him. "I'm packed and ready to go."

"How did you sleep last night?" asked Cheryl.

"Not bad, was a little tired this morning though," he confessed.

"So was I," she replied.

"Okay, Miss," he said, looking at Caleigh, "let's go see some tropical fish." She held his hand as they started to leave. "We will see you back here around three," he said as they walked away.

"See you then," replied Cheryl. They watched them walk out of sight. Cheryl turned to Arietta. "Spa!"

"Spa!" replied Arietta.

When they arrived at the spa, they gave their names and were taken to a change room, then into the massage room. Cheryl had booked a room with two beds, so they could talk. They lay on their stomachs and looked at one another.

"This is going to be incredible," said Arietta as the massage began. "Oh, before I forget, all the stuff arrived for Caleigh's party, and everything is set to go."

"She is going to love it, and if it's anywhere close to the ceremony you planned, it's going to be amazing and a day she will remember forever," Cheryl replied happily.

"I can't wait either; it's going to be incredible!" She hesitated for a moment, not knowing whether or not to ask, but it was just the two of them, and it was a girls' day out, so she thought, why not? "What did you guys talk about last night?"

"Well," replied Cheryl, thinking, "James told me about the wedding, and how much fun it was, and how you had planned it perfectly."

"He did?" she asked and was happy to hear he had talked about her.

"Yes, he told me it was unbelievable," she replied, thinking it may open her up. "Then he said I could ask him questions about his life, you know, personal ones."

"Really," she said enthusiastically. "So, tell me!"

"He told me he got married twelve years ago and was married for five, and that she left him, and it seems like he took it extremely hard. He said he is single because he doesn't want to go through all that pain again. I asked him if he would ever fall in love again, and he said he didn't know. So, I asked him, what if the right person came along? Someone who understood what he went through and was guaranteed to be there for him and never leave."

"What did he say?" asked Arietta, wanting to know the answer.

"He said there were no guarantees."

"Oh," she said, a little disappointed.

"He also said he lost his faith and blamed God for her leaving, and that he has never entered a church since the day she left." Then Cheryl remembered. "Well, until now, until the ceremony." Cheryl then proceeded to tell Arietta about going through a similar experience with Caleigh when she was very sick.

"I can see questioning your faith when you're facing losing your child but over your wife leaving you seems odd. I mean, lots of people are divorced these days, and I'm sure they don't all walk away from their faith. You would think it would be stronger than that one person."

"I know what you mean. I found that a little strange, too."

Arietta thought. "Maybe he really loved her, and she did something bad like fooled around on him."

"Maybe he caught her in their bed or something," added Cheryl. "That could push someone over the edge."

"Yeah, maybe," said Arietta but something didn't seem right.

"I guess separation affects everyone differently," probed Cheryl.

"I guess so. Hopefully, he had his family's support during that time. They are the only ones you can count on and can give you the advice you need. Friends are good in all, but they always take your side and want you to rake the ex over the coals, so you're best to keep them out of it."

On that note Cheryl realized that Arietta wasn't going to open up to her and changed the subject talking instead about clothes, hairstyles, and the resort. After the massage, they had a manicure and pedicure, then ended their day with an afternoon tea and quaint sandwiches in a charming garden, before heading back to Cheryl's patio to wait for Caleigh and James.

"Mom, Mom," called Caleigh from a table by the pool. "We're over here," she said, waving and pointing to James sitting next to her.

Cheryl and Arietta walked over to them and sat down.

"What are you eating?" Cheryl asked her.

"It's a brownie sundae; it has vanilla ice cream, brownies, chocolate sauce, whipped cream and sprinkles," she explained before taking a mouthful and swallowing. "It is so yummy…it's to die for," she said, looking over at James as they both broke out in laughter.

Cheryl and Arietta laughed too.

"An inside joke," stated Cheryl. "How was your afternoon?"

"We had sooo much fun! We took a taxi to Trunk Bay which is in the Virgin Islands National Park; did you know that?"

The women both shook their head and said, "No."

"It is and it's the 'Jewel of the Virgin Islands,'" she said, happy with herself. "It has lifeguards, snack bars, a beach, and beautiful clear blue water. So we got our snorkeling stuff," she stopped and had a mouthful of her sundae, "and James helped me put it on, and we went into the water. Guess what they have?"

"What?" they asked her.

"An underwater trail you can follow. It was so cool. We saw parrot fish, sea turtles, coral, and French…" She looked at James.

"Grunts," he said.

"Grunts," she repeated, "and…"

"Tangs and wrasses," he added.

"Tangs and wrasses," she said. "It was so awesome." She went back to her sundae.

"Tell them how you held your breath," said James.

"I almost forgot. I held my breath and dived deep into the water and swam with the fish. It was like I was one of them," she said cheerfully.

"Wow!" said Arietta. "That would have been something to see. I'm going to have to give that a try."

Caleigh nodded her head. "You should," she replied, finishing off her ice cream. "Make sure you go to the snack bar and ask the guy how everything is because all he says is…" She looked at James and together they said, "It's to die for," and broke into laughter. "So we had burgers, fries, and Cokes."

"And, was it to die for?" asked her mom.

"It was!" said Caleigh and laughed. "Then we decided to come back here and have dessert by the pool, well, dessert for me."

"Your mom said you received all your invitations back, and everyone is coming," said Arietta.

"I did. I'm so excited, and I can't wait! It's going to be fabulous! I can't believe it's tomorrow!"

"Yes, it is," said Cheryl. "That means it's an early night tonight…swim, television, and then bed."

"I know," replied Caleigh.

"Well, I should probably get back to my room," said Arietta, standing up. "I may have a quiet night myself."

"I'll walk with you," said James. "I could do with a little siesta." He stood up and pointed. "Her bag is on the chair, and we got an underwater camera; it's in the bag."

"I forgot about that, Mom. I can show you the pictures tonight," said Caleigh excitedly. "We can look at them on my tablet."

"I can't wait to see them," said Cheryl enthusiastically, smiling at her daughter.

Arietta looked at Cheryl. "That was wonderful today, just what I needed. Thanks for inviting me."

"It's what we both needed, and I'm glad you came," said Cheryl and turned to James. "Thanks for watching her and giving her a fantastic day."

"It was my pleasure." He looked down at Caleigh. "Anytime, right!"

"Right!" she replied and stood to give him a hug. "Thank you." She walked over and gave Arietta one. "Maybe we can spend some time together?"

"I would love that," said Arietta.

"Pinkie promise," said Caleigh, and they entwined pinkies and shook them.

Arietta and James said goodbye and walked back to their room.

"What you going to do tonight?" asked Arietta.

"Maybe put my feet up and take it easy."

"Do you want to do something with me?" she asked. "Something relaxing."

"That would be nice," he replied. "What do you have in mind?"

"I don't know now, but I'm sure I will come up with something good," she said.

"I forgot," he said, smiling. "I am with the 'Queen of Planning.'" He bowed his head. "I place myself in your capable hand."

"Well, thank you," she said playfully. "Call me after you had your siesta, and I will give you further instructions."

"Give me sixty minutes," he confirmed.

Chapter 14

He walked over to her patio, and Arietta was waiting for him. She handed him a glass of wine. She was casually dressed, with a New York T-shirt, shorts, and sandals, and, as per her instructions, so was he in a NYU T-shirt, shorts, and deck shoes. He looked over at the table and smiled; she had covered it with a Statue of Liberty beach towel, and on top were two place settings.

"Cheers," he said and took a sip of his wine.

"Come inside," she said, grabbing his hand and taking him into her room. "I want to make sure I hear the front door."

He sat on the bed, and she sat next to him.

"How was your nap?" she asked.

"It was just what I needed. Soon as I hit the pillow it was lights out; I'm glad I put my alarm on."

"Or else, I would have come knocking at your door." As she said that, there was a knock on hers. She opened it; the hotel staff wheeled in the cart. "Please put it over there by the patio door," she said and gave him a tip as he left. She walked over to the cart and picked up the Caesar salads, carried them outside and placed them on the table, sticking her head inside. "Come on." James followed her out, and they ate. She took the dirty plates inside and came back out. "Main course," she said. "New York strip, potato gratin, and green beans." She placed the plate in front of him. "I noticed someone eating it in the restaurant last night and thought, I just have to try that." She cut a piece of the steak and put it in her mouth. "Oh, this is so good! It melts in your mouth!"

"It's so delicious," said James. "I can never get mine to taste this good."

"Do you cook at home?" she asked.

"Most of the time," he replied. "I enjoy cooking."

"Same here, I love to cook," she said. "If we would have been in Manhattan, I would have had you over and cooked you an unbelievable meal," she revealed and sipped on her wine.

"I will have to take you up on that offer one day."

"Consider it an open invite," and took a bite of her food. "My mom and dad love to cook, and it's like a competition between them to see who can outdo the other. I learnt everything from them. My dad always says, 'good company and good food, is good for the soul.'"

She was so carefree with her hair tied back in a ponytail, no makeup and casual attire but strikingly beautiful and natural, thought James. He was glad she could be this way around him. "Here is to good company and good food," he said, raising his glass and touching hers. He took a drink and watched her do the same.

"That was a pleasure for the senses," she said, smiling.

James stood up to take the plates.

"No, no, you sit down, my night, you're my guest." She took the plates inside and came out with two cups of coffee. "We will have dessert in a few minutes." She placed the coffee on the table and went inside to grab the cream and sugar and came back out.

James told her about bumping into Father Bartholomew and how he had just come from seeing Rio and Gio about the money they had given him, and how Gio was going to send some of his best men down to oversee the replacing of the roof.

"That is so great! It's so nice of him to send men down to help. I heard Gio owned a big construction company in New York, and that his sons run the business now." She grinned at James. "Now for the best part, dessert!" She went inside and came out with a plate that was covered to hide the contents. "This is for us both to share, and I thought since we both live in Manhattan, I would ask the kitchen to make us a taste from home." She lifted the cover. "Tarte Tatin for two!"

"Wow, this looks incredible," said James. "You know, I have been craving this." Then he gave her a puzzled look. "How did you know I live in Manhattan? And how did you know I love this dessert?"

She gave him a mischievous smile. "It's my job to know these things, how else could I plan," she said and gave him a wink. "Let's dig in."

It was devoured in no time.

"That was delectable," said Arietta.

"It was," agreed James.

"I am so full."

"I know what you mean," said James as he reached down with his hand and patted his stomach.

She looked over his shoulder. "Do you want to go for a stroll on the beach and walk it off?"

"Love to," he replied.

"First, let me clean this table off," she said, putting everything on the cart and then pushing it outside the front door. She came back out onto the patio. "Okay, let's go."

They took off their shoes and walked along the beach away from the resort.

"How did you know I live in Manhattan?" he asked curiously.

"I can't reveal my secrets or my sources," she said jokingly. She put her arm through his. "Unfortunately, it is not as clever or sinister as it sounds," she said. "I saw the airline code, JFK, on your luggage and made an educated guess."

"Well, you are very astute and very clever…And the dessert?"

"That was more of a given. I figured anyone living in Manhattan must have tried the tarte Tatin at Gotham's at least once, if not five or ten times!"

"I think I'm past the ten-mark!" he said.

"Add me to that list," she confessed and laughed. "This is such a beautiful place; I love it here. How long are you here for?"

"I am here for another eleven days."

"Good," she replied, squeezing his arm. "Me too."

"My family is coming here for a week," revealed James.

"They are?" she asked, interested. "Who?"

"My brother, his wife and daughter…and my sister, her husband and daughter. They both have sons, but they are travelling together in Europe, backpack thing."

"Is your family staying here?" she asked.

"No, they are staying in Charlotte Amalie. A group of my niece's friends will be here too. They all graduated this year and they're all here to celebrate; plus, it's my niece's birthday this month so it's a double celebration for her, well, party."

"When do they arrive?"

"Friday, the party is on Saturday in Charlotte Amalie." He went quiet for a moment and looked at her. "If you're not doing anything Saturday night, you're more than welcome to come."

She smiled. "I would like that, and I would love to meet them…and party!"

"Oh, trust me, with my niece and her friends, you won't be disappointed."

"Sounds like it will be fun." She was delighted that he had asked her.

They turned around and walked back, letting the warm water gently brush against their legs.

James stopped and turned to her; he had something on his mind.

"You okay?" she asked.

"Can I ask you something? It's actually a favor," he said, looking into her eyes.

"Anything," she said. "All you have to do is ask."

"When I was talking to Father Bartholomew, he asked me about going to him for confession, so I've been thinking about it and was wondering, actually hoping, if I did go would you come with me?"

"Of course, I will," she said without hesitation. "When were you thinking about going?"

"I'm not sure yet, maybe sometime next week."

"Once you have it figured out, let me know."

"I will."

She put her arm through his again, and they continued to walk. They arrived back on her patio and wiped the sand off their feet and went inside. She pulled the duvet down and stacked a few pillows on either side of the king-size bed. "These beds are so big you can get lost in them," she said and looked at James. "I thought we would watch a movie?"

"That sounds great."

"Now…you can lie on one side, and I can lie on the other, or if you're uncomfortable about sharing the bed, you can pull the armchair over here, sit on that and put your feet up on the bed."

"The bed is fine."

She put the television on, and they picked out a movie. She turned off the lights and lay next to him.

As the movie started, James reached down and pulled the comforter over them both.

"Thank you," she whispered. "I was getting a little chilly."

The next morning, she woke up and James was gone. He had left a note on the pillow:

> *Arietta,*
> *Thanks for the lovely evening,*
> *James*
> *P.S. You snore!*

She laughed at it and got up.

Chapter 15

Arietta walked out her front door, holding the birthday present and waited for James.

"Sleep well?" he asked.

"I'm so sorry for falling asleep on you so quickly," she said apologetically. "I couldn't keep my eyes open."

"No need to apologize. I was falling asleep, and I figured I better go before I did," he said. "Besides, your snoring kept waking me up."

"Aren't you funny, I don't snore," she said and swung the present, hitting him in the stomach.

"Ouch," he said, being over dramatic and grabbing his abdomen.

"Oh, please," she said and laughed.

He mimicked her snoring.

She laughed louder. "Will you stop…you make me sound like a pig snorting."

They walked to the same area where Rio and Gio had their cocktail reception. There was a tent set up, and it was half the size and open on three sides. They went inside, and James looked around. The side that was covered had three long tables, one for the gifts; the second had chips, cheese puffs, pretzels, vegetables, fruits, cheeses, and dips; and the third had plates, napkins, ketchup, mustard, sliced pickles, lettuce, tomatoes, onions, and several salads. Next to the tables was a drink dispenser that was set up to serve pop, juice, and water. The round dining tables were set up inside and outside and were covered in pink and purple linens, the center pieces were a bouquet of balloons. Around the tent were birthday decorations and a big sign that read 'Happy 12th Birthday Caleigh.' Arietta took James outside. In between the tent and the beach were two big barbeques cooking food.

"Hot dogs, hamburgers for the kids, steak, and chicken for the adults," said Arietta. She took him to a table, and in front of every seat was an itinerary listing the party activities and where they would be taking place. "Look over there," she said, pointing to a corner; it was D-Mon. "Girl's got to have music at her party, especially for the party games."

"Arietta, you are without a doubt the best planner ever," said James as he looked around, stopping at her eyes. "This is truly unbelievable."

She grabbed his hand and squeezed it gently. "Thank you."

It was eleven thirty, and all the children had arrived. Arietta called Cheryl, and a few minutes later Caleigh walked into the cheer of 'Happy Birthday!' Her face lit up. Then Cheryl walked around with Caleigh and the children and pointed everything out.

"Caleigh, girls and boys, Moms and Dads, our birthday girl has arrived, and the first activity of the day is lunch. I know you have all missed breakfast and brought your appetite with you, and you won't be disappointed; there are hot dogs, hamburgers, steak, and chicken. I ask that we let Caleigh and her mom go first, then the children, and then the adults…and after everyone is fed, it's…" He walked over to Caleigh and put the microphone close to her mouth, and she shouted, "Party time!" The children cheered. "Enjoy your lunch," said D-Mon.

Once everyone had eaten, it was time to play games. The first one was the stand-still game, where music was played and when it went off, the children had to stand still as quickly as possible and not move. The next was musical chairs. After that was a treasure hunt, where the children were put into several small groups and assigned an adult leader. They had twenty minutes to find the items on a treasure map that were hidden around the resort; the first group back won. When that ended, everyone was hot, so it was time to play water balloon toss. The kids were paired and faced one another and had to throw a water balloon back and forth without it breaking, and if they caught it, they each moved one step back. Everyone got wet. They had a fifteen-minute drink break and finished off the afternoon with games on the beach. At three o'clock the children were asked to line up. They followed Caleigh and her mom around the resort and stopped at two cabanas by the pool. The children were ushered inside where several women applied face makeup to make them look like pirates. The third and fourth cabanas had pirate costumes for the children to wear and keep; the adults received pirate bandanas and eye patches. Once they were ready, they marched around the pool, past the bar and were met by the meanest pirate ever, Blackbeard.

"So ye think ye are pirates?" he asked.

"Yes," said a few of them.

"I can't hear ye," he replied. "Ye are going to have to be louder than that. Are ye pirates?" he asked again.

"Yes," they all shouted.

He went over to Caleigh. "What be ye name, young lass?"

"I'm Caleigh…I mean, I'm Captain Caleigh."

"Well, Captain Caleigh, is this ye crew ye have around ye?"

"Yes, they are, these scallywags is me crew."

The adults were laughing at the banter and Blackbeard himself was trying not to laugh at her responses. "Well, then, I see ye, Captain, I see ye crew of scallywags…Where be ye ship?" asked Blackbeard, looking around.

Captain Caleigh looked around. "We don't have a ship," she replied.

At this time all the people around the pool had either swam up or walked over to listen.

"Ye wouldn't be lying to me now would ye, lass?" he asked. "Because I need to sail around the harbor and find a good spot to bury me treasure."

"No, Blackbeard," she said.

"Well, follow me." The children and the adults followed Blackbeard around the corner and through the bar toward the dock and stopped on the beach and looked as he pointed. "Then whose ship would that be?"

The children looked over and saw a big pirate ship. They all screamed with excitement.

"Do we get to go aboard?" asked Captain Caleigh.

"Why, this be ye ship to take me around the harbor," he replied. "Lead the way."

They followed Caleigh, boarded the pirate ship, and met the crew. The boat left the dock and headed out to sea. On board, the kids looked for Blackbeard's coins that he had lost, and those pirates that had stolen them were thrown in the brig. They attacked the adult pirates with buckets of water and learnt and sang pirate songs. They looked over the side and watched the dolphins swimming next to the ship and waved to the people on the boats passing by. Two hours later they approached the dock.

"Apparently ye have some mutineers aboard, Captain Caleigh," said Blackbeard.

"Yes, we do," she replied. "I have their names here on my list, and when I call them out, you scallywags bring them to me."

"Aye, aye, Captain," they replied.

"First Mate James." The kids ran over and pulled him in front of the Captain. "Second Mate William," she said, and the kids grabbed him. She named three other fathers. "Ye have all been convicted of mutiny and will have to walk the plank…and that spit of land that ye see behind ye…is your new home," she said, playing the part of Captain Caleigh perfectly.

"James," she said, "walk the plank."

All the kids yelled, "Walk the plank! Walk the plank!"

James slowly walked down the plank. He turned and begged for mercy.

Captain Caleigh turned and said, "Blackbeard."

Blackbeard stomped onto the plank, making a motion to go for James who quickly jumped in. One by one, the fathers jumped off the plank. Now that the men were in the water, the kids that wanted to, were allowed to walk the plank, and jump off. Captain Caleigh went first followed by the rest of the children, and then a few adults. They splashed around and played in the water for a while, then headed to shore. On the beach the hotel staff met them with towels. They waved goodbye to the pirates on the ship as it sailed away, and then the children headed back to their rooms to change into pajamas for the evening event.

An hour later everyone arrived back at the tent; the side facing the beach had been covered up intentionally. There were hot pizzas and a long table set up for all the children to sit at. When they were finished eating, everyone sang Happy Birthday, and a big pirate ship chocolate cake was brought out. Caleigh made a wish and blew out the twelve candles. The cake was cut and handed to the kids and adults. After the cake was done, Caleigh opened up her presents; she received toys, clothes, DVDs, CDs, and money. Caleigh and Cheryl thanked everyone for the gifts.

Cheryl looked at Caleigh and the children. "Are you ready for the last activity of the evening?"

"Yes," replied all the kids.

Arietta gave a nod to the hotel staff, and the flaps on the tent were removed to reveal a big movie screen. In front of the screen were rows of chaises that had pillows and blankets on them, and behind them rows of chairs. At the back was an old-fashioned popcorn maker and next to that was a long table with small bags full of candy and small bowls filled with fresh popcorn.

"Caleigh let's go enjoy your movie under the stars," said Cheryl.

Caleigh's chaise was highlighted with birthday decorations. All the other kids jumped up and ran over to claim theirs. The kids got comfortable, and the adults took the seats in the back. The staff handed out bags of candy and bowls of popcorn to the children; it all went quiet and *Pirates of The Caribbean: On Stranger Tides* started. And under hundreds of stars, Caleigh and her friends watched the movie.

The movie ended and so had the party. The children and parents thanked Caleigh and Cheryl for an amazing day and slowly walked to their rooms. Caleigh asked James to carry her, which he did, and she fell asleep on the way. He put her on her bed and went outside with Arietta while Cheryl tucked her in. Moments later Cheryl came out crying.

"What's the matter, Cheryl?" asked Arietta.

"This has been such an unbelievable day for her, and me; I'm just so happy. I don't know what words I could use to thank you," she said, hugging them both.

"You don't have to," said Arietta. "We know."

Cheryl let go. "I guess I should go in and snuggle with her; it's been a long day," she said and thanked them again before she turned in.

Arietta and James walked towards their rooms, and James turned to her. "Cheryl is right, that was an unbelievable day. It was perfect. How do you do it?"

She smiled at him. "Well, it wasn't too difficult. The hotel already had the tent, tables, linens, barbeques, screen, and cabanas; I just told them how to set it up and what food they needed to cook and when. I made the itinerary with Janice. "And on our trip to St. Thomas, you and I ordered the decorations, candies, balloons, and costumes; and we hired D-Mon, the makeup women, and the pirate ship and crew. The staff put the decorations up and the candies in the bags…simple."

"Simple?" he questioned. "I think you have a real talent for this. You did a fantastic job not only today but with the ceremony, too. Don't underestimate yourself."

"Thank you," she said. "You know, James, it may seem like a lot of work to most people and maybe it is, but for me it was so much fun, and I loved every minute of it. Watching Caleigh and Cheryl, and the faces on the children and the parents was so rewarding."

"Well, I think you deserve a celebratory drink for an excellent day," said James.

"I will take you up on that," she said, and they went into the bar where James ordered them a drink. They sat on a couple of chairs close to the beach and looked out at the sea. "Thanks for walking the plank. It was nice of you and the fathers to volunteer."

"No need to, that was great, I've never walked the plank before," he said, "and I loved the way Caleigh took to her role; she really pulled it off."

"Spit of land," said Arietta, "straight from the mouth of Captain Jack Sparrow."

They both laughed and continued to talk about her performance and her day. They finished their drinks and walked back to their rooms.

"We are going to meet my family and my niece's friends at the Banana Tree Grille for dinner around six. The party starts around eight."

"That's fine," she said.

"With the party going late and it being on St. Thomas, before I had asked you to come, I had booked a suite at the Marriott Frenchman's Reef Resort so that I wouldn't have to worry about getting back; that's where my family is staying, and knowing them they will probably end up continuing the party in someone's room and dragging me along, and I wanted to have a place of my own to crash. The suite is bi-level and has a sofa bed on the main floor and a bedroom upstairs. So…" He wanted to make sure what he was going to ask came out right. "If you want, we can share the suite? You can have the bedroom upstairs. Or I can get another adjoining room?"

She smiled at his thoughtfulness and consideration for her. "I think I'm okay with sharing a suite."

"Are you sure?" he asked.

"Positive!" she replied. "This actually works out better."

"It does?"

"Well, now we can head over there early, check in, and spend time with your family at the resort. Then we can get showers and get ready in the room."

"What time do you think we should leave?" James asked.

"Well, it takes forty-five minutes to get to the island…so let's meet for breakfast at ten and be on the ferry by eleven thirty."

He smiled at her.

"What?" she asked. "Why are you smiling at me like that?"

"You are without a doubt the best planner ever!"

"Thank you," she said beaming.

"Goodnight," said James.

"Goodnight." She went inside and into the bathroom. While washing her face, she looked at her reflection in the mirror. She suddenly realized her success at planning these two events had given her an immense feeling of personal satisfaction and happiness, and not only that; she had also given those adults and children that attended these events a wonderful lifetime memory. She smiled at her reflection.

Chapter 16

They arrived at the Marriott Frenchman's Reef lobby at twelve thirty, James registered, and then they went up to the eighth floor and walked into their Royal Suite. The main floor had a full bathroom, a sitting area with a sofa bed, an armchair, a flat screen television and a mini fridge. They walked through the sitting area and opened the balcony door and walked out.

"Oh, this is unbelievable!" said Arietta. "You can see the sea, the harbor, Charlotte Amalie, the cruise ships…You get another perspective of how beautiful it is from up here."

"That's for sure," replied James. "It's spectacular."

"We are going to have to sit on these chairs and see it at night," suggested Arietta. "With all the lights I bet it looks incredible."

James agreed.

"Come on, let's see the upstairs," she said and grabbed his hand. They went back through the sitting area and climbed the spiral stairs to the loft. There was a huge king-size bed and television, and when she opened the French doors, they revealed a full bathroom with a large separate shower and a whirlpool tub for two. She jumped on the bed and lay down. "This suite is amazing." Then she thought for a moment. "You should have the upstairs, and I'll take downstairs."

"This is yours," said James, grinning. "Let me get your bags." He went downstairs and brought up her things, placing them on the floor.

"I love this room," she said, jumping off the bed. "Thank you."

"I know you do and you're welcome," James replied. "Well, let's get ready and meet my family." He went downstairs and changed and was looking out at the view when he heard Arietta come down. He turned around and watched her glide down the stairs, wearing a sexy cobalt blue bikini and a sheer matching wrap. "Wow! You look stunning!"

"Thank you," she said, smiling. She liked the way he always complimented her. "Let's go."

They took the elevator down and walked out to the pool area.

"Just look for a big crowd of people, most of them young girls in their early twenties," suggested James.

"Uncle James," cried out a voice.

"Uncle James," cried out another.

Both nieces ran up to him and covered him in hugs and kisses.

"I'm so glad you are here," said Stephanie.

The other niece looked over at Arietta. "Hello," she said.

"Arietta, this is Elizabeth, my sister's daughter, and this is Stephanie, my brother's," said James as he pointed at them.

"Hello," they both said.

"I love your name," said Elizabeth.

"Thank you," she replied.

"I'm glad you are coming to my party tonight; it is going to be so much fun," Stephanie said as they walked over to where the rest of the family and friends were sitting.

"James!" they all called out.

"This is my friend, Arietta," he said, looking at her. "Arietta, this is my sister, Sophie and her husband Ken."

"Hi, Arietta," they said in unison.

"This is my brother Richard and his wife Karen," said James.

"Hi, Arietta, just call me Ricky."

"Hi," said Karen. "Come and sit down." She motioned to a seat next to her and watched Arietta sit.

"Arietta, these are my friends Emily, Brittany, and Taylor. The others are either in the pool or not here yet, you can meet them later," said Stephanie.

"And this is my friend, Caitlin," said Elizabeth.

"Hello," said Arietta to them.

"Hello," they all replied.

"So, you girls ready for your graduation party?" asked James.

"We are!" they screamed.

"It is going to be so much fun; we can't wait," said Stephanie.

"And you're going to be a big twenty-two as well," said James.

"I know, I'm getting so old. I remember when I was seventeen," she said, tongue-in-cheek.

"Oh, to be twenty-two again," said Sophie.

"Here, here," agreed Karen.

"You guys look great," said Stephanie and went around and gave them each a hug.

"James how is St. John?" asked Ricky.

"It's beautiful," said James. "The beaches, the water, snorkeling, food, it's incredible."

"Are the women as gorgeous as you?" asked Sophie, looking at Arietta.

"Well…" She didn't know how to answer. "There are a lot more attractive women than me; our friend Cheryl could be a model."

"Where is she?" asked Elizabeth. "Why didn't you bring her?"

"We asked her, but she has a daughter who is twelve, and she didn't want to leave her alone all day and night."

"You guys are staying over?" asked Ken with a teasing grin.

"Yes," replied Arietta slowly and a little embarrassed.

"Ken, stop it!" said James.

Sophie hit Ken's arm and said, "Don't worry about him, Arietta; he likes to stir the pot and cause trouble."

"I do," replied Ken, having successfully done so.

"If you must know all the nitty-gritty details, we are staying over," confirmed James. "Friends, own rooms."

"That's great," said Stephanie to Arietta. "Now you can party with us all night."

"Your uncle has told me about your late-night parties," said Arietta. "That's why we are here," she said, smiling.

"All right," said Stephanie excitedly. "Hear that girls, Arietta is with us to the end!"

The girls cheered, lifted their glasses, and drank.

"What about you, Uncle James?" asked Stephanie.

"Do I have a choice?" he asked.

"No," she said without hesitation. "To Uncle James."

"Uncle James," the girls said and drank some more.

"You guys don't have a drink," noticed Stephanie and took off with her friends.

They came back with a tray of drinks, placing them on the table and everyone grabbed one.

"To the graduation class," said James. "Congratulations."

"Graduation," replied the girls.

They all drank.

Ricky, Sophie, and Ken started talking to James about the flight while Stephanie and her friends went into the pool.

Karen turned to Arietta. "How did you two meet?"

"The first night they had a manager's welcome reception at the pool bar, and I met him there." She took a drink and changed the subject. "How did you meet Ricky?"

"I dated Ricky in high school, and we went to the same college." She whispered, "I got pregnant the last year of college, so we got married and Ricky's parents helped us raise Stephanie until we got on our feet."

"That must have been difficult?"

"It was but when I look at the end results, two great children and a wonderful husband, well, most of the time," she said, laughing. "It was all worth it." She looked at Ricky. "We've known each other for twenty-seven years and been married for twenty-three." She looked at Arietta. "Have you ever been married?"

Arietta went silent.

"Oh, I'm sorry, that's none of my business," she said apologetically.

"It's okay, just that I'm going through a—"

"Arietta, come in for a swim," said Elizabeth who had been talking to her friend but listening in. She took hold of Arietta's hand and pulled her out of the seat. Everyone looked at Arietta as she took off her wrap and revealed her bikini body. Ricky and Ken looked over at James who ignored them.

"Wish I had friends like that," commented Ken who was slapped on the arm again by Sophie.

Sophie looked at James. "She seems nice."

"She really is."

"She is very beautiful and has a perfect body," added Karen. "I don't think I like her," she said good-humoredly.

James bragged about Arietta and the wedding and birthday party she had planned and how incredible they were. He talked about Cheryl and the cruise and her daughter and her battle with cancer. Then Ricky and Ken talked about the resort and the bars, while Sophie and Karen talked about the restaurants and the rooms.

"Sometimes Aunt Karen can be a little inquisitive," said Elizabeth. "She means well."

"Oh, so you saved me?" asked Arietta.

"For now," she replied. "They are very protective of Uncle James since he got hurt really bad. I'm not supposed to talk about it outside the family, but I'm sure you know."

"Yeah, I guess," replied Arietta and wondered why the secrecy. "Do you go to college?"

"I do, I'm in my second year, and I love it," she said enthusiastically. "I'm studying English just like my uncle. He helps me with my papers and Stephanie's too."

"And mine," said Caitlin.

"Well, that's nice of him," said Arietta, not really seeing Ricky as the literary type but thought, you can't judge a book by its cover, and laughed to herself at what she just said.

Stephanie and her friends swam over to them. "What are you guys talking about?"

"College," replied Elizabeth and Caitlin.

"So, what did you get your BA in?" asked Arietta.

"English and minored in history," replied Stephanie. "I'm starting teacher's college this fall."

"That's wonderful. What age do you want to teach?" asked Arietta.

"Elementary, I love younger children, they are sponges for knowledge." She looked past Arietta. "Uncle Ken, Uncle James, over here," she called, waving her arms.

They swam over.

"Have you noticed anything?" asked Sophie, looking at Ricky and Karen.

Ricky shook his head. "No."

"He seems different," said Karen.

Ricky shook his head. "You are reading too much into it. Look at this place, look at the friend he is with; he is just happy. Who wouldn't be?"

"Ricky," said Sophie in an uneasy voice, "you know why we are concerned."

"I know," replied Ricky. "Just stop worrying about him for a moment and let him be."

"You said that before," said Karen, "and remember what happened to him."

"Karen don't bring that up, you know I don't want that to happen to him again," said Ricky, getting upset.

Karen grabbed his hand. "Sorry, honey, I know you thought you were doing the best for him; we all did."

Ricky glanced over at James. "Look at him, he's enjoying himself and he is smiling," said Ricky. "To me that's a good thing."

Sophie and Karen looked over at James and agreed.

"So, I am going to go and be happy with him. Excuse me, baby," he said, kissing his wife on the cheek. "And big sis," and kissed Sophie on top of her head and left.

"Maybe he's right," said Karen.

"Maybe," said Sophie as they watched Ricky jump in the water and swim over to his brother. "I'm glad to see James happy; I just don't want to see him get his heart broken again."

"James, Ken, let's get a drink at the pool bar," said Ricky. "I love that we can stay in the pool and drink at the bar."

"Not without us," said all the girls.

"Come on then," said Ricky, and they all swam to the bar.

James stopped, looked over at Sophie and Karen, and waved to them to come in. Minutes later they swam up and joined them.

"I really like your family," said Arietta as she sat down next to him on the balcony. "They are really nice."

"They like you," replied James.

"How do you know?"

I can tell," he said. "My nieces think you're beautiful, have an incredible body, and are smart."

"What about their uncle?" asked Arietta.

"I'm pretty sure Ricky and Ken think the same," he joked.

"You know what I meant, mister," she said and let it go. "I'm glad everyone decided to go to their room and have a break before meeting for dinner. I can use the rest."

"I know what you mean," he replied. "Are you going upstairs to have a lie down?"

"I think I need to." She looked behind him at the sofa. "That doesn't look very appealing."

He turned around and looked at it. "I'm sure it's more comfortable than it looks."

She laughed and so did he. "The bed upstairs is huge; I'm sure I can loan you half of it for an hour."

"Really," he said, "and listen to you snore."

"I do not snore," she said and playfully hit his arm. "Well, I'm going up to the bed, offer still stands." She stood up and left. Arietta took off her wrap and bikini, threw them on the floor, and got under the covers. She hoped he would come up but didn't think he would, otherwise she would have put something on. Moments later he came and lay down next to her on top of the sheets. She smiled and drifted off to sleep. When she woke up, he was gone. She put on a robe and went downstairs and heard him in the shower. She went back to her room and got ready. She came down the stairs, wearing a sexy, purple dress and heels, makeup, and her hair straight.

"You look gorgeous!"

"Thank you, and you look very handsome," she replied. "Shall we go?"

Arietta and James arrived at the Banana Tree Grille and were seated with James's family and their friends. They ordered a special Sunset Cocktail and talked about the restaurant being on Bluebeards Hill and the beautiful view it had of the harbor and the island, and about Bluebeard's Castle; then ordered their food. The appetizers consisted of Mediterranean Seafood Cocktail, Mussels and Pancetta, Lump Crab Cakes, and Rich

Mozzarella Burrata, and from the breadbasket menu they ordered the Gorgonzola Loaf. The selection of main courses was incredible and ranged from pasta, steak, seafood, pork, duck, and chicken along with your choice of several sides. Everyone agreed that the meal was delicious. They left the restaurant and headed down to Veterans Drive to the Haven Bar. Arietta and James looked at one another and smiled. They went upstairs and were seated inside in a reserved section.

"Hello, everyone, my name is D-Mon, and I just wanted to come over and personally welcome you. Tonight, we have live music and during the breaks yours truly will be your DJ, so if you have any special requests, please let me know. The waitress will be over in a minute to take your drinks," he said as he looked round at the group. "Arietta! James!" He went over to them. "You guys out again and ready to party like the wedding?"

The group looked at them.

"Of course," said Arietta, "although we have some tough competition tonight with these young ladies."

"Ladies," he said, turning to them, "don't let these two fool you; they were the last two dancing at the reception. I had to kick them out," he said with a laugh. "You guys have a good time." He looked over at Arietta and James. "I know these two will," he said, winking at them. "Let's get this party started!" he yelled as he walked away. The girls cheered in agreement.

The drinks started flowing, the band started playing, and the girls started dancing; the party had begun and went on all night. Arietta danced with the girls, James's sisters, and brothers, but mostly with James, which didn't go unnoticed. The night came to an end, and they said goodbye to D-Mon and the staff, thanking them for a great night. They jumped into the taxis waiting for them outside and headed back to the resort. They took the elevators to Sophie and Ken's room, which was also on the eighth floor, but had a view of the ocean. Arietta and James went out on the balcony with his nieces.

"This place is so beautiful," said Stephanie.

"You can see the lights of the boats out in the water," said Elizabeth, "and all the stars in the sky."

"I wonder what Charlotte Amalie and the harbor looks like?" asked Stephanie.

"That's what our view is," commented James.

"You and your friends should drop in and a have a look before you go to your rooms," suggested Arietta.

"I would love that," said Stephanie.

"So would I," added Elizabeth.

"We haven't seen it yet either, so we can all see it together," added James.

Before she left for dinner, Sophie had pre-ordered room service, so a light buffet of sandwiches, vegetables and fruit had been dropped off. As people ate, champagne and glasses were brought out and a toast made to all the graduating girls. After they drank the champagne, beer and wine were served, music was put on, and dancing began. Early in the morning the party ended, and people drifted off to their rooms. Stephanie, Elizabeth, and their friends picked up their drinks and followed James and Arietta to their room. Everyone went on the balcony and witnessed the glittering light of Charlotte Amalie and the harbor; it was beautiful. They talked for thirty minutes about the view and the island after which the girls' said goodnight and left. Arietta and James went back outside and sat on the balcony. Ten minutes later there was a knock on the door, and James opened it. There was no one there, but on the floor was a bottle of champagne and two glasses. He picked it up and brought it in.

"Who was it?" asked Arietta.

"No one, well, no one was there when I opened the door," he replied, walking out onto the balcony. "But they left us this," he said, showing her the champagne and glasses.

"Well, let's have a drink and enjoy this view a little longer," suggested Arietta.

James opened it, poured two glasses, and handed one to her. He put the bottle down on the ground and sat next to her.

She moved her seat close to his. "Cheers to a great night and a lovely family."

"Cheers and thank you," he replied.

They drank their champagne, sat in silence, and took in the view. After a while Arietta put her head on his shoulder and fell asleep. He picked her up and carried her upstairs, pulled down the duvet and sheets, put her on the bed, and covered her up. He went downstairs and pulled out the sofa bed.

Arietta woke up the next morning and realized she was in bed and still had her dress on. She got up, changed, and went downstairs. James was still sleeping, so she lay next to him and drifted off to sleep. A while later she felt him move and opened her eyes. "Good morning," she said. "I'm guessing I fell asleep, and you carried me to bed?"

"Morning," he replied. "I did," he said, a little confused she was there.

"Don't worry, I just came down twenty minutes ago. I didn't want to wake you, so I thought I would lie here quietly and dozed off."

"Oh, okay," he replied, still half asleep.

"I will make some coffee," she said and jumped out of bed.

He watched her in her shorts and T-shirt walk back and forth to get the water. "How did you sleep?"

"Slept good," she replied. "My dress was a little uncomfortable, kind of woke me up." She looked over at him. "Thanks again for carrying me to bed."

He smiled at her. "That's okay." He got up and walked over to the balcony and went outside and sat down. He noticed the empty bottle of champagne and glasses and stood up and put them to one side. He leaned over the railing and down at the harbor. It was a busy sight with cruise ships docking and boats and yachts leaving.

"Here you go," she said, handing him his coffee and standing next to him. She noticed the champagne bottle. "I wonder who dropped that off?"

"Your guess is as good as mine," he replied, unsure himself.

"Well, whoever it was, it was very much appreciated," she said and smiled, "and it finished me off!"

"You and me both," he added.

They dressed, had breakfast, and caught the ferry back to St. John. On the way they talked about his nieces and their friends. It went quiet for a moment as she looked at him thoughtfully; she decided she needed to know for herself. "How come you are still single?"

He looked at her, a little surprised by her directness but realized the question was eventually going to be asked. "I was married once for five years, and seven years ago it ended painfully for me. I didn't want to go through that pain again, so I decided to stay single."

"Do you believe in love?" she asked.

He thought for a moment. "I do but not for me."

"Are you planning on staying single?" she queried.

"I guess so," he replied honestly. "It's safe and best for me."

"I'm sorry you were hurt so badly," she replied. "Maybe one day you will let it go and maybe fall in love again." She felt sorry and sad for him but most of all a little upset that he had led her on.

"Maybe," he replied. He looked at her for a moment and wanted to ask her about her situation with Graham, but from what she had said to Cheryl at the spa, he thought better of it and changed the subject. "So you can't make the fishing trip tomorrow?"

"No, I wish I could. I would love to go, but I need to take care of some personal business."

Since she offered no more information, he let it go and talked about last night instead.

Chapter 17

It was a beautiful, hot, sunny morning. James, Cheryl, and Caleigh boarded the fishing charter at the Cruz Bay dock and went to the right side of the boat, each claiming a rod. Once the boat left, the captain welcomed everyone aboard and explained that his crew would be around to help out with rods and the unhooking of fish. He also informed them that there was food and drinks available in the galley, and that they would fillet your fish for a nominal charge when they returned to the dock.

Cheryl looked at Caleigh, who was talking to a young girl next to her, and turned to James. "I didn't get a chance to thank you for the pirate ship, that was incredible; it really made her day."

"I'm glad she enjoyed it."

"Oh, she did! I think everyone did, it was a big hit!" She looked out at the water. She had something on her mind and turned and whispered, "The night of the cruise I was a little drunk and woke up in bed naked. I know I have a habit of taking my clothes off in the middle of the night when I'm in bed, because they get constraining…"

"So you think that's what happened?" he asked teasingly.

"Ah…yeah," she replied.

"Okay, that's what happened," said James, looking away from her.

"Tell me," she said and nudged him.

"Okay, okay," he said and told her what happened.

"Good," she said, relieved. "That's what I thought, thank you." She looked at Caleigh still talking and turned to him again. "Did you notice Arietta was a little quiet last night during dinner?"

"Really," he said. "She seemed okay."

"I don't know if she is, she is usually more involved and animated with her conversation," suggested Cheryl. "She just didn't seem to be herself."

He thought about what she was saying. "Now that you mention it, I guess so."

"And in the pool, she was really quiet and didn't stay long," continued Cheryl. "Something is bothering her."

"Maybe the personal business she needs to take care of today was weighing on her mind."

"Maybe," she said, thinking. "Was she okay with your family on Saturday?"

"Yeah, she had a good time, everyone did."

"I know," replied Cheryl. "I'm so," she looked over to make sure Caleigh was still occupied, turned, and whispered, "sorry I missed that, you guys had such a good time."

"Well, they are planning another one soon. I think it's going to be karaoke, maybe you can make that one?"

"Karaoke!" she said excitedly. "That will be so much fun. When is it?" she asked.

"I don't know yet, but as soon as I find out I will let you know."

"Okay," she said appreciatively.

"You're still meeting my family tomorrow and hanging out with us?" asked James.

"Of course," she replied. "I'm looking forward to meeting them. Arietta said she would be there, too." She realized she had been talking about Arietta before she got side-tracked. "I guess you're right; it must be the personal thing she has going on today, poor girl."

"I hope it goes okay," said James, concerned.

"I'm sure it will," said Cheryl.

The boat came to a stop, and a crew member came around and put bait on their hooks. Everyone casted, and within several minutes people were catching bonito, jacks, yellowtail snapper, grouper, Spanish mackerel, and kingfish. Their fish was taken off their hooks and placed in a bin assigned to them. James noticed how much attention Cheryl was getting from the male crew members with her bait, fish, and rod; he was pretty much left on his own, which he didn't mind. He just thought it was comical watching these men falling over one another to help her, and with them being around, Caleigh got all the help she needed, too. The boat went to cays, lagoons, and reefs around the islands where the water was calm, and the views were picturesque, and the fishing was good. Four hours later they disembarked and watched the crew fillet their fish. They took their catch to Woody's Seafood Saloon in Cruz Bay where the chef offered to cook it for them for lunch. They sat inside and had a drink while they waited.

"Look," said Cheryl suddenly to James and motioned out the window.

It was Arietta walking down the street; she met Graham, exchanged pleasantries, and went inside a restaurant.

"That's a good sign," acknowledged Cheryl.

"It is," said James.

The chef had cooked each variety of fish in his own secret recipe and served it to them as samples to share, along with portions of sides; it was delicious. Caleigh ordered a dessert while Cheryl and James drank coffee.

"I see you got lots of help on the fishing trip," James said jokingly to Cheryl.

"I know, and I watched you left all on your own struggling to get your fish off your hook," she said, laughing.

"Oh, you think that's funny," he said, smiling at her.

"I liked it when you kept dropping them on the deck and were running after them, trying to pick them up," said Caleigh, laughing along with her mom.

"Oh, both of you now," he said.

The waiter came by, dropped off Caleigh's dessert and her attention went to that.

"So, Cheryl, do your parents live close to you in upstate New York?" he asked.

"About thirty minutes away. It's nice because they can come down and help me when I need it, and they love Caleigh visiting on the weekends."

"Do you like where you live?" he asked.

"I do, it's nice," she said. She looked at Caleigh eating her dessert and not paying them any interest. "But if I could, I would love to live somewhere like Manhattan. That's where you live?"

"Most of the time," he replied.

"Do you like it?" she asked enthusiastically.

"I do. What's not to like?"

"I know," she said. "Shopping, restaurants, shows, sports, concerts, and the list goes on." She whispered, "If I had a good job with great pay so I could put her into a private school, and I could get a place with an extra bedroom for my parents to use when they visited, if I had that, I would move there in a heartbeat," she said, smiling at the thought.

"Did you always want to work in a medical office?" he asked.

"Well, kind of, I was walking to my job at the bar and I noticed they were looking for help on the weekends, so I got a part-time job filing and doing odd jobs, and they told me they were always looking for assistants, so I figured I would get my diploma, work full-time and make more money."

"Sounds like it's challenging?" he asked.

"It was at first, but once I got things organized, over time it's become very mundane. Don't get me wrong; I love interacting with the patients, doctors, hospitals, and clinics, that's the fun part. It's just that I am particularly good at organizing, prioritizing, and multitasking, and once you get a handle on that, the challenge is gone. I guess it would be nice if new things were needed to be done or taken care of, something different." She thought about it for a moment. "Something more challenging and rewarding." She stopped and looked at Caleigh. "But I can't complain too much. I get lots of time off with her, as well as connections through my doctors with the hospital and staff."

They heard loud voices outside; it was Arietta and Graham. Arietta had walked away from him and had her back to them, but her body language suggested she was terribly upset. She hailed a taxi and got in. Graham raised his arms to the sky and shook his head. He turned around and continued down the street towards the ferry.

"That's not good," said James.

"That's not good at all," said Cheryl.

They finished lunch and went back to the resort. James went to his room, changed into his bathing suit, and dropped by to pick up Caleigh and took her to the beach, while Cheryl went to see Arietta.

Arietta walked down the street and saw Graham standing outside La Tapa restaurant. They greeted each other warmly and went inside. They sat in a secluded area and ordered some drinks and appetizers. As they ate, Graham talked about the ferry ride and Manhattan. The plates were taken away, and new drinks were brought.

"So?" asked Graham.

She knew what he was asking. "So what?"

"So… What is your stand on the merger?"

"I think it's a bad idea," she replied.

"Why?"

"I think you want this merger based on your relationship with Violet, not on what's best for the company."

She is all business, he thought and sat back in his seat, frustrated. "Over the last several months, we have done our homework on this, you know that; marketing suggests that this is a good move for us. It will give us a significant increase in sales, we will be pulling in a new clientele of customer and reaching out to a wider demographic…It's a win-win for us."

"What about our company? Our tradition? What we exemplify? What we are to our current clients? Do we just push that to one side?" she asked in a strong tone.

"We still have that," he replied, "and they will always be there. Violet is adding a different dimension, look, feel, and option. We will be catering to our current clients' children, grandchildren, nephews, and nieces. We need to forge ahead and attract new clients, new money."

"And what happens if it fails?" she asked. "What then?"

"If we don't take the chance we will never know," he said and paused for a moment. "If we don't do this someone else will."

Arietta laughed. "And what happens if the love of your life works for the competition? Will you still be at her side?"

Graham looked at her, a little taken aback by her remark. "We will always be at each other's sides, it's called love, something you gave up on a long time ago."

She glared at him, furious at what he had just said but kept her cool. "What happens if the merger goes through, and you fall out of love? What then? We are stuck with her and have to deal with her every day."

Graham sat back and looked at her. "Business is business, she is a professional, as am I, and we will perform as such. Our personal life we will figure out and is none of your business, so back off."

"If it affects our company, then it's my business," she said in a loud, stern voice.

Graham looked at her and softened his approach. "You have all the information on the merger, and everything points to a green light. Why are we talking about me and Violet?" He stopped and thought for a moment. "Is this about you and Vincent? Are you comparing us to that?" He wished he hadn't said that and could take it back.

She calmly finished her drink, stood up, and made for the exit.

Graham quickly left money on the table and followed her outside.

"No merger, go home and don't come back," she said.

"Arie," pleaded Graham.

"Go home," she shouted.

She stormed off, her head down to hide her tears, not even sure if she was heading in the right direction.

Graham watched her walk away and get into a cab. He threw his arms up in exasperation, shaking his head he turned around, walked to the dock, and took the ferry back to St. Thomas. He wished he had never said what he did; it was uncalled for and cruel. He also knew without her support the merger would never happen. He decided he would fly back to New York tomorrow and wait until Friday afternoon to tell Vincent and Violet the bad news.

Arietta got in the cab and did her best to stop crying. She went back to the resort and straight to her room where she pulled the drapes closed and fell on her bed, weeping. A while later there was a knock on the door. She decided not to answer it but changed her mind when they knocked again. She dried her eyes and opened the door a little.

"Hey, thought I would just check on you and see if you are okay? See if you want to come to the beach?" asked Cheryl.

"I'm fine," she replied. "Just a little tired, and I'm not feeling well, think the late nights are catching up with me. So, I'm just going to stay in my room, relax, maybe get a bath, and watch a movie."

"Okay," said Cheryl. "We will be on the beach, if you change your mind, or call me later if you want to meet for dinner."

"I will," she said and watched Cheryl walk away. "Cheryl," she called and waited for her to turn around. "Thanks."

"Enjoy your rest," replied Cheryl, gave her a smile, and left. She went to her room to change and met Caleigh and James on the beach. They went in the water for a swim, and while Caleigh was busy playing, she told James what happened. "Her eyes were very red like she had been crying a lot," revealed Cheryl.

"Guess she needs her space," said James. "You can't do much more than you did."

"I know," said Cheryl sadly, wishing there was something more she could do but realizing there wasn't.

They swam and played on the beach all afternoon. For dinner they decided to order room service and have it on Cheryl's patio. They ate pizza and then went for a quick swim. Once out of the pool, they dried off and James bid them goodnight. He walked past Arietta's room and contemplated knocking but talked himself out of it and went on to his room. He was tired and thought he should go straight to bed but decided to get a shower, put on his shorts, pour a glass of wine, and go outside for a while and enjoy the night. He lay on the chaise and gazed at the stars.

"Can I join you?" asked Arietta. "Or do you want to be alone?"

"No, come over and lie down," he said, pulling the other chaise next to him. "Want some wine?"

"Please," she said as she lay down.

He came out and handed her the wine. She wasn't herself. "How are you doing?"

"I'm doing okay," she said quietly.

"Did you want to talk about anything?" he asked.

"No, just want to watch the stars. It's just nice knowing I have someone next to me," she said and reached over, taking his hand. "But you can talk, I like listening to you, you have a nice voice…Tell me about the fishing."

He spoke about fishing and the men helping Cheryl and him chasing his fish on the deck, which made Arietta laugh a little, about the restaurant, and the beach.

She listened and sipped on her wine but said nothing. Inside, she was struggling to keep herself together and realized she wasn't going to make it. She finished her wine quickly and started to cry as she stood. "I ha…have to…to go," she said and left.

He could hear her sobbing all the way back to her room. He put his glass down and decided to go check on her. The door was open, and he could hear her crying. "You okay?"

"I will be," she said.

"Okay. I will close the door and come by in the morning," he said and was about to go.

"James, can you stay with me tonight, please? I don't want to be alone right now."

He thought for a moment.

"Please, don't leave."

He went over to the bed, her hand reaching for him; he gently took it and allowed himself to be pulled down next to her. He lay down on his back, and she put her head on his chest. He put his arms around her and held her, soon she was asleep. Early next morning he got up and went to his room. She woke up when she heard the door close and knew he had held her all night. She smiled and fell back asleep.

Chapter 18

James met his family at the dock. As they all walked onto the beach, he pointed out the Island Waves Bar and Grill, the pool, and the Terrace Restaurant. Then turned to his left and pointed down the beach to his room.

"This is a beautiful place," said Sophie as she sat on her chaise.

"Sure is," replied Ken.

"Stephanie and her friends don't know what they are missing," added Karen.

"Hi, James," said Caleigh with Cheryl steps behind. "Is this your family?" she asked.

"It is," he replied. "This is Caleigh and her mother, Cheryl."

They all said hello as Caleigh sat on the sand with Elizabeth and Caitlin, and Cheryl sat on a chaise between Sophie and Karen.

"Uncle James, can we go in the water?" asked Elizabeth.

"Of course, you can," he replied.

"Caleigh, do you want to come?" she asked.

Caleigh turned to her mom. "Can I?"

"Yes, but not too far," she said and watched her walk off with Elizabeth and Caitlin.

"Where's that bar?" asked Ricky.

"I'll show you," said James as they stood up.

Ken, realizing he would be left with the women, jumped up. "Coming too," he said.

"Won't see them for a while," said Sophie and turned to Cheryl. "Arietta told us about Caleigh; that's so sad and so young."

Cheryl explained when Caleigh was first diagnosed, the treatment she went through, and talked about the remission and how she has been clear for quite a while now.

"That's great news," expressed Sophie. "I'm sure it's all in the past now."

"We believe so," said Cheryl. She then told them about their trip being paid for by 'Make-A-Wish Foundation.'

"Really," said Karen. "James has a fund set up that he puts money into every year, and he even hired a person to oversee it, and throughout the year organizations like Make-A-Wish, will contact her regarding individuals whose wish it is to go away on vacation, and in turn his fund gives the family the money they need to pay for their trip. Sometimes it's done directly with the family, or it goes through Make-A-Wish or whomever the organization is. It depends on the situation, and how she is initially contacted." She looked over at Sophie. "How many kids and their families does he pay for?"

"I believe it's up to fifteen families," replied Sophie. "The lady that runs it, what is her name?" asked Sophie and started to think. "Joanne, that's her name! She takes care of it; everything is done through Joanne. James never meets the families or knows their names; he prefers to stay anonymous. They send thank-you notes to the fund, well, to Joanne, and she replies to them."

"He gets some special requests too, right, Karen?" asked Sophie.

"Almost all the families want to go to Disney World, but the odd times the child wants to go somewhere different, and because Joanne only has so much allotted per person per family, and the cost tends to be more, she contacts James and lets him know."

"And?" asked Cheryl.

"He never refuses," answered Karen. "He sent one child on a special trip this year and helped her mother by paying off her medical bills. Apparently, the mother had to borrow the money, and it was going to take her years to pay it back."

"That is so nice," said Cheryl, and she thought about him offering to pay for the party and her unpleasant response to him and felt bad. "He never mentioned it to me," said Cheryl. "That's wonderful."

"He likes to keep things private, so maybe best if you wait and let him bring it up."

"I will," replied Cheryl.

"Hello."

"Hello, Arietta," they replied.

"Let me guess? The men are at the bar!" she said.

"Yes, they are," replied Sophie. "That means peace and quiet for us."

"Have a seat here," said Karen, pointing to the empty one next to her. "How have you been doing since last time we met?"

"Okay," she said. "I had a lot of fun Saturday."

"We all did," replied Karen.

"I heard you, James, and the girls were on your balcony for a while, enjoying the view of the harbor and the lights," said Sophie. "They said it was beautiful."

"It was, and your girls are so nice," complimented Arietta and talked about the view from the balcony and their daughters.

The men came back with a tray of drinks, and they sat and talked about the resort and the island. James and Arietta decided to go for a swim, and Ricky joined them.

"Think I will go see the girls," said Ricky and swam off to play with them.

"Thanks for last night," said Arietta.

"Not a problem," replied James. "How are you doing?"

"Doing better, especially now that I'm out of the room and around you and your family," she said.

"I did knock, and there was no reply," he mentioned to her.

"I know, I was just getting out of the shower, and you were gone by the time I answered."

"That's okay," said James. "Are you staying around and having dinner with us later?"

"Yeah, was planning on it," she replied.

"We are just going to the Island Waves Bar, everyone wants to stay casual," said James, "so no need to get dressed up."

"That works," said Arietta. "Kind of looking forward to a casual night."

They went back to their seats and spent the afternoon on the beach talking, swimming, and drinking. Before dinner, Sophie and Karen went to James's room to get freshened up, while Arietta and Cheryl went to theirs; the men went to the bar. Arietta was the first one to join them, followed by Cheryl and then Sophie and Karen. They decided to sit close to the beach and order appetizers and finger foods to share.

"It's great that Elizabeth and Caitlin are watching Caleigh tonight," said Cheryl. "It's nice to get out for a few hours."

"I think Caleigh is doing them a favor, means they don't have to hang out with us old folks," surmised Ken.

"Who are you calling old?" replied Sophie.

Ricky noticed the women and Ken were talking and leaned over to talk with James. "You seem to be happy. How've you been doing?"

"I am," he said, "and I'm doing okay."

Ricky noticed he looked a little uncomfortable. "James, I'm your big brother, we talk about everything, are you okay?"

James looked at him and gave him half a smile, then told him about the encounters with Lily.

"She said your nickname and gave you the necklace, that's eerie," said Ricky as he shook his head and felt a shiver run down his spine.

"There's something else," said James and told him about the dreams he had been having.

"James, that freaks me out a little, especially the one about the water and the funnel, that's messed up. No wonder you are a little uneasy talking about it."

"I know," replied James. "I've been trying to put it all out of my mind."

Arietta had been talking with Cheryl and overheard James talking about Lily. Already knowing the story, she zoned it out, but when Cheryl had turned away to speak with Sophie and Ken, hearing James talk about his dreams, Arietta listened in again.

Ricky had noticed Arietta had stopped talking and changed the subject. "Looks like we need some more drinks," he said and called the waiter over.

"You seem a lot better?" asked James.

"Thank you," replied Arietta. "Feeling better."

"If you want to talk, I'm here, anytime," he offered.

"Thanks," she replied. "Same goes to you, too."

James was caught off guard by her reply but let it go.

The waiter brought the drinks and food to the table, and shortly after they finished eating, a band started to play. They danced throughout the evening, and everyone was having a lot of fun, especially Arietta and James.

"Now we are going to slow things down for a song or two, so you love birds can get a little closer on the dance floor," said the lead singer.

James asked Arietta to dance, and Sophie and Ken also stayed on the floor.

Arietta looked at James and smiled; he smiled back.

"I really like you, James," she said.

"I like you," he replied.

"No, I mean I really like you…a lot," she confessed and moved forward to kiss him on the lips. He pulled away before she did, and she immediately felt embarrassed and humiliated, and even more so when she realized Sophie and Ken had witnessed her failed attempt. She rested her head on one of his shoulders and hid until they finished the dance. She rushed away from James and sat back in her seat. Grabbing her drink, she tossed it back.

"I'm sorry," he whispered, "I just don't think it's a good idea right now, you're going—"

"Really," she said in an upset voice that made people around the table stop and look at her. She glared at James, stood up, and strode away from the table and onto the beach.

James followed her, and Cheryl followed him.

"Arietta," called James.

She stopped and turned around.

"What's the matter?" he asked.

"What's the matter?" she repeated. "Here I am throwing myself at you, and you keep on pushing me off to one side. Does it mean nothing to you what we did this week? The time we have spent together. The wedding, the birthday, the dinners, the breakfasts, the church, the special, romantic meal; one night I even left my door open for you to join me, and then I lay next to you in bed at the Marriott, and nothing. And on top of that you're playing me and Cheryl off against each other. Do you think this is some kind of game? Do you think you can toy with people's feelings? You humiliated me in front of your whole family!"

"Arietta," said Cheryl, trying to calm her down.

She looked at Cheryl's pleading face and then went back to James. "You lay with me last night, and tonight I attempt to kiss you, and you shoot me down! How dare you!"

"Arietta, I don't think you—"

"What, James, understand?" She looked into his eyes. "Oh, I understand. I understand that poor James here got his heart broken when his wife decided to leave him seven years ago, and every day since that he wallows in self-pity and seeks the attention of his family to feel sorry for him. You think you are the only person in this world that has had their heart broken. You think you are the first person in this world whose spouse has left them. You think you have the market on pain, suffering and what it feels like to be empty and alone. No, you don't! But you milk it for all you can…You have sat there for the last seven years feeling sorry for yourself, missing her, loathing her. You are a self-pitying and selfish person! You need to get over her, get yourself together and start living your life! Who says they don't believe in love? It's an excuse to hide and not take a chance and deal with the realities that surround you…like me, right here, right now, right in front of you." She grabbed his hand and put it to her heart. "I'm real, not some ghost from your past haunting you." She threw his hand away. "You're pathetic…Newsflash, James, she left you seven years ago and she's not coming back!" Arietta burst into tears and ran away. Cheryl went after her.

James watched them leave and stood there for a while thinking, before returning to the table and his family.

"You okay, James?" asked Ricky.

"I don't know," he replied.

"James, don't let what she said get to you," said Sophie.

"She doesn't—"

"Understand, Ricky?" asked James. "Oh, I think she does." He paused for a moment. "She understands more than you know." He put his hands over his face and was deep in thought and when he removed them had a distant look. "She's right."

"What do you mean?" asked Ricky.

"She's right about everything. For too many years I have been sitting around feeling sorry for myself, living in sadness, grief, and misery." He looked at his family. "She's not coming back, and she never will." He took a long drink. "At first, I didn't know what Lily was talking about. I thought she was crazy, and these dreams I have been having, I blamed them on this trip, this place," he said, looking around at the resort, "and I thought to myself I should never have come here." He looked over at Ricky. "But Lily's not crazy, it's not this trip, this place, this island. It's none of them; they are excuses…It's me."

His family was quiet.

"I'm going back with you on the ferry tonight to spend a night or two on St. Thomas…I need some time alone." He stood up and looked at them. "You have all been there for me, and you have supported me through some very rough and very bad times." He shook his head. "I really don't know how you put up with me…but I know the only reason I am standing here in front of you today, is because of all of you, and I want you to know that there isn't a day that goes by that I don't think and thank each and every one of you." He looked off in the distance towards Arietta's room. "But she is right," he stated and left them stunned in utter silence.

The family looked around at each other, and for the first time in a long time decided to leave him be.

"Arietta, wait," called Cheryl, as she followed after her and watched her go into her room and close the door behind her. "Arietta," she begged, knocking on the door.

"Go away," she sobbed.

"Arietta…"

"Leave me alone!" she moaned. "Please, just leave me alone."

Cheryl looked at the door. "Okay, call me if you want to talk." There was no reply. Reluctantly she started back along the path and ran into James. "You okay?"

"Yeah, I guess."

Cheryl really didn't know what to say to him. She kind of thought Arietta was right but, at the same time, so was James. Arietta was going through a separation.

"I'm going with my family on the ferry to St. Thomas tonight."

"Are you staying with one of them?" she asked.

"No."

"Same resort?"

"No, I need some space and time alone," he said, leaving her alone on the path. He hurried off in the direction of his own room.

Cheryl arrived back at the table and grabbed her handbag. "It was nice meeting you all."

"You too," they replied.

"I'm going back to my room. The girls are fine staying with me until you are ready to leave," said Cheryl.

"Our ferry leaves in forty-five minutes," replied Karen. "I will come by and get them in thirty minutes."

"Okay, goodnight," replied Cheryl, taking off. "Did you girls have fun?" she asked as she walked in. She listened to them talk about their evening.

"Mom, I almost forgot, Grandma and Grandpa called and asked that you call them back straight away," said Caleigh.

"I will," she replied and wondered what it was about. She picked up the phone, went onto the patio, and called their number. "Hi, Dad, are you and Mom, okay?" she asked nervously.

"We are both fine dear," he said to her in a comforting voice.

Cheryl was relieved. "What is it?"

"Well, two things, I went to your place today and picked up your mail, and there was a letter from Make-A-Wish, and it said urgent, so I opened it up, and inside was a letter and a cheque."

"What did it say?" she asked.

"Basically, they are going to cover the additional cost of your vacation and that you shouldn't have to incur any out-of-pocket expenses," he said, summarizing the letter in his hand.

"Dad, how much is the cheque for?"

"Three thousand dollars," he answered. "But that's not all, and this is the second thing: we also received a letter from the same place today and guess what?"

"They're paying off your mortgage," she said with a blank look on her face.

"What…Why, yes…How did you know?" he asked.

"Dad, do you have your letter with you?"

"One second and I will get it." He went away and came back. "I have it."

"Dad," she said, "is the first name Joanne in either of the letters?" Please say no, she thought, please say no. Seconds felt like minutes.

"Yes, yes, it's on both of them," he confirmed. "It says the fund she oversees is responsible for the donations."

"Thanks, Dad," she said.

"Me and your mom felt like we won the lottery," he said happily.

She could hear her mom's voice in the background, and then she came on the phone.

"Isn't that a wonderful surprise, honey," she said.

"It sure is, Mom," she said. "I have to go now, take care, love you both." Cheryl hung up and took the phone into the room. "Girls, I'll be back in a few minutes," she said and took off to James's room at a brisk pace.

From inside his room, James heard a frantic banging on his door. "One second," he called and opened it; he could tell by her face something was wrong. "What's happened? Come in."

She stormed inside. Turning around, she froze him in her sights; she was furious. "Who do you think you are?" she yelled at him.

"What?" he asked, bewildered.

"I am such an idiot. Here I am thinking, here is a really nice down-to-earth guy, loves kids, thinks Caleigh is wonderful and could be a really terrific friend for me. He doesn't want anything from me, he helps me out financially with my daughter's birthday, he helps make a memorable vacation for me and Caleigh." She stopped and took a deep breath. "Arietta is right; this is all just a game to you. What do you do, James? Pray on helpless, financially struggling mothers whose daughters are sick and then throw some money their way, hoping to win them over, maybe hop into bed with them, then move onto the next helpless victim, or do you just get off messing around with them?"

"What are you talking about?" he said, even more confused.

"I was speaking with Sophie and Karen at the beach, and they told me about your fund and how you contribute every year and help all these families; my heart was filled with happiness and pride knowing that the man who was responsible for that was a good friend of mine. Then they went on to tell me how you also help kids who wanted to go on special vacations, and there was one child in particular who you helped out as well as her financially struggling mother, and I thought that was so nice for him to do that. I wanted to run over to you and give you such a big hug and tell you that I thought it was so great what you were doing."

"Okay, so what—"

"Oh? So, what's the problem?" she asked. "I will tell you the problem. I just got off the phone with my father, and I received a letter and cheque from your fund to cover the additional out-of-pocket expenses I incurred on this trip, and my parents, and this is really smooth, received a letter saying that their mortgage is being paid off." She walked right up to his face. "What do you think I am, some sort of charity case that needs handouts from some pathetic, emotionless, loveless jackass? I told you when we talked about Caleigh's birthday that I didn't want charity or handouts." She paced away from him, then came back and stood in front of him. "Do you know what sacrifices I made for Caleigh? How difficult it was to save up money? How much time I took off work? How I had to work twice as hard to make it up? The sacrifice my parents made? They were supposed to have retired and been mortgage-free; now they have to keep on working because they have this huge mortgage which I have to help them with. But do you know what? When I look at Caleigh, it was all worth it." She stopped for a moment and was fighting back her tears. "Then you came along, and you were like a father, an uncle, that Caleigh has never had, and I thought this is good for her, she needs a male figure in her life…And the way you were with her…how happy she was going on that pretend date with you…You know, she still has that flower you gave her pressed between her favorite book; she plans on putting it in an activity album along with photos of her party, the fishing trip, and the underwater photos…and…" She started to cry. "And I think about how sweet it was that you went through all that trouble to make me feel comfortable with you paying for her party, and for me to know it wasn't charity, but a donation."

"Cheryl, you have this all wrong," said James, trying to comfort her.

"Get your hands off me," she shouted and stumbled backwards. She gathered her thoughts and quietly said, "I also thought you would be a good friend for me, too. I don't have any male friends. The ones I had only wanted to lay down with me, and I quickly found out that those who were treating Caleigh nice were just doing so to get to me." She looked into James's eyes. "Then I met you and I saw how wonderful, kind, and thoughtful you are, how you let a woman feel special by pulling out her chair or complimenting her on her outfit, her hair, her eyes, and her smile. And not only me, I overheard you a few days ago complimenting these two older women on their hair as they came out of the salon, and you went on your way, and they walked by me smiling and giggling like schoolgirls. You made their day; you make everyone's day…I know you have issues with your ex-wife, and I really do feel sorry for you and wish you would have opened up and spoken to me about it, as a friend." She swiped her eyes. "And I know I have Caleigh, and she needs me, and I know I don't have time for a romantic relationship right now, but I did have time for a really good friend." She stopped for a moment, thoughtfully. "Arietta is right; you are self-pitying and selfish, and you have played us both, but we are not here for your amusement, and I am not your personal charity case. I deserve you to respect how hard I have worked and the challenges my family and I have faced, and face, every day." She stopped and regained her composure. "I told you my financial situation as a friend, and you turned it around and used it to take advantage of me, my daughter, and my family. When I get home, I am going to rip up the cheque and re-mortgage my parents' house and send your money back." She started toward the door. "I know Caleigh needs me right now and has to come first, and I wanted you to be a good friend to my daughter and me, but now all I want is for you to keep away from us both!" She opened the door and turned to face him. "Here's some advice. Stop trying to make other people happy and concentrate on yourself." With that, she stormed out, slamming the door.

James sat on his bed and ran his fingers through his hair, deep in thought. After several minutes he got up, finished packing and made two phone calls; he then wrote a note and placed it in an envelope, writing a name and a room number on it and carefully sealed it; he then went to the front desk and dropped it off. He walked to the dock, met his family, and took the ferry to St. Thomas. On the way he talked to his niece and her friend about their night but discussed nothing with the adults. When they disembarked, James told them he was going for a walk. Saying goodbye, he headed off in the other direction.

"James, James," Ricky called and caught up with him. "You want some company?"

James looked at him. "No, not tonight, think I need some time to myself."

"Where you going to stay?" he asked.

"I phoned and made a reservation at Hotel 1829. It's not far from here," he assured him. "Just don't tell the family where I am. I'll call you tomorrow sometime…I'll be fine."

"Okay," replied Ricky. After giving his younger brother a hug, he turned to join the group in the taxi.

"Ricky, thanks for the bottle of champagne on Saturday night," called James.

Ricky quickly walked back to him. "How did you know it was me?"

"I know you want me to be happy again, fall in love, and have someone to share my life with; you have never given up on that dream for me. Only you would give me a gentle push with your subtle gesture of romance," replied James, smiling sadly.

"Sometimes all it takes is a gentle nudge."

"Arietta and I both enjoyed it immensely, just the two of us, looking out at the harbor. It was very romantic."

"I'm glad you enjoyed it and that it made a nice end to your night," he said cheerfully.

"Before we left, I went to grab the bottle and glasses from the balcony, you know as keepsakes, but I guess Arietta put them outside for housekeeping." He looked behind him at the taxi and his family waiting inside. "You should go. I'll call you tomorrow."

Ricky looked back at them, then at James. "All we want is for you to be happy," he said, "and I have to tell you I have never seen you as happy as you were Saturday and today, with her."

James nodded. "She is a very special woman."

Ricky grinned, gesturing for him to elaborate some more.

James laughed and gave him a slight push. "Get out of here, you."

Ricky walked away but before he jumped in the taxi he turned around to James. "Love ya." Then someone said something from inside. "Sorry…we all love ya." The taxi door closed shut.

James watched the taxi drive away.

Chapter 19

James sat on a bench and gazed out at the harbor; he could see a sprinkling of lights coming from the cruise ship, boats, and yachts. He thought about what Arietta had said to him and didn't know where to begin to fix it. Then about what Cheryl had said.

"Hey, James," said a familiar voice.

Startled, James looked behind him. "Hey, D-Mon, how are you doing?"

"I'm doing well," he replied. "Lily said I would find you here on this bench and right at this time."

"Wow!" exclaimed James. "She is good!"

D-Mon smiled. "She's helping me out at the bar tonight and saw you from the balcony," he said and turned towards the bar.

James followed his gaze and saw her leaning over the deck. She waved to him, and he waved back. James laughed.

"She said you would get a kick out of that. Why don't you come in, and I'll get you a beer?" he offered.

"I don't know," he said hesitantly.

"We have a better view than this bench, and it's somewhat busy," he said with a wide grin. "Come up and listen to some Caribbean music; it's good for you and what ails you."

James stood, picking up his overnight bag. "Do you ever think about a job in sales?"

D-Mon laughed. "I actually thought about it, but realized I already am in sales." He looked over at James. "You should know that."

"You're referring to your job as a DJ, working at the bar, and getting your family hired and their merchandise bought."

"Yeah, but that's just the sales part of it. When I'm working as a DJ at the bar, I want to make sure people are happy and feel good about themselves, and if opportunities come along where I can help my family make some money so that they can be happy and feel good about themselves too, then so be it."

They crossed the street and walked up the stairs. When they arrived at the top, he stopped and turned to James. "The sales part is just a means, it's to what ends that is important."

He looked at D-Mon. "Really?"

"It's a philosophy I live by," he replied.

"It's as simple as that?"

"Why complicate things? Keep everything simple," he said, grinning. "Let me give you an example: if the music I play doesn't make people happy, dance and sing, then the music I'm playing is the problem, not the people." He walked James to a seat. "Here, you have a beautiful view of the bench and the harbor," he said, laughing.

James laughed at his joke and watched him walk away. He looked out at the harbor; how peaceful it looked.

"Here is your beer," said another voice that he recognized but was slightly different.

"Hi, Lily," he said and waited for her transformation.

"Hi, James, how are you doing tonight?" she asked.

He was a little surprised. "I'm doing okay."

"I'm finished up here in a few minutes, mind if I join you for a drink?"

"No, please do," he replied.

She smiled. "Okay, I will see you soon."

Sipping his beer, he took in the bar; it was busy with tourists and locals. All of a sudden, a voice came over the speakers.

"Okay, ladies and gentlemen." It was D-Mon. "Tonight we are going to spice things up a little with our local music…The more you dance the longer we play…In the true words of Rio and Gio…let's get this party started!" Music came through the speakers and several girls and couples got up and started to dance.

Lily came down, sat opposite James, and put her beer on the table along with two shots of rum; she passed one to James. She lifted hers up. "Cheers," she said, their glasses clinked and together they drank the shot. Lily took a sip of her beer and took in the view of the harbor. "It's a beautiful night."

"It is," he replied anxiously, still waiting for her metamorphosis.

"No need to worry, James," she said with a shy smile. "No more transformations for you."

James was relieved. "That was a funny joke with D-Mon, knowing I would be on the bench and at that time," said James.

She laughed and grabbed his hand. "I couldn't resist, and I knew you would appreciate the humor in it."

"I did," he said and laughed with her. "So, no more transformations?"

"Let me answer that with a question," she said and looked at him. "Who are you worried about right now?"

James thought. "Arietta, Cheryl, and Caleigh," he replied.

"That is why." She spoke softly.

James sat back and looked perplexed.

"Okay, let me help you out. Before you arrived here and put your foot on the tarmac, who were you worried about?"

He thought about sitting on the plane and what he was thinking of at the time. "Her and me."

"Not anymore," she added, giving him a long look. "James, what were you feeling when you were sitting on that bench?"

He thought again. "Sad, unhappy, and alone."

"Is it because of Arietta, Cheryl and Caleigh?"

He nodded his head. "Yes."

"That is why there is no need for it, for my transformation; you are on a different path, a healthy path," she said.

"A healthy path?" he asked with uncertainty.

"Those feelings you have for those people that you can see, touch, and talk to, are good for you, for your health, and for everyone involved. You are only living if you feel, otherwise you are just a shadow, a ghost," she said. "Memories are a part of what makes us human, we all have them, but we must move on from them, so we can continue to live our lives to the fullest...yes?"

"Yes," agreed James, smiling. "Can I ask you something personal?"

"Of course," she replied.

"Why is it that you never really say anything, you just ask a lot of questions?"

"You should know the answer to that," she said.

"You see what I…" James realized she was joking with him. "Ha, ha, very funny."

"We need another shot," she said and raised her hand to the bar. The shots arrived, and together they threw them back. "To answer your question, most people already know the answers, you just need to ask them the right questions to help them find them." She looked into James's eyes. "And sometimes others need a little more persuasion," she said, grinning. She looked over at the people dancing. "Want to dance?"

"I don't know, I'm not sure I'm up to it," replied James.

"You know, D-Mon put this music on for you," she said. "Plus, it would make me happy."

James suddenly realized it wasn't always about him. "Then I guess I can't disappoint you…or him…and have him blaming his music," said James.

"Oh, he told you his philosophy," she said and laughed. They stood up and went to the dance floor.

"James and Lily are in the house, ladies and gentlemen," announced D-Mon. "Now it's a party!"

After they danced, they moved to the bar and chatted with D-Mon. James was the last one to leave, and they walked him to his hotel. He got his key, and they escorted him up the three flights of stairs to his room. D-Mon gave him his bag, and Lily a hug. He went into his room, flopped onto the bed, and passed out.

Arietta was crying hysterically when she arrived at her room. She went inside, closed the door, and fell on her bed. There was a knock at the door; it was Cheryl. She told her to leave her be. Cheryl left, and all was quiet. Her life was a disaster. She thought about packing up and going home but realized that was the life she had left to come here to give her time to think about starting a new one. What a mess she had made with James. Now she didn't even have him, and his family, they must think I'm a nutcase, she thought. Then there was Graham. She knew what she wanted to do, had to do. Why was she acting this way towards him? She didn't want to think about it anymore and, feeling sorry for herself, finally fell into a deep sleep.

She woke up the next morning hoping it was a bad dream but quickly realized it wasn't. She lay in bed and thought about her situation. She was too upset to see James and almost certain she was the last person he wanted to see, but she didn't want to be alone today. She called Cheryl and asked if Caleigh wanted to get together today. She could hear her asking and Caleigh screaming yes in the background. Thirty minutes later she arrived at Cheryl's room and knocked on the patio door.

Cheryl answered. "She's almost ready. She is just putting on her favorite dress for you." Cheryl stepped outside and closed the door behind her. "You okay?"

"I'm okay, just a lot of things going on," she said and tried to smile. "Thanks for letting Caleigh come with me today."

"You're kidding, she is so excited, she can't wait," said Cheryl with a half-smile.

"You okay?" asked Arietta. "You don't look it."

Cheryl's eyes welled up, and she told Arietta about the phone call from her parents and her confrontation with James. "I don't know if I overreacted or not. I guess I wish he would have asked me. I just feel ashamed, like he is treating me like a charity case. Why didn't he ask me? Why would he do something like that and embarrass me? Why would he do it behind my back? It bothers me."

"I think you have a right to be upset. He acted inappropriately, and I'm not saying that because of what I'm going through; he should have spoken to you first." Arietta noticed something else was bothering her. "What, there is something else?"

"Well, I went on and on about me hoping he would be my friend," explained Cheryl.

"Yes, and…?"

"I never gave him a chance to talk, I never gave him the opportunity to tell his side of the story, and I had condemned him before I even listened to him. What kind of friend am I?"

"Maybe you should go over and talk to him today while I have Caleigh," she suggested.

"I can't," she replied.

"You can't, why not?" she asked nervously.

"He went on the ferry last night with his family," Cheryl answered. Breathlessly she asked, "Is he leaving?"

"No, he was only packing a small bag, for a night or two." She looked at Arietta. "You know I don't think James has been fair to you, and I think you are right to some extent, but he has been up front and honest about how he feels and what he has gone through, whether you think it's right or not…and…"

Arietta waited. "And?"

"Well, don't you think you need to sort out your life, too?" asked Cheryl.

"Sort out my life?" asked Arietta, at a loss.

"Isn't that the reason you are here and left New York," stated Cheryl.

"Oh, I see," said Arietta. "You mean my life, and you mean with Graham."

"Yes," she confirmed. "Don't you think it may be part of the reason why James has kept his distance?"

"Well," Arietta thought for a moment, "I never really thought that could be part of the reason. Maybe you are right, maybe I do need to sort that out."

Cheryl was a little mystified. "I think that may be a good idea." Not really sure why Arietta hadn't realized this earlier.

"But I think that's only part of the reason," said Arietta, "and I don't think it's the real reason." The door opened behind Cheryl. "Here she is. You look beautiful!"

Cheryl turned around. "Oh, you look adorable," she said, noticing something else. "What's with the bag?"

"Arietta and I are having a girl day and night; in my bag are my pajamas, toothbrush, swimsuit and a change of clothes."

"Young lady, it's for the day, no one said anything about the night. Leave the bag here," said Cheryl, pointing to the room.

"Please, Mom." She batted her eyes at Arietta.

"It's okay with me if it's okay with your mom?" said Arietta.

"Are you sure?" Cheryl asked.

"I'm sure." She looked at Caleigh. "Come on, let's go drop your bag off in my room." She held out her hand to Caleigh. "Are you ready for a fun day?" she asked.

"I am," she said, grabbing Arietta's hand. "Bye, Mom."

"Bye, honey, enjoy your day," replied Cheryl. She went into her room and decided to go for a swim. She dressed in her bikini and was ready to leave when she noticed an envelope had been slid under the front door. Cheryl picked it up and opened it. It read, 'Joanne Harris, please feel free to contact her, I told her to expect your call.' It had her phone number and was signed, 'James.' She went to the phone and called the number.

"Good morning, Joanne speaking," a voice answered.

"Hello, Joanne, this is Cheryl, Cheryl White."

"Hello, Ms. White, Mr. Davenport said I should expect your call. What would you like to know?"

"What would I like to know?" she said, repeating the question back.

"He told me that you were the recipient of funds from him and that you had some questions. Usually, Mr. Davenport is very anonymous about this sort of thing, but he mentioned you are at the same resort with him and that you had some concerns, so I am here to answer any of your questions."

"I want to know when James, I mean Mr. Davenport, contacted you this week?"

"I'm sorry, I'm a little confused, this week?" she asked, looking for clarification.

"Well, he had to have contacted you this week so you could send me the funds. How else would you have known?"

"I'm confused, Ms. White, known what?" she asked.

"To send me the money," said Cheryl.

"Oh, you want to know why and how you and your parents received the additional money?" asked Joanne.

"Yes," said Cheryl.

"You know Ms. Smith?" she asked.

"Yes, she is the person I spoke with from Make-A-Wish."

"You told her about your trip and how you were going to pay the difference and about your parents mortgaging their home," she said.

"I did," she replied.

"Well, she knows me very well and the fund that I oversee. That is how you received the initial money for your vacation, so she contacted me again and told me about your situation. I in turn contacted Mr. Davenport."

"But that was over six weeks ago," Cheryl admitted.

"Well, I spoke with Jane, I mean Ms. Smith, about four weeks ago, by the time I got in touch with Mr. Davenport, and he approved it, it was two weeks ago. We tried to get the cheque to you before you left for your trip, but we were too late, but Ms. Smith said you already had made up the difference, and it would be a pleasant surprise for you when you returned home."

"So this was arranged weeks ago?"

"A month ago. Mr. Davenport's approval is just a formality; he has never refused anyone…ever," she said.

"Then how did he know it was me?" asked Cheryl. She was feeling very uneasy.

"When I talk to Mr. Davenport and tell him these special situations, he never knows who the family is, their names or where they are going. I just give him the amount, and that's just out of respect for him." There was silence on the other end of the phone. "The only way he would know about you, your name and what you received would only be from what you told him, otherwise he is unaware."

"Oh no," cried Cheryl, sitting on the edge of the bed. "What have I done?"

"Ms. White, what have you done?" she asked.

"I have to go," replied Cheryl and was holding back her tears when she said thank you and hung up the phone; she fell to the floor in a heap and cried. Minutes later she stopped and dried her eyes. "I know what I have to do," she whispered. She stood up, showered, put on a dress, and went to the dock.

"This is a really nice room," said Caleigh as she dropped her bag on the floor.

"Look at this," said Arietta, opening up the drapes and the patio door. They walked outside.

"You can sit here and run back and forth to the beach," said Caleigh excitedly. "That's awesome."

"It is," replied Arietta. "Is there anything special you want to do?"

"Well, sightseeing, swimming, eating at a restaurant, shopping, and getting an ice cream," she said.

"Okay, first on the list, sightseeing. Let's go to the lobby and see what we can find out." They went to the front desk and ended up talking to the rental agency and hiring a jeep for the afternoon. "We need to go back, get our swimsuits, sunglasses and suntan lotion," said Arietta. And as they went by the bar, Arietta noticed Cheryl in the distance, wearing a pretty dress, walking onto the dock. I wonder where she is going? she thought.

Cheryl walked off the ferry and grabbed a cab to the Marriott. She walked around the pool area looking for any of James's family but had no luck. She was about to give up when she saw Ricky and Karen walk off the elevator.

"Hi, Ricky, hi, Karen," she said.

"Hi, Cheryl," they replied.

"Is everything okay?" asked Karen.

"I'm not really sure," she admitted. "I was hoping I could talk to you for a few minutes."

"We were just going to have something to eat. Come and join us."

They went into the restaurant, sat down, and ordered lunch.

"What's wrong Cheryl?" she asked.

"I have done something awful, and I need to fix it straight away. I don't know where to start. I feel so embarrassed and ashamed," she said.

"Why don't you start from the beginning?" said Ricky.

Cheryl told them about meeting James, the birthday party and his donation, the phone call with her parents and the confrontation she had with him, and how she never gave him a chance to talk or explain himself, and finally about the conversation she had with Joanne. "I told him that all I want is for him to keep away from us both." She was almost in tears but didn't want to make a scene and desperately fought to hold her composure. "I feel so awful."

"There, there, dear, don't fret; it was an honest mistake," reassured Karen.

"I just need to talk to him and straighten this out; he told me he wasn't staying here. Do you know where I can find him?"

"Sorry, Cheryl, we don't know."

"I do," offered Ricky.

Karen turned to him. "You do?"

"He promised me not to tell the family," he revealed. "He is going to call me today, and I was hoping to go see him and make sure he was doing okay. I was going to tell you after he called, I swear."

Karen smiled. "You're a good brother and a good husband, and I know you were," she said, kissing him on the cheek.

Ricky looked at Cheryl. "He's staying at Hotel 1829."

James dressed, had something to eat, and decided to visit some of the places that Caleigh and her mom had. As he walked, he thought long and hard about everything that had happened and decided what he needed to do. At the Emancipation Gardens he called Ricky and agreed to meet him at four. He arrived back at his hotel a few minutes early and pulled up a chair at the rustic bar and waited.

"James."

"Hey, Ricky," he replied.

"What did you do all day?" he asked.

"Sightseeing…I visited some of the historical places close to here," he said and turned to the bartender and ordered Ricky a beer, "as well as doing a lot of reflecting and soul-searching."

"Come up with anything?" Ricky asked as he took the beer off the bartender.

"I need to go back to St. John. I feel like I'm hiding out over here," he said.

"Running away, I think is more accurate," suggested Ricky.

James smiled. "You are right…running away."

"What are you going to do?"

"Go back tomorrow and see if she will talk to me," said James.

"Who will?" asked Ricky. He already knew the answer; he just wanted to hear him say her name.

"Arietta," he replied.

"And if she won't," he asked.

"Then I really can't do more than try," he speculated.

"You can try really hard," said Ricky, half-joking. "On the phone you mentioned something about Cheryl?"

"You know she called me a jackass," said James and laughed a little.

Ricky almost spit up his beer laughing. "Seems like she has you pegged."

"She does," he replied and grinned at his brother wiping the beer from his chin. "She told me she never wants me to see her or Caleigh again." James was looking at Ricky and didn't notice someone sitting down beside him. "Let me tell you what happened." He was about to tell him the whole story when Ricky interrupted.

"Listen, I just wanted to stop by and make sure you are okay, but I have to go," said Ricky.

"But you just got here, stay for one more," he pleaded.

Ricky finished his beer. "Don't worry, you're in good hands, call me," he said and literally ran out the door.

James turned to the bar and thought, that was odd…in good hands. He felt the eyes of the person sitting next to him and turned around to see it was Cheryl.

"Hello, James."

"Hi, Cheryl," he replied.

"Can I buy you a beer?" she asked.

"I guess."

She ordered two beers and waited for the bartender to put them on the bar and walk away. "James, I am so sorry for what I said to you the other day. I was so wrong to have judged you so quickly without letting you tell me your side of the story. I feel so awful."

"It's okay, you reacted to what you thought was the situation. It's understandable."

"I know, but I said horrible things to you and called you names and put you down. I'm so ashamed of what I said." She started to cry.

He stood up and put his arms around her and held her gently. "Listen, no need to apologize; it was an honest mistake, no harm done."

"You mean that?" she asked and pulled away, looking at him.

"Of course, I do," he said, smiling. "Friends fight."

"They do, and I really want us to be good friends."

"I'd say we already are." He sat down again and handed her a napkin.

She wiped her eyes, then picked up her beer. "To good friends," she said.

"To good friends," he replied and looked at her for a moment. "You know, I am in awe of you," he confessed.

"You are?"

"All that you have done for Caleigh, all the sacrifices you have made, and all the hard work. I am so impressed with you. You are a great woman, a great mother, and a good friend." He raised his glass.

She smiled as tears rolled down her cheeks. She knew he had every right not to talk to her ever again, but instead, here he was, giving her tremendous compliments. She took a drink, then kissed him on the cheek and whispered, "Thank you."

He handed her another napkin. "No more tears."

"No more," she replied and wiped them away.

"Your parents seem like very special people," he commented.

"They are," she replied. "Helpful, generous, caring, and as honest as the day is long." She thought for a moment. "They are both financially savvy. Guess it has to do with their backgrounds; they're both accountants. They helped me with mine and they got to see, first-hand, the difficulties and challenges I faced. They said it would be nice to help other parents with children with cancer who are struggling financially, you know, get them access to funds or loans at an extremely low interest rate. They even talked about opening a business to help them."

"You are lucky you have them. Few people are as fortunate as you."

"I know, they are a blessing," she said thankfully. "Some people have no one to help them, and I guess that's what they were thinking," she replied.

"How did Caleigh like hanging out with Elizabeth and Caitlin?"

"She loved it," she replied happily, and told him about Caleigh's night with them. "She is with Arietta today and is having a sleepover in her room tonight. She is so excited."

"I bet she is, that will be fun," said James, and then talked about his night with Lily and D-Mon.

They moved to the restaurant and sat on the open-air patio to have dinner. Cheryl listened as James spoke about an idea he had for Caleigh.

Arietta and Caleigh drove to the Annaberg Sugar Plantation, then walked the Reef Bay Trail and saw the petroglyphs, and then they stopped off at Hawksnest Beach for a swim. After, they went to Cruz Bay and walked around the boutiques, where Arietta bought Caleigh a dress, sandals, and a matching handbag, and then stopped in at Driftwood Dave's and shared a hamburger and baby back ribs. They went back to the resort, had another swim in the pool, then dried off and each had a chocolate ice cream sundae. They went back to Arietta's room, put on their pajamas, and watched a movie; they both fell asleep well before the movie ended.

Chapter 20

James checked out, picked up his bag, and walked with Cheryl through the iron gates and down the steps.

Cheryl stopped and looked back at the front of the hotel. "I love this hotel; the rooms are quaint, warm and cozy, the rustic bar area, and dinner on the patio with the amazing food and view." She turned and walked away with James. "It's very romantic."

"It is that" he agreed and walked with her to the ferry.

Cheryl turned and gave him a big hug and a kiss on the cheek. "Thank you for last night and for what you are going to do for Caleigh, it's amazing. You have made me so incredibly happy I can't take this smile off my face."

"I like you much better when you are smiling than crying," he said.

"Or yelling at you," she added, and they both laughed. She boarded the ferry and waved goodbye.

James took a taxi to the Marriot Resort. He had called his family before he left his hotel, and they agreed to meet him in Sophie and Ken's room. He knocked on the door and went inside. They sat and had coffee as they listened to what he had to say regarding Caleigh, and Cheryl's parents.

"I thought this morning we would call room service and have breakfast on the patio, and we can run back and forth to the beach," suggested Arietta.

"I would love that," replied Caleigh.

"But first let's get dressed and go to the lobby so we can return the keys to the jeep." Arietta got up, picked out some clothes and went into the bathroom to get ready. When she came out, Caleigh was already dressed. "Okay, little lady go brush those teeth." She watched Caleigh go into the bathroom and walked outside onto the patio. She looked over at St. Thomas and thought about James being somewhere on the island. She hoped he was doing okay. For some reason she felt scared, scared like the time she decided to walk out of her office and come here. She wondered if he was thinking of her and if he was scared too. Deep down she missed him, she missed being with him, she missed talking with him, she missed his smile, the way he made her laugh, the way he danced with her, the way he made her feel; she missed everything about him. But unfortunately, it wasn't reciprocated, because he was still in love with someone else.

"I'm ready," said Caleigh, cutting short Arietta's thoughts.

"One second," said Arietta and went inside to grab the keys. "Let's go." They went down the path, by the bar, past the pool and to the lobby. Arietta handed the keys to Caleigh; she went inside the rental agency, dropped them off and came back out.

"Breakfast and beach," said Caleigh, holding her hand.

"Breakfast and beach," replied Arietta. They walked back the same way they came, but this time, when they reached the bar, something caught Arietta's eye, stopping her. It was Cheryl walking down the dock to the resort; she was wearing a big smile and the same pretty dress she had on yesterday. Arietta went numb and froze.

"Come on, Arietta," said Caleigh, pulling on her hand.

Arietta felt Caleigh pulling her hand and turned around and walked back with her to the room. They ordered room service and changed into their bikinis. The food arrived, and they placed it on the patio and ate, played on the beach, swam, and ate some more.

Cheryl walked off the ferry and was smiling at what had happened. She looked up and saw Caleigh and Arietta walking down the path and thought about catching up with them but decided to let them enjoy their morning. She went back to the room, showered, and put on her bikini.

Around noon, Caleigh packed up her things and walked with Arietta back to see her mom. When they arrived, Cheryl was lying on a chaise, sunbathing.

"Mom," shouted Caleigh, running over to hug her. "We had so much fun. We drove in a Jeep and went sightseeing at the plantation and walked on a trail; we went swimming at the beach, we shopped in Cruz Bay, and Arietta bought me a dress, sandals, and a bag; we ate at a cool restaurant called Driftwood Dave's, we swam here at the pool and had ice cream, and we watched a movie in bed. And today we ate on the patio, played on the beach, and went swimming. It was fun, fun, fun."

"Wow! Looks like you two had a wonderful time together," said Cheryl, looking at Arietta. "Thank you."

"Sure," said Arietta coldly. "Here is your bag, Caleigh," said Arietta with a smile, handing it to her.

Cheryl noticed something was off. "Caleigh, can you take your bag inside and unpack it for me?"

"Okay, Mom." She went over to Arietta and gave her a big hug. "Thank you," she said, going inside.

"Was she okay? You seem as if something is wrong?" she asked, sitting up.

"She's fine, she's an angel. What about you?" Arietta asked in an aggressive tone.

"What do you mean by that?" replied Cheryl, now on the defensive.

"I saw you heading to the dock yesterday. Where did you go?" she asked.

"I went over to St. Thomas," she replied. "Why?"

"I was about to ask you that same question," she said.

"I went over to find James and to talk with him," replied Cheryl.

"And did you?" she queried.

"Yes, with the help of his brother," she replied, baffled.

"Did you make it back here last night?" she enquired.

"No, it was too late, and I stayed…" All of a sudden, she realized where Arietta was going with her line of questioning.

"You couldn't wait to go see him and get your hands on him, so you dump your child with me and take off to have a good time. I saw you this morning getting off the ferry, wearing your sleazy smile and the same slutty dress that you wore yesterday," accused Arietta in an upset voice. "What kind of mother are you to do that to your daughter? And what kind of person are you to do that to your friend?"

"You have it all wrong," said Cheryl, trying to explain.

"I don't think so," replied Arietta. "Stay away from me, you bitch." She stormed off.

Minutes later Caleigh came out of the room and saw her mom upset. "Is everything okay, Mom?"

"Everything is fine," she said. "Come over here and give your mom a hug."

"Why?" she asked.

"Because I need one," she said, and held her daughter tightly to her chest so she wouldn't see the tears that were rolling down her face.

James stepped off the noon ferry and onto the path that led to his room. He saw Arietta walking towards him from the direction of Cheryl's room and stopped as she approached him.

"You bastard!" she yelled and strode past him to her room. She went inside, fell on the bed, put her face in the pillow and cried.

Confused, James walked slowly to his room. He threw his bag on the floor and lay down on his bed; he looked up at the ceiling and closed his eyes, rubbing his hands over his face.

After an hour of crying, Arietta decided that she wasn't going to spend the last few days hiding in her room. She put on her bikini and decided to go for a swim. She went to the other side of the pool to avoid walking into Cheryl and picked out a chaise that was in the sun. She put her towel down and went in the water. In front of her, she could see Cheryl's room, and soon after noticed Caleigh coming out in her swimsuit, Cheryl following behind. Arietta froze for a moment in fear that they were going to come into the pool, but they turned and headed in the direction of the beach. Caleigh was happily walking in front while Cheryl walked sadly behind her. Arietta swam for a while, then got out of the pool, lay on the chaise, closed her eyes, and sunbathed.

James jumped in a taxi and went to Cruz Bay. He walked around and did some window shopping for an hour, then went and sat on a patio that overlooked the beach and the harbor. He sipped his beer and watched the children playing in the sand and looked out at the boats leaving the bay. When he stepped off the ferry his original plan was to knock on Arietta's door and hope she would give him a chance to speak, but after her last comment it seemed that she had seen enough of him for a while, maybe forever. He thought about her, wondering what he should do.

The warm sun felt good on Arietta's body. With her eyes closed she tried not to think about James, but it was difficult. The time they had spent together and the way he made her feel was consuming her thoughts, and she wondered if she had done the right thing. Maybe she should have spoken to him in private and not within eyesight and earshot of his family, but in her defense, she knew they had seen him reject her attempt to kiss him, and she had been embarrassed and humiliated, and they needed to know what had happened between them to make her want to kiss him and act the way she did. She wondered how he could feel nothing for her and then go and spend the night with Cheryl. Maybe that wasn't their first and only time? But it had to be. And why did they? Did she go to talk to him, and one thing led to the next? She didn't know, and then it hit her; she didn't know and maybe it was time she got some answers. She decided she needed to put her emotions and feelings aside and talk with James, but how could she; he probably wouldn't want to see her again, never mind talk to her.

Cheryl went to the beach and pulled the chaise under the shade of a palm tree. She watched Caleigh build a sandcastle with her friends and thought about James and how great he was with her and about the time Caleigh told her and Arietta that she was on a date with him and the flower he had given her. She wondered whether she should tell James what Arietta had seen and said to her or whether she should try to talk to Arietta herself. Arietta wasn't talking to James, and she realized she was left with only one option; she would have to talk to Arietta. She thought about Arietta and how she took Caleigh for the day sightseeing and bought her a beautiful outfit and had her for a sleepover. The spa day they spent together and laughed as she recalled the two guys trying to pick them up and them standing up at the same time to leave. She thought about Arietta for quite some time and suddenly realized something and sat up.

Arietta went and cooled off in the pool. She thought about Graham and wished that things had gone better between them. She figured Graham would tell Violet and Vincent tomorrow, during their weekly luncheon and cocktails, about what she had said to him. She thought back to that time in her office when she made the decision to come here to fix her life and put it back on track; how ironic, she thought. She stayed around the pool for the afternoon, then went to her room.

James had some lunch and spent a few hours talking to a few of the locals. He said goodbye and grabbed a taxi to the resort and went to his room.

Cheryl and Caleigh spent the afternoon at the beach. It was getting late, and they decided it was time to get ready for dinner. They packed up their belongings and headed to their room. They dressed for dinner and went upstairs and sat looking out at the harbor. They talked about what they were going to do later on tonight and tomorrow. All of a sudden, Cheryl noticed Arietta walking into the restaurant and pretended not to see her. Someone called Arietta's name, and she spoke with him as he led her to his table. Arietta was far enough away where they couldn't see one another or make eye contact. Cheryl concentrated on Caleigh and talked to her throughout the evening. After dinner they went for a walk.

Arietta showered and dressed. She put on her dress and heels and decided she would eat at the Terrace Restaurant and enjoy a view with dinner. She went up to the restaurant and spotted Cheryl and Caleigh sitting outside. The only empty table was the one next to them. She wondered if she should turn around and leave or if there was a table inside that was free.

"Arietta," called a voice off to her far left.

She looked over to see Gio walking towards her. He came up to her and kissed her on each cheek. "How are you, my dear?" he asked.

"Doing well," she replied.

"Where is James? Are you dining alone tonight?" he asked, looking around for him.

"He is back at the room," she replied nervously. "He's resting."

Gio could sense something wasn't right but ignored it. "Well, come dine with us. We just arrived," he said and pointed at several tables occupied by his family and friends.

"Okay," she said shyly and took his arm and walked with him to a seat next to Rio.

"Hello, Arietta, my dear," said Rio. "Good to see you again."

"Thank you, same to you...all of you," she replied as she looked around the table.

"I just wanted to say once more how beautiful our day was. We talked about it the whole time we were away," said Rio. "It will be a day I will never forget."

"Thank you," said Arietta, remembering back to that day, but somewhat sadly now because it reminded her of James and the fun they had and how he made her laugh and smile. "When did you get back?"

"Yesterday, we left Wednesday afternoon and were there for seven nights," she explained. "We all went to the British Virgin Islands; they are beautiful. If you get a chance, you and James should visit before you leave."

Arietta gave a half-smile. "We should try," she forced out.

They told Arietta all about the British Virgin Islands, about The Baths and its rock formations, and huge boulders and cave; about the beautiful beaches at White Bay, Devil's Bay, and Savannah Bay; the reefs at Smugglers' Cove and the shipwreck and marine life at the Rhone National Marine Park and the Bubbly Pool.

"That does sound wonderful," she said and was glad she had joined them; it had taken her mind off of pressing matters and the problems in her life.

James ordered room service, sat on his patio, and ate in silence. After he finished, he poured a glass of wine and looked out at the lights flickering on the boats and yachts. He gazed up at the hundreds of stars in the sky, and all of a sudden, he felt very lonely and alone. He realized he needed to be around people and decided to go to the bar. He finished his wine, took a shower, and dressed.

They finished their dinners and decided they would go to the bar. They found several tables close to the band and talked. Arietta sat facing the main entrance and was talking to Rio when something made her look up at a figure walking in. Her heart sank; it was James. He looked over at her and calculated that sitting at the end of the bar, close to where he came in, gave them ample distance. He sat down and ordered a drink. She continued talking to Rio, who had seen what had caught her eye and the resulting sad expression that came over her face but said nothing and pretended she hadn't noticed. And all was fine until…

"Look who we met ordering a drink at the bar," announced Rocco and Joey.

"He wasn't going to come over because he thought it was a family thing," said Rocco, "but we told him he was family and that his lovely girl had already joined us."

Joey grabbed a seat and put it right next to Arietta.

"You needed a little nap?" asked Joey.

"Yeah, been a long day," he replied.

"Well, that's good that you are all rested, because we are all here to have fun tonight," said Joey, sitting down next to him and began regaling him with stories about the British Virgin Islands.

Arietta never spoke to James, and he never spoke to her; with everyone else they were polite and cordial. Everyone was so busy talking and having a fun time that no one even noticed the silence between the two of them, no one that is, except for Rio and Gio. The band played, and people began dancing and moving between tables to socialize. After an hour, James said goodnight and got up to leave. Arietta stood up as well and said she would walk with him to the room. They both walked out of the bar and hadn't gotten far when she turned to him.

"Why did you do it?" she asked.

"Do what?" he asked, wondering which 'it' she was referring to.

"Sleep with Cheryl last night?" she asked.

"What? What are you talking about?" he said.

"Did you see Cheryl yesterday afternoon? Did she stay in Charlotte Amalie?" she questioned.

"Yes, and yes," he replied. "But that doesn't mean that—"

"Did she stay in the same hotel with you?" she continued.

"Why would you think we were together?" he asked. "Where did you come up with this?"

Arietta told him about seeing Cheryl the day before, leaving on the ferry and returning early the next morning and the only person she was with was him.

"So, you automatically assume that we slept together?" he asked.

"Yes, I do," she said honestly.

He looked at her and thought for a moment about how to answer her. He could be upset with the accusation and let her have it; instead, he remained calm. "Cheryl did come to see me, we talked, she did stay over at the hotel, we did not sleep together, I got Cheryl her own room."

"Sure," she said, unconvinced.

"Why did you bother to ask me?" he asked.

"What do you mean?"

"You ask me a question, I give you the answer, and you still don't believe me. Why did you bother to ask me if you are not going to believe me?" He leaned into her and whispered, "I haven't been intimate with a woman in over seven years."

Arietta looked at him. "Oh, I forgot…you're still in love with your precious ex-wife."

He looked at her and shook his head. "Maybe you should worry about your own life first and take care of that before you start worrying about everyone else's."

"What's that supposed to mean?" she asked.

"Goodnight," said James and left.

Arietta watched him leave and turned around and sat at a secluded table by the beach and ordered a drink. She wasn't there long when someone sat next to her.

"How are you doing?" asked Rio.

She was going to lie and say fine but had the feeling her and Gio were aware that something was going on. "I've been better," she replied.

"You want to talk about it?"

Her first reaction was no, but she changed her mind and told Rio what had happened since they were away.

"My impression of James is that he seems like a very down-to-earth and honest person," commented Rio.

"He is," replied Arietta. "That's one of the things I like about him."

Rio gave her a puzzled look.

"What?" she asked.

"If he says he didn't, then why don't you believe him?" asked Rio.

"I don't know," replied Arietta, confused. "I guess these feelings he still has for his ex-wife are strange to me. After so many years, she still has this awful grip on him, and he seems like he doesn't want to pull away from it and…"

"And?" Rio asked.

Arietta paused. "Love again."

Rio looked off in the distance and told Arietta a story. "When I met Gio I knew straight away he was my true love and that I wanted to be with him forever. There is not a day that goes by that I don't look at him and realize what a wonderful, loving, kind, generous and thoughtful man he is. He makes me smile and he makes me laugh. Now, don't get me wrong, we have had our moments and our fights but that is just a part of growing together as a couple, and you have so many good times that those not-so-good times are few and far between, and funny enough, when we both look back on some of those not-so-good times, we think about how trivial they are today." She stopped for a moment and gathered her thoughts. "And as you get older you worry about different things."

Arietta moved closer to her. "Like what?"

"Like dying, I don't mean dying and what's next, I mean dying and leaving the other person you love alone in this world. I know if anything were to happen and I lost Gio, I would never be with anyone else. To me, he is my world and irreplaceable. I would enjoy my family, my grandchildren and tell them all about him. He would always be in my conversations, in my memories and in my thoughts until it was time for me to move on." She paused, and this time looked at Arietta. "I feel so lucky that the person I loved from the first time I set eyes on him has been a part of my life all these years. I don't know what I would have done or how I would have felt or reacted if I lost him only a few years after we were married." She stopped talking and waited for Arietta's reaction.

Arietta was looking at Rio, but her mind was racing, and all the conversations with James played in her head. Then suddenly it hit her. "Oh no!" she cried, standing up, her face drained of color. "Oh nooo."

Chapter 21

She knocked on his door, but there was no answer, so she went around the back to see if he was on his patio; he wasn't, just an unopened bottle of wine and a glass on the table. She looked around, and, in the distance, she saw a silhouette walking on the beach. She kicked off her shoes and walked towards it, hoping it was him.

"James," she called.

He turned toward her.

"Tell me about your wife?" she asked.

He started to walk away from her, and she didn't know what to do. He turned around. "Come and walk with me."

She did, and they walked for a while in silence.

"Around fourteen years ago when Stephanie was about nine, Ricky and Karen would call me up a couple times a week and ask me if I could pick her up from elementary school. The school had a playground, so after I met her, we would go there, and I would watch her and her friends play, and push them on the swings. One day I was at the school waiting for Stephanie. She had run back to her classroom to get something, and I started talking to the grade-two teacher…"

"So you are the Uncle James that she talks about all the time," she said.

"That would be me," he replied with a smile.

She liked his smile. "My name is Clair; I teach grade two."

"I'm Uncle James, the struggling writer," he replied.

"Do I have to call you Uncle James, too?" she joked.

"No, you don't," he replied, a little shy and embarrassed.

"Can we go to the park?" said Stephanie as she ran toward him.

"Yeah, let's go," said James. "It was nice meeting you, Clair."

"It was nice meeting you, James," she replied.

"If you want to come to the park, that's where we will be," he said timidly.

"If I finish up early enough, maybe I will."

"I took Stephanie to the playground, and fifteen minutes later Clair joined me, and we sat and talked for thirty minutes. Before she left, we exchanged numbers, and I called her up, and we started dating. I was twenty-six at the time, and she was twenty-five. She was a beautiful girl, with long blonde hair, and an attractive smile. She was kind, considerate and gave without ever thinking twice or ever expecting anything in return. She loved kids, and she was a great teacher…Everyone loved her, my family, my friends, and all the children she taught. I had taken English at college and wanted to be a writer. At that point I had sold articles to local magazines and wrote some stories in the local papers. So, she pushed me to write something on a bigger scale, like a novel, so in between these articles I started to write my first novel and within eighteen months it was published. We got engaged, and ten months later we were married. During the day she would go to her teaching job, and I would write, and everything was going really well. We had rented a little place and had talked about buying a house when we had a little more money, and maybe then we would start a family, but in the meantime, we just enjoyed each other and the little we had…" James stopped for a moment; he was getting emotional.

"You okay? You want to stop?" Arietta asked.

"I'm okay, just give me a moment," he said and composed himself. "We had been married for almost four years, and, in this time, I had published two novels and had just finished my third. We had more money now, so we moved into a small house and were trying to have a family. She had always talked about going away, but we had put it off because we never seemed to have the time or the money to do so, so we decided it was now or never, and agreed to go away. She told me she was going to book the trip; she always dreamed about going to the US Virgin Islands and to St. John and knew everything about the place, so she wanted to plan it all and surprise me; she was so happy." He paused for a moment and continued. "One Saturday morning we were fooling around on the bed, and I fondled her breast, and she gave out a small cry in pain, like you do when you bang your arm or leg on something. She thought that maybe they were just sensitive, but I urged her to get it checked out. The following week we were called into her doctor's office. She was told she had cancer in one of her breasts and that they needed to remove the tumor. They told us that it was the only place the cancer had been found, so they operated and removed it successfully. A few months later they found another one in her other breast, but this time when they did some further tests, they had found that it had spread throughout her body, and they gave her six months to live." He stopped talking for a while and wiped tears from his eyes. Arietta grabbed his other hand and held it tightly. "They said there was nothing they could do for her now, and in the next few months, they would give her something for the pain. Since there was no need for her to be at the hospital, she stayed at home, and I stayed with her and took care of her. We also had a nurse come in a few days a week to check on her, and my family helped out as best they could by getting groceries, dropping off meals, and taking care of the day-to-day stuff, like laundry, and making sure bills were paid." James stopped walking and looked out at the water. "One day we were sitting at the house watching a movie, and she turned to me and said she would like to see the children in her class one more time before she stopped looking like herself. So, I arranged to have them come in one morning to see her, and really to say goodbye. They all brought in pictures which we put up on the wall. Then they gave her a special gift that they had made; each one of the children had painted one bead, some were one color, others were multicolored, some had polka dots, some had stripes, but each had its own personality like each of the twenty-four children, and each bead had been threaded through a string to make a necklace. They stood around her, and each said their name, pointed to their bead and described it. The children had also written on a piece of paper, their name, and a description of their bead, and called the poem, 'Twenty-Four Children.' They gave the necklace and poem to her. Clair cried, I cried, and the children cried. I put the necklace on her, and she gave the children each a hug and a kiss on top of their head. She never saw them again and never took that necklace off. She would always touch it and smile, and I knew she was thinking, not only about those children, but all the children that she had taught." James started walking again, and Arietta said nothing, giving him the time he needed to collect his thoughts. "One day, Clair asked me to make her a promise…"

"When I'm gone, I want you to live and enjoy your life and meet someone. You deserve to be happy. You have such a big heart; please don't waste it grieving over me. You will always have our memories and the life we shared. I want you to know that I am so glad I met you, and you are such a big part of my life. I love you so much…You're my James in shining armor."

"I love you," he said as tears rolled down his eyes. "I don't think I could ever be with someone again."

"James, it would make me sad if you spent the rest of your life alone, missing me and unhappy. Eventually you will have to let me go and find someone else to share your life with." She looked at him. "James, I love you, but you will never find her if you don't let me go."

James cried on her chest. He didn't want her to go anywhere. She stroked his hair; she loved how soft it was, especially when it was messy, and how she loved running her hands through it. "James, look up at me," she said and waited until he did. "I always talked about going to St. John. I want you to go for me, for us both. I want you to go and feel the sun on your face and the clear blue water on your feet. Promise me you will go for me, for us?" she said.

"I don't know if I can."

"Look at me, James," she said, and she waited for him to look at her. "Promise me you will go when the time is right."

"How will I know?" he asked.

"You will," she replied.

"I promise," he said and kissed her softly on the lips.

James slowed down and stopped again, facing Arietta. "Another day, she was playing with her necklace, so I asked Clair…"

"What are you thinking about?"

She started crying, and I went over and held her. "I didn't know how or when to tell you this, but I know I want to and I need to," she said, in between tears.

"Clair, you can tell me anything," James said.

"I'm worried that you may not be able to take it, and it scares me. I don't want you to hurt any more than you already do, but I want you to know," she said, crying.

He waited for her to calm down. "I promise you I won't."

"You promise?" she asked.

"I do."

"When I had my blood tests done the second time and they found the cancer, the doctor also told me that I was several weeks pregnant and that because of my condition the baby would stop developing…so she is going to be going with me to Heaven."

James held her tightly. "Well, I know you will take care of her there," he replied and held her for a long time. Eventually he got up and went into the kitchen to make some tea, and she could hear him crying. When he returned to her, he had wiped his eyes and acted like everything was okay.

"Put down the tea, James," she said, "and come over here." She held him in her arms. "Please don't cry on your own."

He cried in her arms, and she cried with him.

James looked into Arietta's eyes. "Over the next six months, I watched this beautiful woman, full of life, shrink to someone I barely recognized. For everything in my life to die, and be taken from me, made me angry and hateful. I stopped believing in God and lost my faith. Clair and I went to church every Sunday, but the day they carried her coffin out those church doors was the last day for me. I went off the deep end. I went on drinking binges, slept all day, and I stopped seeing my family and friends. My brother Ricky told them to give me some time alone, until one day Sophie and Karen came by and found me on the bathroom floor. They thought I had killed myself; I had just passed out from drinking too much. They started coming over more frequently to check on me and take care of me. They would clean my house, do my laundry, and prepare meals for me. Then Sophie said something to me one day…"

"James, when are you going to start writing again?" she asked from the next room.

"Never, I don't have anything nice to write about anymore…I just want to die," he replied.

James never heard her response but could hear her sobbing and went in to see if she was okay. "Everything all right?" he asked.

She looked at him. "Why do you say things like that? Do you know, everyday Karen, Ricky, Ken, and I walk in here to see how you are doing, and we have this awful fear that when we open your door, we will find you lying on the floor, dead." She looked directly at him. "Clair is gone. We all miss her, and we all loved her, but I miss you and I love you, and I'm worried for you. I don't want to lose you too. You need to talk to someone…"

James looked away from Arietta and down at the sand. "My sister had this look of despair and helplessness on her face that I will never forget. I never realized until that point what I was putting them through. They had all put their lives on hold for me, to help me out, and I was just taking it from them and not helping myself; I was making their lives a living hell. They had children that needed their attention, and I was taking it away from them. I knew I had given up on life, on me, but my family didn't deserve to be pulled into that." He put Arietta's arm through his, and they started to walk again, and he continued. "I walked over to my sister and gave her a big, long hug. When I let go, I went to the kitchen and placed the liquor and beer in a box and put them at the front door. I put the dishes in the sink and started to clean them…"

Sophie walked in. "What are you doing?" she asked.

"Helping to tidy up," he replied. "Can't expect you to do it forever."

"What's with the box by the front door?" she asked.

He walked over with her, and they looked down at the box of booze. "I was going to do the symbolic thing and pour the booze down the drain to show that I was cleaning myself up and taking a break, but realized Ricky and Ken would probably be upset with me for throwing it out and not giving it to them," he said and managed a small smile.

It was the first time Sophie had heard him joke in a long time and that smile on his face was a much-welcomed surprise. She held her brother, and for the first time in a long time had a feeling of hope for him. James helped her tidy up, showered, and called a psychiatrist…

They turned around and headed back. "So I went and talked to someone. We met every other week for a few months, and we talked for thirty minutes; she really helped me come to terms with what I was going through. We talked about my writing, and she suggested that maybe I should use these feelings I had and transpose them down on paper. Which I did, and it helped me a lot. Over the last six years, I ended up writing an additional three novels; the last one has just gone to print. I also started going to the gym and taking care of myself again, and several years ago I set up a fund under Clair's name, the 'Clair Davenport Fund.' Its main purpose is to give people diagnosed with cancer or recovering patients a chance to go on their dream vacation, something Clair was unable to do, and I know would have been happy to support. I only wish we would have gone away." James stopped and put his hand over his face and cried. Arietta put her arms around him and held him for a while. He regained his composure, and they started walking and he continued. "A few months ago, I decided it was time to go through her clothes in the closet. As I was putting them in bags, I came across a suitcase in the very back; I almost didn't see it. There was a sticky note with her writing on it; it read, 'Open me, James.' I opened it, and inside was a letter from her, and it basically said, 'if I was cleaning her closet and giving her clothes to charity, that it was time for that vacation, hope you like the suitcase, love Clair.' There was also a picture of St. John and the resort she had picked out and an envelope and on it read, 'This is my treat.' I opened it up, and inside was ten thousand dollars. I cried, put everything back in the suitcase and placed it in the back of the closet and closed the door. I started to walk away but stopped and went back into the closet and pulled the suitcase out and placed it on the bed. I called my sister and my brother, and over the next couple of days, I booked and paid for a vacation for me, my brother and sister, their spouses, my nieces, and their friends. I used Clair's money for my trip and paid for the others with my own. The reason I came to this resort by myself, is because this was the one she had wanted us to come to…" He managed a smile. "Plus, I knew my family would want to be somewhere that was more of a party place and closer to the action."

They arrived at his patio, and he went inside, brought out another glass and a corkscrew. He grabbed the bottle of wine and the glass from the table, and they walked to the beach and sat on two chairs. He opened the wine, poured it, handing Arietta a glass.

"I feel so awful about what I said to you; I didn't know she had passed away. I am so sorry. I didn't mean it. I am so ashamed for saying that to you, and your family they must think I am heartless and cruel."

"You don't need to worry; you didn't know," he said. "After you left, I went back and told them you were right."

"I was right about what?" she asked.

"Everything," he said and looked at her. "I have never truly let her go. I kept on holding on to her and talking about her as if she was a living person, and I made it difficult on everyone, mostly on me."

"It's understandable," she said, comforting him.

"It is, but not seven years later; it's unhealthy," he said. "After I arrived here, weird things started happening to me, and I had these dreams, and this tremendous feeling of being lost. I felt extremely guilty about being happy and spending time with you, but I have come to realize it was my own self-pitying heart and thoughts betraying me. Clair never wanted me to grieve or feel guilty; she wanted me to be happy."

"By weird things, do you mean Lily?"

James nodded his head. "Yes."

"It is strange what she said about you being Clair's knight in shining armor and the necklace."

"How she knew all that is beyond me," he replied, shaking his head. "But I don't think I'm going to spend any more time trying to prove that scientifically; just going to put it down as Lily and Clair giving me a push in the right direction." He sipped his wine. "You know, the dreams have stopped."

"Really," said Arietta.

James then told Arietta about his meeting with Lily the night before. "So, no more surprises from her, no more dreams…I guess I'm on my own."

"You are not on your own," she said, squeezing his hand.

"That's nice to know."

"So, you haven't been with anyone for seven years?" she asked.

"No, the last person was Clair."

"Oh!"

James noticed the concern on her face. "What's wrong?"

She told James about her confrontation with Cheryl. "I basically called her a slut and a terrible mother."

"I am sure you can work this out," he said reassuringly. "Maybe tomorrow you can go talk to her and straighten everything out," he suggested. James then told her everything that happened with him and Cheryl in St. Thomas, what they talked about in regard to Caleigh, and how he met with his family and what he talked about with them in regard to Caleigh and Cheryl's parents. He also told her about the conversation Cheryl had with him during lunch, after the fishing trip, about her mundane job and how she was looking for something challenging and more rewarding, how she talked about working and living in Manhattan. "I just want you to know everything I know about her before you talk to her. Cheryl doesn't know about Clair yet; I wanted you to know first. I think after you talk to her, I need to spend some time with Cheryl and Caleigh and let them know everything, too."

"You do," replied Arietta and squeezed his hand. She looked up at the night sky and was happy they had talked. She hoped Cheryl would be as understanding and forgiving as James.

"It's getting late," he said, standing up. He picked up the bottle and corkscrew, and they went back to her room. Arietta said goodnight, and he watched her climb the steps to her patio. "Arietta," he said. She stopped, and he walked up the steps and gave her a hug and a kiss on the cheek. "I'll see you tomorrow morning."

"Tomorrow morning," she repeated. Smiling, she went into her room.

Chapter 22

The phone rang, waking Arietta up. She looked at the clock. "Ten," she said to herself and picked up the phone. "Hello," she answered.

"Hello, Arie, it's Graham."

"Hello, Graham, what do you want?" she asked in a tired voice.

"We need to meet," he said in a confident tone. "Today."

"Well, you're in New York, and I'm here so unless you learnt how to—"

"I'm here," he said.

"Where?" she asked as she sat up.

"I'm on the beautiful island of St. John and staying in one of the villas," he replied, sure of himself.

"What villa?" she asked.

"One of the spacious and breath-taking villas that the resort you are staying at offers," he replied.

She was silent.

"You there?" he asked.

"I told you not to come here," she said in a stern voice.

"We need to talk, which means we need to meet, and since you won't come to New York, I came to you or should I say, we," he said with an air of confidence.

"We," said Arietta.

"Yes," he replied smugly.

"What do you want?" she asked.

"To meet today for lunch?" he asked.

"If I say no," she replied.

"We are not leaving the resort until we do," he replied.

"Okay, lunch it is!"

"We will see you at twelve," he reconfirmed, "at the Waterfront Bistro in Cruz Bay."

"Twelve," she confirmed, "and Graham…"

"What?" he asked.

"Let's hope for your sake you brought the right 'we' with you," she said, knowing that would rattle him. She hung up the phone, sat on the bed, and thought. "James," she said. She put on some shorts and a top and went to James's room and knocked on the door. It took him a few moments, but he opened it, and she went in. "I need your help," she said.

"Okay," he replied. "What do you need me to do?"

"I'm meeting Graham at twelve, and I want you to come with me?" she asked.

Don't you think you should meet him on his own?" replied James, a little unsure.

"No, he has someone with him, and I want you to be with me. I don't want to go alone," she explained.

"A lawyer?" asked James.

Arietta looked at him. "I don't think so, probably Vincent," she said.

"Who is Vincent?"

"His right-hand man, his best friend," she replied.

"Why would the guy you are going through a separation with bring his best friend?" asked James, totally confused.

"Separating with? What are you talking about?" asked Arietta, now also confused.

"Graham, your boyfriend, common law, husband…I'm not really sure who he is."

Arietta looked at him and laughed. "What makes you think that?"

James was unsure why she was laughing but told her about the phone call he overheard, him showing up on her patio, and then seeing her with him in Cruz Bay.

"You and Cheryl saw that?"

"Yeah," said James.

She walked up to James. "Graham is my brother. He also works for me in the company my parents own. We were talking about a merger, and I left New York because of it, well, partly."

"Your brother," replied James and sat on the bed. "Well, this place is full of surprises."

Arietta sat down next to him. "All this time you thought I was here because I was leaving him and his showing up was his attempt at reconciliation?"

"Well, I thought you may have had other personal things going on also, but yeah, mostly," he said.

"Cheryl too?" she asked.

"Yes," he replied.

She thought for a moment. "Is this another reason why you've been keeping your distance from me and why you stopped me from kissing you the other night?"

"Yeah, I thought you needed to sort things out with Graham first," replied James. "Cheryl and I weren't sure what was going on between the two of you, and we felt that you were trying to deal with it as best as you could on your own, so we decided not to ask or interfere."

"That's why Cheryl and you were telling me to sort my life out. It all makes sense now. I guess I should have said something to the both of you sooner, especially to you, but it never occurred to me that it looked that way," she said sadly.

James put his arm around her. "We both should have."

"Yes, but I don't think either of us has been in the right frame of mind to open up about it, until now." She smiled at him. "But I think that has changed."

"I believe so," he said, smiling back at her. "So, how can I help?"

"I want you to come with me, and just be there. You don't have to say anything," she assured him. "Just be there, with me, next to me."

"Okay," he replied.

Arietta and James met at eleven thirty, took a taxi to Cruz Bay and walked into the Waterfront Bistro. Arietta spotted Graham and his group sitting at a table that had a beautiful view of Galge Cove and headed their way.

"Arie," said Graham, standing up to greet her and give her a hug and kiss on the cheek.

"You remember James," she said.

They both said hello and shook hands. The three of them walked to the table where Graham introduced Violet, Vincent, and his wife Sara, to James.

"What is she doing here?" asked Arietta.

Graham was uncertain whom she was referring to and guessed she meant Sara. "This affects her too, and she needs to be part of this discussion."

"I would prefer it if I wasn't," Sara said. "I don't think this involves me at all."

"I agree," said Arietta coldly to her.

"She needs to stay," said Vincent.

"What's he doing here?" asked Graham, looking at James.

"He is here with me," she replied in a calm voice, "as an observer."

"Would you like me to sit over there with Sara?" asked James.

"No," replied Arietta. "This won't take long."

Sara looked at James, and all of a sudden, her face lit up. She contained her excitement.

Graham spoke. "I will keep this simple and to the point just the way you like it." He opened a satchel and pulled out two legal documents. "This is mine and Vincent's letters of resignation. Next week we will go to the meeting, tell them what a mistake it is not to approve this merger, and that we can't work for a company or person who is blind to that. If the merger is rejected, we will resign, effective immediately, and pursue other opportunities. I have spoken with you about the studies that have been conducted that conclusively state that this merger will significantly contribute to our company's financial growth and market share, but from what I understand, you have a different take on them, and thus, are not willing to approve the merger."

Arietta picked up the letters without looking at them and glanced around the table, her eyes stopping directly on Graham's. "Is there anything else?"

"Does there need to be?" he asked boldly.

She smiled at him, which made him nervous. "Then we are done here," she said, about to get up.

"Before you go, Arie," said Graham, turning to James. "James, I told Arie the last time we met that I have seen you before, and I will be damned if I can't remember where."

James shook his head and said, "I don't know."

Sara knew the answer and couldn't hold it in anymore. "He is James Davenport, fictional writer of contemporary romances such as—"

"No, I got it!" said Graham. "You're the writer James Brian."

"No," said Sara, looking upset at Graham for cutting her off, then turning and smiling at James. "You are James Davenport?"

"I am," he said.

"You wrote, 'Hold Me In Your Arms,' 'Kiss From Heaven,' and 'My Heart Is In Your Hands'?" she asked.

"I did," he replied.

"I can't believe it is you, and you are sitting right in front of me. My girlfriends and I have a book club, and we have read each of your books more than once." She looked over at Violet, then at Arietta and spoke to her. "We all had a crush on him, and we made a bet on who would be the first one to meet him and get their picture taken with him."

Arietta smiled at her for being so excited and honest and directing the conversation to her. "What was the bet?" asked Arietta.

"Oh, what was it now?" She thought for a moment. "The fact that you got your picture with him, and bragging rights would have been enough for anyone of us…but the winner got dinner for two at 'Daniel' in Manhattan."

Graham looked puzzled. "You're not James Brian?"

"I am," replied James.

"So, you wrote under two names," he said, suddenly understanding.

"I had to because of the different genres of books; my publisher wanted me to be seen as two different authors. Brian is my middle name."

"Vincent and I read your novels; most businessmen in Manhattan have. What am I saying, most businessmen in the world probably have," said Graham, now just as excited as Sara. He looked at Violet. "He wrote a trilogy, only two are in print. The third is due out…" He looked at James.

"Thursday," he replied.

"The first one was called 'Genesis', and it talks about the birth and growth of the perfect man, superior in every aspect, physically and mentally. He is corrupt, greedy, and self-absorbed, and at the end of it, he takes over his protégé, not by killing him, but by ruining his life to the point where he ends up committing suicide. The next book, 'Paradise' the character rises to the top of the corporate world but does it in such a way that no one suspects him, and even if they did, couldn't prove it. He is ruthless and considers himself the God of this paradise that he has created. The third is called 'Demise' and I'm only guessing it's the demise of him and, or his paradise." He looked over at James for a hint.

Vincent interjected. "I don't want to know anything," he said. "I want to read it."

"I didn't realize you wrote under a different name and wrote those books," said Sara. "Vincent has had them at home for ages, and I never bothered looking at the author's picture." Then Sara remembered. "You stopped writing romantic novels because of your wife, and I heard that they offered you movie deals, but you refused because of her."

James looked at Sara, and by her sad face he understood she knew what had happened to Clair, and although he continued looking at her, what he was about to say was for the benefit of the other three. "Yes, Sara, that's true. My wife, Clair, died of cancer seven years ago, and at that time I stopped writing completely. I had planned not to write again and became somewhat of a recluse, and at that time I realized if they made movies out of my novels, I would have the public's attention put back on me, which is something I didn't want. Plus, those books were written when Clair and I were together, and at that time I couldn't bear to be reminded of her, of my loss, and have people ask me about it. A while later, and under someone's advice, it was suggested that I write about something completely different, so I did."

They were all silent.

"Sara, if you would have opened Vincent's books up, it wouldn't have helped you."

"Why is that?" whispered Sara.

"There is no picture of the author," answered Vincent quietly. "It was supposed to give the reader the allure that this person was living amongst us and could be any one of the businessmen you dealt with, which worked well from a marketing and sales perspective, but I realize now that the reasons were totally different."

"I was curious to see what the writer looked like," said Graham, "and I have a friend who is an editor at the same publishing company, and also one of our clients, and he showed me your picture one day as a favor to me. It was a very brief glimpse and a long time ago, which is why I had a tough time remembering where I had seen you." Graham looked around at Violet, Vincent, Sara, and then at James. "I promise you your secret is safe with us."

The group nodded in agreement, and the table was quiet again for a brief moment.

"I loved your romantic novels, and I miss you not writing. I hope one day you will write another one and come to our book club and talk about it," said Sara. "I can't wait to text my friends I met you."

Arietta stood up, and so did James.

"I will be in touch," Arietta said to Graham.

James leaned over and whispered in Sara's ear, and she screamed excitedly.

Arietta and James headed for the exit. "They will never break that promise," Arietta said as they walked outside, "because these days you are only as good as your word, and a kept word goes a very, very, long way."

"That's comforting to know," replied James.

Arietta looked at him. "What did you whisper in Sara's ear?"

"I told her if she holds off, she can get a picture with me back at the resort, so she can have the bragging rights, and win that bet."

"You are so kind and thoughtful," she said. "You know, she writes for the local town paper and online. She does a literary column, mostly on book reviews and authors." She put her arm through his as they walked down towards the dock and squeezed it. "Thanks for coming."

Chapter 23

They arrived at the dock and decided that they should find a place to get some lunch. Arietta noticed a sign, 'three-hour boat cruise with buffet, lunch and drinks' and they decided to go on it. They ate lunch and ordered a beer, then ventured upstairs to the main deck and stood at the back, watching Cruz Bay shrink into the distance.

"Do you want to talk?" he asked.

"I do," she said and nervously smiled. "I was trying to decide on where to start." She collected her thoughts for a moment and began. "My parents met in New York City back in 1972. They were originally from England, my mother was from Liverpool, and her trade was a seamstress, something that she had learned from her mother. With the sudden death of her mother, and her father having passed away a few years earlier, she contacted some relatives living in New York City, and her and her brother decided, in 1972, to immigrate to the States. My father was born in London, as were his parents, but my great-grandparents were from Italy. In Italy, my great-grandfather was a tailor and moved to England to make a name for himself, and during that time he taught his son the trade, who in turn taught his son, my father. So, my great-grandfather, grandfather and father were all tailors. Everything they sold was tailor-made: suits, pants, shirts, even jeans, and they catered exclusively to men. After my grandmother passed away, my grandfather decided he would retire and go back to Italy, and during this time my father had met an older man who owned a tailoring business in New York and had asked my father to come work for him. So, in 1971, my father immigrated and worked in New York City for this gentleman named Sol. Sol was a sole survivor from the holocaust and had moved to the States during the war, and as he had no family, he treated my father like his son. In 1972, my mother is in New York City looking for employment and saw an advertisement for a seamstress and applied. Of course, you can guess who was looking to hire?" she asked as she took a sip of her beer.

"Your father," answered James.

"Yes, my father." Laughing, she continued. "Well, my father hired her without actually seeing if she was a good seamstress or not. He said he fell in love with her right then and there. Lucky for him, she was an excellent seamstress. Sol taught my father everything about the business and introduced him to all his contacts, at which time my mother and father became not only romantically involved but also took on more of the responsibilities of the business. Over the years, the business grew and flourished. In 1975, my father proposed, and in 1976 they were married. They had a very small wedding, during which Sol announced that he was going back home to Europe to retire and giving the business to my parents as a wedding gift; my parents were overjoyed." Arietta stopped and laughed a little. "They didn't have a lot of money, so they ended up spending a week camping in the Adirondacks for their honeymoon. They had it all planned out where they were going to camp every night, except the last night, and decided on the way back to the city that they would just stop off at a place and camp for the night. So, the last day they packed up their tent and were driving down NY-8 towards Piseco Lake. It was getting late, and they noticed a sign for the Lakeview Lodge that said it had shoreline campsites. They pulled into this beautiful rustic lodge and spoke with the owner about getting a site for the night. The owner informed them that there was a major storm approaching from the west and that it wouldn't be safe for them to camp but would give them a cabin for the same rate, which they accepted. They talked to the owner for a while about New York City and their wedding and that they were on their honeymoon. My parents then drove down to cabin C2 and were unpacking a few things when shortly after there was a knock at the door; it was the owner. He had brought down a picnic basket and told them it was compliments of him and his wife and to enjoy their honeymoon. They opened the basket and inside there were cheeses, crackers, a loaf and fruit, a bottle of champagne and two glasses. They finished unpacking and sat on the porch and ate and drank the champagne. It was a beautiful evening, but, in the distance, they could see the storm approaching. My father went inside and got a sleeping bag and came out and laid it on the porch. They both stripped naked and lay on top of the sleeping bag and started to make love as the calm sun set. Shortly after, the lightning started to flash across the dark sky and their naked bodies, and the thunder roared, and the rain started to pour. My father picked my mother up and carried her down the steps and out into the storm. They made love as the rain fell on their naked bodies; my father gently placed my mother down, and they continued to make love on the ground. When they had finished, they walked hand in hand inside the cabin, showered off the mud and made love in bed. The next morning, they sat on the porch and drank their coffee. The sun was out, and the ground had dried, and they could see the imprints of their feet and the outlines of their bodies in the dried mud, and they looked at each other, laughing as young lovers do. They packed up and went inside the lodge to drop off the basket and glasses and to thank them; the owner and his wife turned around and gave them the glasses and the empty bottle to remind them of their honeymoon and their night at lodge." Arietta drank her beer and looked at James. "My parents still have those glasses and that empty bottle of champagne. My mom said it was the first champagne they shared alone, and since that day, they use those glasses every anniversary, and the bottle is on their dresser in their room and has a melted candle where the cork used to be."

"That's romantic," said James.

"It's so romantic," she replied and continued with her story. "So, they jumped in their car and got back onto NY-8 and my father noticed my mother touching her stomach with her hand. He asked if she was okay, she tells him that she thinks she is pregnant, and he smiles and puts his hand on hers. They are waiting to turn onto NY-10, and my mother reads the name of the town they are in and falls in love with the name and turns to my father and says, 'That is what we will call her.' The town was called 'Arietta' and nine months later they had me."

"Wow! That's incredible," said James.

"I know, I love that story," she said and looked at him, misty-eyed.

James held her hand, and they walked over to the side of the boat, and he waited for her to continue.

"Two years later they had Graham, and we were a happy and close family growing up, and when I was old enough, my mother taught me how to be a seamstress. So, in the summertime I worked under my mother as a seamstress during which time my father also taught me the tailor and business-side. Their customers were primarily high-end; men looking for custom-made suits, dress shirts, pants, and jackets, and women wanting evening gowns, business suits, pants, and skirts. My favorite part of my job was watching the customer's reactions after they put on their clothes," she said with a smile. "At college I took business, and I realized I didn't want to do what my parents were doing; that was their dream, but after I graduated, my father's health was poor, and he needed me to help him run the business, so I did. My father's health improved, but he still needed me to run the business part of the company, so that he could run the client and tailoring end, while my mother helped out the seamstresses. My plan was that my brother would take over from me once he received his degree, so after Graham graduated, he ended up helping out my father with the client and tailoring, and I taught him the business side, but it seemed there was never enough time for him to replace me and take over, so I ended up staying on." She stopped and thought. "In hindsight I should have told my parents that I was done, and that Graham needed to take it over."

"Why didn't they just hire someone?" asked James.

"I'm telling you this now, but I never told them about my plan for Graham replacing me. They thought I was happy, so there was no need to hire someone. Looking back, I know now I should have said something." She paused for a moment. "Graham has a best friend whom he met in college, and his father was also a tailor, and his clothes line was custom-made casual summer attire, you know, for golfing, sitting on a yacht, dressing for summer parties at the Cape, but unfortunately his business was running into financial problems, and he didn't have the energy or desire to tackle them, and felt that his son was too young to take on that sort of responsibility. So, he asked if he could merge his business with my father. My father would take over it, buy him out and own it. His only condition was that his son was guaranteed at least a vice-president position in my parents' company and would be an employee until he either retired or quit. My father was hesitant because of that. On paper, the merger was a win-win for my father and taking on his son as a VP was well worth the gamble. I told my father to take his offer; it was a sound and profitable business decision." Arietta took a long pause and finished her drink. "Also, during this time I had been dating his son for several months. We both were businesspeople, and he enjoyed going to restaurants and cocktails after work, that lifestyle, and I guess I got caught up in it too. But I, we, did something we shouldn't have. With my father being hesitant, we thought if we were married, the business would have a family connection and that would put my father's concerns to rest, so we married. The merger went through, my father ended up buying him out, and his son-in-law became a vice president. My father kept their brand name for three months before changing it to his." She looked at James. "A year later we were divorced, and we both agreed it was a terrible mistake. The merging of the companies was a big success, but what we did to make it happen was a big blunder. I guess he loved the business, and the lifestyle, and I really couldn't fault him for that; but I didn't."

"Vincent?" asked James.

She nodded her head and grabbed his hand as they walked to the bar to replenish their drinks. They continued to the front of the boat and saw Cruz Bay in the distance. "A year after we were divorced, he met up with his high-school sweetheart at a party. They got together and, eighteen months later, were married, and are still very happily married with three children." She shook her head and looked down like she was going to cry but maintained her composure and looked at James. "I was bitter, you know that vengeful bitterness, and I felt like I had been betrayed. I was working in a job I didn't like, for a company I didn't care for, and now sitting in the same room as my ex-husband, and most of all, hearing him go on about his happy life. So, I decided to be a total bitch to him, his wife, and his kids. At work I did my job and treated everyone else with the utmost dignity and respect, but at the end of the day it was always my way. I was incredibly angry and hurt and worst of all, I was alone..." She stopped and started to cry.

James put his arm around her and held her close.

Arietta wiped her eyes. "I used to be so happy and carefree, I loved being around people and making them smile and laugh, but I soon realized that that person had disappeared and gone away, lost somewhere, somewhere out here at sea, never to be found." She started crying again. "The sad thing is no one knew how unhappy I was, except one, my mother." She stopped and wiped her eyes. "A month ago, she came to visit me in my office unexpectedly. She started telling me how I was conceived on the most beautiful of all nights, how it was sunny and calm one moment then dark and stormy the next and during it how her and my father made love as gentle as lambs then as fierce as lions. I asked her if she had come in to share her sex story with me again, but she didn't laugh. She told me that when I was a young girl, and before I started working for the company, I was sunny, calm, happy and a beautiful person; since then, I had become troubled, dark, and stormy. My mother stood and went to the door. That's it, I said to her. She looked at me and told me that I needed to find myself, be happy and get through this storm and leave it behind. She walked over to me and held me, and I cried long and hard in her arms. She wiped my tears and told me that she and my father both loved me and wanted me to be happy, that I had been a good daughter to them and had helped them out and took care of them, and for that they were thankful, and that I would always have their love and support. She kissed me on the cheek and walked to the door. I stopped her and asked her what the weather was like after the storm. She smiled and told me it was sunnier and more beautiful than ever." Arietta put her head on James's shoulder. "In my mind I already knew what I had to do, what my mother had said to me had just given me that little push I needed to do it, and a week last Friday I decided I had to go and find me. So, I walked out of my office and the merger meeting with Graham and Vincent, shopped, packed, stayed at an airport hotel, and got the first flight out to a hot, sunny destination."

"You coming here was by accident?" asked James.

"I guess that depends on which way you look at it," she replied.

"There is something I don't understand," said James. "You don't want to work at your company anymore?"

"I don't."

"The sooner you leave the better for you?" he asked.

"Yes, the sooner the better."

"Then why do you care about the merger…unless it's a really bad idea?"

"Violet is an unbelievable fashion designer, and she wants to merge with us but keep her brand name. She wants to design prom dresses, evening dresses, suits, dress pants, dress shirts, and so on, for the daughters, sons, granddaughters, grandsons, nieces, nephews of all our clients. It's a brilliant idea, and she is a brilliant designer. The studies we have conducted suggest it's a win-win for us and her."

"Okay, now I am really confused."

She smiled at him. "I needed Graham to do two things: the first is to show to me that he was doing this for the best interests of the company and not because they are a couple and think it would be cute, and during our meeting in Cruz Bay, he made it quite clear to me that it wasn't the case. The second was to stand up to me, call me out, and tell me I was making a mistake to the point where he felt so strongly about it, he would quit. Trust me, if he can stand up to me, he can stand up to anyone," she said and laughed. "My stormy side, I mean."

"Why didn't you tell him this today?" asked James.

"He has to learn to sweat it out and not cave in, so he better not call me, or when I call him, tell me that he has changed his mind."

"I can see that…and I understand that, but either way you are going to approve the merger and leave, so, why are you stalling?" he asked.

She turned and held him in her arms and whispered, "I'm scared. I know what I have to do, but I'm scared to do it."

"Why?" he whispered back.

"I don't know what I'm going to do, after," she said, "after I leave."

He looked at her and thought for a while. "Arietta, what has made you the happiest this week?" he asked.

"You want me to list them?" she asked.

"Sure…"

"You, Cheryl, Caleigh, planning Rio and Gio's ceremony, planning the birthday party, being here…"

"Now, take away the people and the place," suggested James.

"Planning the ceremony…planning the birthday party…Event planning!" she said. "You know, I have been so caught up in you and me, and Cheryl, and Graham, I forgot about how happy that made me." Her mind was racing. "And it was so much fun, and it was like I…I was my old self…I made people happy…kids happy…and I met so many people…I felt so much personal satisfaction…I felt alive." She had a big smile on her face. Then she started to think about it a little more, and her smile started to fade. "But how could I do that in Manhattan?"

"Arietta, if you could plan both those events with limited resources here and make them spectacular, I'm sure Manhattan will be a walk in the park."

"But there is strong competition there, and they have regular client bases, and they get referrals," she said.

"Arietta, think," said James. "Think about who you are, where you work, and who you know?"

"You mean," she said.

"Yes, I mean."

"That sounds like stipulation number one," she said.

"Number one?" asked James, unsure what she was talking about.

"I need my office, and I need a couple of floors, so there is number two," she said, smiling.

The boat docked, and they took a taxi back to the resort, and they went to her patio. She went inside and came out with her laptop and started planning her new career, her new life.

James walked through the open door to her room and grabbed two beers and came out, passing one to her.

"Make yourself at home," she said, laughing. "Thought you had a fear of open doors?" she teased.

"I used to," he replied, laughing too.

She loved his smile. "I need to make some calls," she said and stopped herself. "I'm really happy with this; in fact, I'm very happy, and I only wish I had some people who I didn't know that were looking for me to plan their events."

"You have just reminded me of something," he said and asked for her laptop and went into Gmail and pulled up two accounts: one was for 'Rio and Gio's Ceremony' and the other said 'Caleigh's Birthday,' and passed the laptop back to her.

"There are thirty-five Gmails under Rio and Gio and fifteen under Caleigh," she said and started opening them up one by one, then started screaming, "I don't believe it! I don't believe it!" She looked at James. "There are engagements, weddings, baptisms, confirmations, birthdays, anniversaries…" She looked up from the laptop. "How?"

"You need to thank Rio and Gio and Cheryl," replied James. "Gio said to me on the day of the ceremony that his family and friends were asking for your name and how to contact you back in New York to plan their special occasions, so I created a Gmail account for you and gave it to him. They sent it out to everyone, and that's what you received within a week."

"You mentioned Cheryl."

"She had a woman approach her at the party, asking about you, and Cheryl told me, so I set up another account under 'Caleigh's Birthday.' I gave her the Gmail account name." He stopped for a minute and gave Arietta a sympathetic look. "The next day she made thank-you notes for the kids and parents just so that she could put your Gmail on there and personally went to their rooms and delivered them…She had already thanked them all at the party."

"Really," said Arietta, feeling awful. She clicked on Caleigh's account and read them out loud. "Birthdays, anniversaries, graduations…Some of these are referrals from the people at the birthday party who have family and friends in New York."

"Word of mouth," said James. "That reminds me: some of the people at the ceremony thought Rio had flown you in from New York to plan it for them. They didn't believe you did that in a few days."

"Really, wow! That's a huge compliment," she said, delighted.

"Don't you have phone calls to make?" asked James as he put his feet on the chaise and drank his beer.

"I do, you just take it easy," she said and went inside. She quickly came back out and kissed him unexpectedly on the cheek. "Thank you."

Thirty minutes later she came out with her phone. "I want you to listen in on this." She dialed a number and lay next to James on the chaise.

"Hello, Graham."

"Hello, Arie."

"I have been going through the documents you gave me and thought I should call you just to make sure you don't want to change your mind."

"Our minds are made up," he replied stubbornly.

"Hmm…" she replied. "Then it seems like you are sticking firm with your demands."

"Yes, we are."

"All right, I will meet with you, Violet, Vincent, and Sara in Boardroom A at ten tomorrow morning."

"We will be there," he replied and hung up.

"I am really impressed with him; he is making it so much easier for me than I thought." She put the phone down and her head on James's chest, and he put his arm around her. "I am going to do this," she said.

Chapter 24

"Arietta will be here in a few minutes," said James to Cheryl and Caleigh as he sat down and joined them at the table. "What have you been up to today, Caleigh?"

"We went to the beach, and I played with my friends," she said. "I've missed you. Where have you been?"

"Caleigh," said Cheryl, "that's not polite to ask."

"Sorry, James, I just missed you," she said with a sad face.

"I missed you too," he replied, making a goofy face that made her laugh. "I had to do yucky grown-up stuff, but I wish I was on the beach having fun like you."

"Good evening," said Arietta.

Caleigh jumped out of her seat. "I missed you, where have you…" She caught herself. "I've missed you."

"I've missed you," she replied. "I've just been busy."

"Doing yucky grown-up stuff too, huh?" she asked.

Arietta nervously smiled at her. "Yes."

"Look, I'm wearing the outfit you bought me. Isn't it pretty?"

"It's very pretty. You look beautiful!" said Arietta.

James stood up and pulled out a chair next to Cheryl. "Arietta, come and sit here."

"Caleigh, I've forgotten something back in my room. Want to come with me for a walk?" James asked.

"Okay," she said.

Arietta watched them walk out of the restaurant and turned to Cheryl. "I am so sorry for what I said to you the other day. I didn't mean a word of it, I promise. I have the greatest respect for you and think you are a wonderful mother," said Arietta. "I have been going through a lot of personal things over the last little while, and it all just caught up to me, and I took it out on you, James too."

"You mean with Graham and the separation?" Cheryl asked.

Arietta tried not to smile but did. "I forgot you don't know…Graham is my brother; he also works for me in the company my parents own." She continued to tell Cheryl the abbreviated version of what she had told James, about not being happy with what she was doing, where she was in her life, why she was here and about Graham and the merger."

"But at the spa day I tried to get you to open up and talk about your separation, and you said that you only talk to your family about those things," said Cheryl, confused.

"I was referring to my separation with Vincent," said Arietta and explained what had happened there. "But that doesn't excuse me for what I said about you, and I'm so truly sorry."

She grabbed Arietta's hand. "I have been looking for you. I went by your place last night and this morning, but you weren't there. I was hoping I would bump into you around the resort," confided Cheryl.

"Why?" Arietta asked nervously.

"After you said those awful things to me, I cried and was terribly upset, and I didn't like you very much. I thought you were someone different than that, not a spoilt brat." She laughed a little. "Sorry, that's what I thought you were, but I went to the beach with Caleigh and started thinking about you and the first night we met and those guys hitting on us…"

"Skippy!" said Arietta aloud, and they both laughed.

"Skippy, I was trying to remember his name…and I thought about all the fun we had, and the birthday party you planned for Caleigh, and you taking her for the day and buying her stuff, and I suddenly realized something."

"What?" Arietta asked.

"That was who you are, not this person who was yelling at James and me, that was someone who was upset, hurt, angry and going through some major issues, so I wanted to see you and ask you if you wanted to talk about it and see if I could help in any way," confessed Cheryl.

Arietta gave a sigh of relief. "I can't believe you. You are the best." She gave her a hug and whispered, "Please forgive me."

"I already have, the day I went looking for you," she whispered back. "Friends fight…best friends forgive, forget and move on."

"Thank you, I have been so upset thinking you would never forgive me and never talk to me ever again," she said as she wiped her eyes dry.

"To best friends," said Cheryl.

"Best friends," replied Arietta. They touched glasses and drank their wine.

Arietta spoke to her in some length about the meeting tomorrow morning, and they had just finished talking when Caleigh and James walked into the restaurant.

"We're back," said Caleigh as she joined them at the table.

James noticed the happy smiles on both their faces and sat down. "Let's order some dinner."

"Are you ready for tomorrow morning?" asked James as they stood on Arietta's porch.

"I am," she replied. "Well, as best as I could be in such little time."

"Knowing you, I'm sure it will be perfect and run like clockwork," he said with a vote of confidence. "You asked Cheryl about tomorrow?"

"Yes, she's going to help me organize and facilitate the meeting; I am so grateful to her. Which reminds me, I can't be standing around while she does all the work. I have to do a few more things myself before tomorrow." She stopped and looked at him. "Maybe you should go and talk to Cheryl and Caleigh while you have some free time?"

"I think I will," he replied.

"Do you need me to come with you?" she offered.

"No, you take care of your stuff," he replied and started to walk to Cheryl's room.

Arietta called his name, and he turned around. She ran and put her arms around him. "Thank you," she said and kissed him on the lips. She started to pull away, but he held her close and kissed her a little longer. As she pulled away, they looked into each other's eyes, and she realized she was blushing. She slowly walked backwards, then turned and walked happily to her room.

James knocked on Cheryl's door.

"Come in," she said. "Is everything okay?"

"Yes and no," he replied and looked over at Caleigh lying on the bed, watching him. "Caleigh, there is something I need to talk to you and your mom about. Do you think you can sit next to her on the bed?"

"Uh-huh," she replied and sat next to her mom.

James sat facing them. "Many years ago, just around the time you were born, Caleigh, I married a girl named Clair and I loved her very much. A few years after we got married, Clair was told she had cancer, and they made her better, and it went away, but a few months later it came back, and this time they told her they wouldn't be able to cure her, and six months later she went to Heaven."

"Oh, James," said Cheryl and reached over to hold his hand.

"She did," Caleigh said. "You must have been very sad."

"I was very sad and hurt, and I felt very alone," he replied. "But during that time, I had my family there to help me, and I also had a friend who I used to meet and talk with who helped me get better and feel better, and not feel so sad. This friend also suggested that I should do some things to help me get over my loss, so I took her advice and set up the 'Clair Davenport Fund.' This fund gives donations to charities, and one of the biggest recipients is the 'Make-A-Wish Foundation.' Do you know what they do?" he asked Caleigh.

"They let people who are sick go on a vacation or make a wish of theirs come true," said Caleigh.

"Yes," replied James. "Clair always wanted to visit here, but before she could, she got sick and was never well enough to take the trip, so her fund allows sick children and older sick people to go on the vacation they always wanted to…Now there are a lot of people who survive cancer, like you, and there are people like Clair, who unfortunately don't, and, in both situations, families can be burdened with a lot of expensive bills to pay, and in many cases those families can't afford to pay them. In addition to that, those families that have lost a loved one may not be able to afford to go see a person who can help them get over their loss. You see, Caleigh, when Clair died, I had enough money to pay the expensive bills and also pay to get the help I needed to get through my loss but not as many people are as fortunate. Do you understand?"

"I think so, survivors of cancer and those that lost someone from cancer, both need help," she replied.

"That's right," he said and smiled at her, "and how I want to help these families is by setting up a special fund that will help them pay off their medical expenses and bills, and also give them the money they may need to go and talk to someone. What do you think about that?"

"I think that's really nice," she said.

"This is where I need your help. I was looking for someone who is a survivor of cancer, is very strong, brave, loving and caring to name the fund after. Can you think of anyone?"

She smiled at him. "You can name it after me. Because I am all those things," she replied, "but mostly because I know it will help people like you and mom."

"Well, your mom and I were hoping we could name it the 'Caleigh White Fund.' What do you think?"

"I would love that," she said.

"Then we will," replied James. "I have something for you, it's a gift." Out of his pocket, he pulled out the necklace that Lily had given him and gave it to her.

"This is so pretty," she said and showed it to her mom. "Can I put it on?"

As Cheryl put the necklace on Caleigh, James told her the story behind the necklace and the 'Twenty-Four Children' poem and handed her a copy of the poem.

"Thank you," she said as she looked at the poem, then up at James. "So there are only two necklaces?"

"Only two, you have one and Clair has the other," he replied, "and I think Clair would be very happy with you having this one."

Cheryl looked at her daughter. "That looks so pretty on you."

"I'm never going to take it off," she said. "I don't have to, do I?"

"Only at bedtime," replied Cheryl.

"Then at bedtime I will put it next to my flower, book, and now my poem," she said, lifting up the paper. "Thank you for the necklace and poem, and my fund."

"You're welcome."

Caleigh stood up and hugged James. "I'm sorry you lost Clair."

James hugged her back, then watched her go over to the mirror to admire her necklace.

Cheryl squeezed his hand gently. "I'm so sorry to hear about Clair; it must have been extremely difficult for you to go through that. I know what it was like for me, but to lose someone. It never occurred to me when you were talking about people dealing with a loss of someone to cancer you were talking about yourself." She thought back to the discussion she had with Arietta about what James's ex-wife had done to him to make him be the way he was, and now it made sense; it all made sense.

"It was difficult, but I realize now why she wanted me to come on this vacation."

"James, you will always have Caleigh and me."

"I know. Thank you," he replied. He looked over at Caleigh, who was still occupied, and looked back at Cheryl. "I wanted to ask you something about your parents."

"Okay," said Cheryl.

"Because this is a private fund, I need to hire someone to oversee the books and take care of the accounting side of it; it's a salaried position, and I will need two people. Do you think your parents would be interested?" he asked.

"Are you kidding me!" she blurted. "They would love that! It would be their dream come true."

"Now, they can still live where they are and either work from home or rent an office close to home, it's up to them. They will have to travel to Manhattan occasionally to meet with Sophie and Karen. They are going to be responsible for receiving and reviewing the information from the families, and your parents will need to be part of the review and approval process. Joanne is going to help out for a while until they get a handle on it."

"I'm sure they will be fine with that. Thank you, thank you, they will be so happy," she said, reaching over to hug him. "When can I tell them? I mean, when are you going to ask them?"

"How about tomorrow evening before dinner," he said. "I'll drop by, and you can call them and tell them."

"Honestly, I would love to see the reaction on their faces, but I don't think I can wait until I get home to tell them; they are going to be so happy."

Chapter 25

"I wish I had a little more time to spend on setting up the room. I wanted it to have a pleasant atmosphere, not just me sitting behind a desk and looking across at them like we were in an office," said Arietta. "I guess I will just have to run with it."

"I'm sure it will be fine," said James optimistically.

"I hope so," replied Arietta as she looked at her watch. "Thirty minutes early," she noted as they arrived at Boardroom A.

Cheryl was at the door, waiting. Dressed in a pretty blue top and floral skirt, she was very similar in style to what Arietta was wearing, and they jokingly complimented each other on their business outfits.

"This is about as close to business-like clothing I have," commented Arietta.

"Me too," replied Cheryl. "Guess this is our Caribbean business-look," she said, and they laughed.

"Thanks for helping me today," Arietta said sincerely and grabbed her hand. "It means I can concentrate on what I have to say and not be distracted shuffling people and papers around."

"Not a problem," said Cheryl. "By the way, last night you mentioned you were concerned about the room looking clinical and like an office, so I had them make some adjustments."

James opened the door, and they walked inside. At one end there were several sofas, a coffee table in the center, and two end tables that had vases on them containing red ginger flowers.

"Follow me," said Cheryl as they walked over to the sofas. "Arietta, I thought you could sit here and the guests opposite you, here and here," said Cheryl confidently. "I had them place the speaker phone on the coffee table, and over there I had them set up a table with some coffee, tea, juices and water, as well as some pastries and fresh fruit, and I had them put it right by the entrance to the balcony, so people can sit outside and wait rather than in the hallway." She looked at Arietta. "I hope it's all okay?"

"When did you do all this?" asked Arietta.

"This morning before I dropped Caleigh off, I came by and talked to the manager and Janice and asked them if they could help me make some changes. The sofas and tables were in the hallway anyway, and I thought refreshments and the flowers would be a nice touch. They originally had a rectangle table set up covered in white linen and some chairs around it; it looked very clinical. That table is now being used for refreshments." She pointed over at the table and then looked at Arietta. "I know how important today is for you, and you have had so much on your mind and so much to do," replied Cheryl. "I thought I would help you out."

She smiled at her and looked around. "This is perfect; it's exactly what I had wanted. I couldn't have organized it any better myself." She gave Cheryl a hug. "Thank you for doing this; this makes me feel so much better."

They poured themselves a coffee and sat on the couch while Arietta explained to them how she was going to conduct the meeting.

At ten o'clock Graham, Vincent, Sara, and Violet walked into the room and were greeted by Cheryl who escorted them to the refreshment table, then outside. She walked back over to Arietta and James.

"Ask Graham to come in," said Arietta. She looked at James. "Don't leave my side."

"I'm not going anywhere," he replied.

Cheryl brought Graham over, and he sat down. She put his juice on the table and then sat on one of the empty sofas.

"This is very cozy and comfortable," said Graham, looking around.

"Glad you like it," she said and took a long look at him. "Anything else before we begin?" she asked.

"No," he replied. "Let's get right down to business."

Arietta took a deep breath and began. "There are a few things I need to tell you, and I'm not sure which is more important so I will tell you them in no particular order, and you can decide that for yourself." She proceeded to tell Graham what she had been going through these last few years, about her unhappiness, and wanting to leave the company and the reasons she stayed on; she told him everything.

"Arie," said Graham concerned and leaning over to her. "Why didn't you say something sooner? Why didn't you talk with me?"

"Prior to me walking out of my office and coming here, I knew I was very unhappy, and that I had some things to think about and decisions to make. I wasn't a hundred percent sure what they were or where they would take me; I only figured that out since I've been here."

"Is there anything I can do to help you?" he asked.

"There is but I will get to that later," she said. "The second thing I want to tell you is how pleased I am with you and your approach to the merger. You coming here to see me and pushing something that you not only feel very passionate about, but feel is very important to the success and growth of the company, to the point where you give me your resignation and an ultimatum, is very impressive. The fact that you didn't crumble under pressure and are now sitting in front of me ready to go toe to toe is the testimony of a true leader; I am very proud of you." As she said this she smiled, leaned over, and held his hand. "I mean that, sincerely."

"Thank you," he replied, overwhelmed by what she was saying.

"Hold on one second," she said to him and let go of his hand. "Cheryl, can you get Vincent and Sara?"

She escorted them inside, and they sat on the other sofa.

"Vincent, Sara, I want to let you know that over these last several years I have treated you both very badly, and I want to apologize." She looked over at Vincent. "You have always been an excellent vice president, and I know that when we hired you, we had made the right decision, and you have proven that all these years. I want to thank you for the tremendous contribution you have made to this company and its overall success." She looked over at Sara. "I have been very cold and unkind to you, and I must confess the only reason I have has been due to my own unhappiness. You are a wonderful woman, wife and mother, and Vincent couldn't have found a better person to share his life with. The way I hear him talk to Graham and the other employees about you and the children is a great compliment to you. I hope one day you will forgive me and allow us to become better acquainted and maybe one day friends," she said and looked over at Vincent. "You too, Vincent."

"I'm sure we can," replied Sara, looking back and forth at Arietta and Vincent.

"Yes," said Vincent, a little bewildered.

"I would like that," said Arietta. "Cheryl, can you ask Violet to join us." Arietta looked around at their quiet faces and was unsure if they believed what she was saying.

Violet came over and sat down next to Graham and Cheryl returned to her seat.

Arietta looked at Violet. "I want to tell you I think your work is brilliant and your designs are inventive, stunning, dramatic, eye-catching and overall amazing."

"Thank you," replied Violet politely and a little taken aback.

"On a personal note, I like the way you and Graham have kept your private affairs to yourself and out of mine and our workplace; it is a credit to you both. Graham told me the other day that your private life is your concern, and no one else's, and he is right. You have drawn a defining line between your private life and what is best for the company, and I admire you and Graham for doing something that I could not." She looked back and forth between Violet, Graham, and Vincent. "The three of you have fought this battle with me tooth and nail based on what you believe is best for the company. This is both admirable and a true indication of the passion you have for this company and its continued success." She stopped for a moment and, looking at Cheryl for a long time, realized there was something she needed to do. "At this time, I am going to ask that we take an unscheduled fifteen-minute break to allow me to speak with Cheryl and James in private." She stood up. "Please refresh your drinks, get some food and some fresh air." She watched the four of them stand and quietly leave, waiting until they walked out on the balcony before sitting next to Cheryl.

"Do you want me to call that number now?" asked Cheryl.

"Not yet," said Arietta. "There was something I was going to ask you after I ended this meeting, but I think I need to ask you now because I would like to know your answer before I continue."

"Okay," said Cheryl, not sure what was going on. "Answer to what?"

"As you know, I have decided to open my own company specializing in event planning, and as it stands I currently have only one employee, me…I want to know if you would like to join me and work with me on this new venture?" she asked.

"You want me to work for you in Manhattan?" asked Cheryl.

"No, I don't want you to work for me. I want you to work with me, be my business partner," she stated.

"Business partner, but I don't have the money to contribute; in fact, I don't even know how much I would need," she replied honestly.

"You won't need to, and neither will I, leave that to me," she replied. "Just trust me, okay?"

"Okay," said Cheryl, unsure. She thought for a moment and asked, "Why me?"

"Well, you have different skill sets than I do; you are far more organized than I am. In your current job you deal with different people every day and all their issues, and you're good at multitasking and coordinating. Don't get me wrong: you won't be doing that for long. Soon you will be directing people under you to do it." She stopped and held her hand. "But most of all you are a good friend, and I trust you with anything." She smiled at her and continued. "Please understand that today, all I am doing is getting us set up, and starting tomorrow, you will have an equal say and input into everything regarding our company."

Cheryl was in shock and didn't know what to say. "But where would I live? What about Caleigh and school?"

"You would need to live in Manhattan," she replied. "Caleigh can attend a private school."

"How can I afford that?" she asked.

"Let me take care of your place to live for now, until you get settled, and if you want to move, then you can, but first, let's get you both there," she said confidently. "Sara has her kids in a private school, and it's not far from where you will live. Sara was also raised in upstate New York, so I'm sure you and her and the children will get along fine. Plus, your parents are only a couple of hours away and will be visiting Manhattan to meet with James's sisters about Caleigh's fund. If they have their meeting on a Friday, they can take Caleigh back for the weekend or stay over, and that doesn't include you or them visiting one another. Also, James and I would get to see Caleigh, and she would get to see us."

Cheryl was overwhelmed, but she was still worried about how she was going to afford to live in Manhattan. Janice interrupted her thoughts.

"Here is that faxed document you have been waiting for from your lawyer," she said, handing it to Arietta.

"Thank you, Janice, perfect timing." Arietta looked at it and passed it to Cheryl. "This is a draft, we can work on the details later, but this is the most important thing," said Arietta as she pointed to the salary, bonuses, and equal split of the profits, "and there are still a couple of signing bonuses that I would like to talk to you about later this afternoon, say at three o'clock."

"Three, okay," replied Cheryl, looking down at the salary. "Are you…" She couldn't get the words out.

"Serious? Most definitely, and our salary is negotiable," Arietta said, smiling, "because we will be making the same."

Cheryl was dumbfounded. "When did you decide all this?" she asked.

"A couple of days ago, I wasn't sure you would consider it until James told me that you had said you wanted something more challenging and rewarding and that you would love to live in Manhattan, and seeing what you have done here today, you have just proven me right." Arietta gently squeezed her hand. "I would love you to join me on this new journey, please, please, say yes."

"Yes, yes, yes…of course…I can't believe it, this is one of the happiest days of my life," she said, hugging Arietta. "Thank you."

"I believe it is me that should be thanking you," she said sincerely. She then looked out at the balcony. "Now, let's bring them in and end this meeting."

"What should I do with this?" she asked, holding the document.

"Let's put it at the bottom of this folder for now, and we can talk about it some more, later."

Cheryl put it in the folder on the end table and went outside and asked everyone in. They all came back and sat in the exact same spots that they had vacated. Cheryl called the phone number, put it on speaker, and placed it back in the middle of the coffee table.

"Good morning, Levi speaking."

"Hi, Levi, it's Arietta," she said to the company's lawyer.

"Hi, Arietta, how are you doing?" he asked.

"I'm doing well," she replied. "All the principals are here," she said, naming them off.

"Okay, thank you. I received your information yesterday, and it seems to be straightforward," he confirmed.

"Good…As you know this is a formal meeting, and the decisions agreed to here today are legally binding and the paperwork you create and we sign, a formality," she said.

"Understood," he replied. "Please continue with your meeting."

Arietta looked at the four of them. "As you have just heard, the decisions we are going to make and agree to today will be considered set in stone, the signing of the documents in Manhattan on Wednesday morning will be just that, a formality."

"Okay, Arie," said Graham, anxious and a little nervous. "Let's talk."

Arietta glanced at them all and stopped at Graham. "I am going to give you my full support of the merger."

They all went quiet as if they didn't hear her. Then it sunk in.

"Really, that is great news, Arie, great news!" He hugged Violet and high-fived Vincent.

She waited for them to finish congratulating one another. "There is more: I will be resigning from the company, and, Graham, I would like you to be my successor, that's if you want to be?"

Graham looked at her in disbelief. "Resigning, why?"

"It's really very simple." She paused and looked at them. "I see the three people in front of me as the future of this company and the people who will take it to a higher level, year after year. You have the drive, passion, ambition, and desire to see this company successful. I love this company just as much as you, but I no longer have or possess those qualities to give to it; my passion lies elsewhere. I am going to start my own company, one in which I help people plan their special events." She proceeded to tell them about the ceremony and birthday party she had planned and how challenging they were and how happy and rewarding they made her feel. "The accomplishment and gratification I received from them was tremendous."

"I heard people talking about how fantastic they were. That was you! That's great, Arie!" said Graham. "So, your minds made up and you are sure this is what you want to do?"

"It is," she replied and paused. "Graham, my position at the company is yours, but before I officially resign and hand the reins over to you, I do have several stipulations, so before you answer me, do you want to hear them first?" she asked. "If not, your acceptance of my resignation will also be your acceptance of them."

"I know you would never do anything to hurt the company," replied Graham, "but I think I must."

"I was hoping you would say that," she replied, happy with his response. "Before I begin, let me introduce my partner in our new company, whom you have met today, Cheryl White."

Cheryl smiled at them, and they smiled back. She then handed Arietta a document.

Arietta took the document and looked at Graham. "I will list them off one at a time. After I do, Graham, you can just say agree or disagree, it's as simple as that," she explained. "If you disagree, we will need to come up with a solution today that we both can agree on."

"Fair enough," replied Graham.

"First, any events that your company will be holding, my new company gets to decide whether or not we will take them on. If we decide not to, you may use anyone else you like."

"Agreed," he replied.

"Second, if a client asks if there is anyone you can recommend to plan an event, you will recommend only my new company."

"Agreed," said Graham.

"Third, I will take over and own, the third and fourth floors of our building for my new company."

Graham looked at her for a moment and thought, she already has the third, and the fourth was vacant; plus, they had more than enough room for the anticipated growth over the next several years. "Agreed," he said.

"Fourth, one of the condo suites that we currently use for our clients will be given to our company free of charge."

Graham again paused and thought, they had three and they very rarely used them, most out-of-town clients preferred to stay in a hotel. "Agreed," he replied.

"Five, you will pay me out five million dollars, as well as my salary and bonuses for the next two years."

Graham shook his head at this one and wondered why the number was so low. "Are you sure, Arie? That seems awfully low."

"I am sure, the pay-out will be enough money for us to start up our new company," she replied, winking at Cheryl.

"Agreed," he replied.

"Sixth, you will set up the 'Clair Davenport Fund' and the 'Caleigh White Fund' as the primary charities for your company, which means they each get thirty-five percent of the total raised."

To Graham, these stipulations seemed too simple and thought she must be working up to the tougher ones. "Agreed."

Pleased, Arietta looked down at the phone. "Did you get those responses, Levi?"

"I did," he replied and went silent again.

Graham looked at her in disbelief. "Is that it?" he asked.

"That is all of them," she confirmed. "And your answer is?"

Graham excitedly replied, "Yes." He stood up and walked around the table to hug Arietta, then went back and hugged Violet, Vincent, and Sara, then shook Cheryl and James's hands.

"There is one final matter we need to discuss and then we are done," said Arietta as she watched them take their seats, and she took hers. "Is there anyone you have in mind to take over your soon-to-be old position?" she asked.

"Vincent," he replied without hesitation.

She looked at Graham, then at Vincent and Sara, smiled and said, "Levi, please add a paragraph that I fully agree to, and support, Graham's choice of successor, Vincent, and that this is my wish and decision."

"Will do," replied Levi.

"Congratulations, Vincent," said Graham and shook his hand.

"Congratulations," said Arietta, then looked at the phone. "You will have the documentation ready to sign, prior to the merger meeting?"

"I will," replied Levi.

She turned her attention to Graham. "On Wednesday morning we will meet and sign the documentation. I will open the meeting Wednesday afternoon by announcing my full support for the merger, then announce my resignation effective immediately, and inform them about Graham and Vincent's promotions and why, after which, Graham, you will take my seat and I will leave the meeting." She paused for a few seconds. "Does anyone have any questions?"

It was quiet.

"I have one request of you before I bring this meeting to a close," she said, looking around at them. "There is a karaoke party tonight in Charlotte Amalie to celebrate Stephanie's birthday, who is James's niece, and it goes from seven until eleven. I have chartered a boat to take us there and back, and it will leave the dock at six and will be back here around midnight. I think it would be a good opportunity for us all to let loose, have fun, mingle, and not only celebrate Stephanie's birthday, but this morning." She stopped and looked at them. "What do you think?"

Everyone agreed it was a great idea, and the meeting came to an end.

They all stood up and socialized, and slowly walked over to the refreshment table. Arietta and James stayed behind.

"Thanks for being here," said Arietta.

"I didn't say a word," he replied.

She smiled. "I know but having you here by my side and your support means the world to me."

"Thanks for putting in the charities as one of your stipulations; you didn't have to do that," said James.

"I know I didn't, but I wanted to," she replied. "For you."

He hugged her and thanked her again, and they joined the others.

Chapter 26

Graham left Violet and walked over to Arietta and James. "I'm really surprised about today; it wasn't the outcome I expected," he said honestly. "I thought we would be going at it all day. Don't get me wrong; I'm glad we aren't," he said and looked at her for a moment. "I thought it was very odd that you were hesitant about the merger but after explaining what you had been going through, I can understand why. I want you to know that what you talked about will stay between you and me."

"I appreciate that," replied Arietta. "How does it feel to have the keys to the kingdom minus a couple of floors?"

"It hasn't sunk in yet," he replied. "It means a lot to me that you trust me to take over."

She touched his arm gently. "You've earned it, and I know the company is in good hands, and it will have many successful and profitable years with you in charge."

"Thank you," he said. "You have that look in your eye when you talk about your new company, and I know you; it's going to be something to look out for. I only feel sorry…" He stopped and looked at her.

"Sorry for what?" she asked.

"The competition in Manhattan when you arrive on the scene," he replied. "You will be a force to be reckoned with."

"Excuse me, James," said Janice. "I have that box you were expecting, and I had them place it on the coffee table."

James excused himself and left with Janice.

Graham watched him walk away. "Tell me about these charity funds. I realize one is for his wife, and the other?" asked Graham as he looked at her. He listened as Arietta explained in detail what they both were and how they came about. "That is kind of him to set those up, and for you to endorse them too. After hearing you describe them to me, I can assure you they are both charities that we will fully support and be glad to be associated with."

"Thank you," she replied and looked over at James looking in the box.

Graham watched her gaze over at him. "Arie, can I say something to you?" he asked.

"Of course," she replied and turned her attention back to her brother.

"You have changed over these last two weeks. I noticed it the first day we met. You were like the Arie I once knew: the young happy Arie, the one at college who was friends with everyone, the one everyone loved…but you lost her…Now standing in front of me, I realize you have found her again and she is back."

"I believe you are right," she said, "and she is back for good."

"I guess this break here on St. John has done you the world of good," he said.

"I believe so," she replied and couldn't help but look over at James.

"I think maybe he has a lot to do with it."

"More than you know," she said, looking at her brother.

"Hope I'm not interrupting," said Sara.

"No, we were just talking about old times," replied Graham. "Please excuse me," he said and gave them some privacy.

"I just wanted you to know that I really appreciated what you said to me, and I'm hoping from this point on we can be friends. It would mean so much to me if we could," said Sara.

"I want us to be, but I feel I have a lot to do to earn it from you," replied Arietta truthfully.

"I'm not one for holding grudges, and I think if we can forget the past and start from here, right now, there will be no need for you to spend any time trying to earn it," she suggested.

Arietta looked at her. "That is very kind of you to want to do that."

"We can never be friends if we can't forgive and forget," she said. "What do you think?"

Arietta glanced over at Cheryl and thought about what Cheryl had said to her, and then back at Sara. "I think you're right, thank you," she said and gave her a long hug. Arietta asked her about the children, and then told her about Cheryl and Caleigh moving to Manhattan.

"I will make a point of speaking with her," said Sara.

"She would love that," said Arietta and looked over at James. "Did you get your picture with James?"

"No, not yet, there hasn't been a good time to ask him, and I decided it may be best to let him come to me, you know, when he has time," she said shyly.

"You must be bursting to tell your friends," said Arietta.

"I am, I almost texted them yesterday but talked myself out of it; a picture says a thousand words," she said excitedly.

"How is your column doing?"

"Good, it's just part-time, and it's just for the local community paper. I post it online too, and the readership is good. Unfortunately, I very rarely get blurbs from an author; it's usually from their publicist. Authors typically have their interviews with the big papers and magazines in New York, not us little ones, but I take what I can. I do my column when the girls are at school or have gone to bed. It's my pride and joy, and I really love it. I guess it helps define me as an individual; you know, me the journalist, not me the wife and mother. It's also made me many friends, most of whom are in the book club; we meet every Wednesday night. Overall, I guess it's a good balance between wife, mother, and journalist."

"Sounds wonderful," said Arietta.

"It is," she replied, "although to be honest with you, I wouldn't mind a little more excitement and challenge on the journalism side. The girls are older now, and they need less of my attention. It would be nice to expand and do it full-time, as a career."

"In journalism?" asked Arietta.

Sara thought for a minute. "That or maybe as a publicist; I think they are both fascinating, so either one."

"Or maybe both," said Arietta.

"That would be challenging," replied Sara as she thought about it, "but exciting."

"Sorry I took so long," said James as he joined them.

"I'm going to go over and talk to Cheryl," said Sara and quickly left.

Arietta looked at James. "There is something I want to ask you to do?"

"Okay, ask away," he said and listened to Arietta for a few minutes. "Consider it done."

"You are the best," she said and almost went to kiss him but caught herself on time. Together they headed to the buffet table, put some food on a plate, and went out on the balcony and stood next to Vincent, who was looking out at the water.

"Vincent, mind if we join you?" asked Arietta.

"No, please do," he said. "I was just admiring how beautiful this place is; it truly is breath-taking."

"It is," replied James as he looked at Arietta.

"I wouldn't mind coming here with Sara and the kids for a couple of weeks."

"You should, they would love it here, and there are lots of activities for families," explained Arietta.

"I have something for you and Graham. Let me get them," said James.

Arietta watched him leave, and she wondered what he had, if anything. It sounded like he was giving her and Vincent some time alone to talk. As she thought this, she watched him walk over to the box; it suddenly struck her that she always looked over at him when he wasn't with her and realized it was because she missed being with him.

"I wonder what he has," asked Vincent, breaking her train of thought.

"I don't know; it will be a surprise to me also," she said honestly and realized she was still looking at him and turned to face Vincent.

Vincent spoke to her about what she had said earlier, and they talked about moving on and being friends. He talked about Sara and the children, and about his hobby as an amateur photographer and videographer, and how he had been going around the resort and the island with Sara taking pictures and filming her and the scenery. Then talked about his promotion. "And I'm extremely happy about it. Thank you for your support."

"You deserve it," said Arietta.

"He deserves what?" asked Graham teasingly as he and Violet joined them.

"To have a wonderful wife, children and be happy," replied Arietta.

"I'm glad you are both here," said James and handed them a copy of 'Demise.' "Before they hit the shelves on Thursday morning."

"Amazing," said Graham.

"I can't wait to read it," added Vincent. Then looked somewhat embarrassed to ask but did. "Can you sign it?"

"Come inside, and we will find a nice pen for me to use," said James. Graham followed them.

"Where are you off to?" asked Violet, already knowing the answer.

"You think I'm not getting my book signed," he replied with a grin.

"While you're at it, why not get your picture taken with him?" replied Violet playfully. She turned and looked at Arietta. "Those two, always trying to outdo the other, sometimes they act like young boys," she said, "but best of friends and would do anything for one another."

"I know," replied Arietta. They both looked inside and watched Graham holding the book and standing next to James as Vincent took the picture; then they swapped spots and Graham took Vincent's, standing next to James. Cheryl told them to get on either side of James and took a picture of the three of them.

"That last one is the one they will have at home. The one of each of them on their own with James will be the one on their desks at work," said Violet. "So they can each brag about who they met."

Sara and Cheryl came out and joined them, and they talked about the island and the party later on and James's family. Shortly after, James, Graham and Vincent came out and stood with them, and when they did, Arietta instinctively moved closer to James. James too was pulled towards Arietta, so close their shoulders were touching. Eventually, Cheryl left to get Caleigh, then Graham and Violet departed.

"When did you want to get that photo and win that bet?" asked James.

"I was hoping this afternoon if that was all right," replied Sara.

"Why not now?" asked Vincent.

Sara shook her head and looked at Arietta. "Do you believe this?"

"I know," replied Arietta. She looked over at Vincent. "If she is going to win the bet, she is going to win it in style."

"In other words: look hot, hair done, makeup and sexy dress," added Sara as she made a pose. "I am not looking like a mother of three," she said, making Arietta laugh.

"Sara, I have an idea," said James who quickly glanced at Arietta, then back at Sara. "How would you like to also do an interview with me?"

Sara's smile on her face disappeared. "Are you serious?"

"I am," he replied.

"Ask you anything," she said.

"Anything," he replied.

She thought for a moment. "What series of books do you want to talk about?"

"We can do one or the other or both. It's up to you."

"I don't know about the second series; I never read it," she said, a little disappointed.

"But I did," said Vincent, "and so did Graham, and between the two of us you should get more than enough material to formulate the right questions to ask."

"That will work," said Sara, her disappointment now gone.

"What about the other series of books, will you be okay?" asked Vincent jokingly. "Or will you need my help?"

She laughed at him. "You may want to leave when I ask him those questions," she said teasingly.

"I'm invited to watch," he said.

She looked at him. "I hoped you would take the pictures and video the interview," she replied, then looked at James. "I mean, if that's okay?"

"I'm fine with that," replied James.

"Really, that would be amazing!" said Vincent.

"And don't worry, honey, I will make sure you also get the credit," said Sara playfully but truthfully. She turned to James and thought for a moment. "If only I had all your books…" she said and started to think about how she could possibly get them.

"Come with me," said James, and they went inside and followed him to the box. He pulled out his six novels. "I was going to give them to you later when we took our pictures."

Sara screamed. "This is perfect!" She picked them up one at a time and looked at them. She flipped through the last one 'Demise' and went to the back cover, then something hit her. "But if you do the interview with me, then everyone will know who you are."

"I know," he replied. "You will be the first to tell all of New York."

"And the rest of the world," added Arietta.

Sara suddenly realized what was happening and this tremendous opportunity now sitting on her lap. "Can we do it tomorrow? The photographs and interview, all of it; I would like more time to prepare."

"Tomorrow it is," replied James.

She put the books back in the box. "Vincent, grab the box. I have to go and start preparing," she said and started for the door and turned around. "Vincent, hurry, I have lots to do." She realized she was caught up in the excitement and stopped and came back over to them. "James, thank you," she said and gave him a hug. "This is incredible." She walked over to Arietta, "thank you," and gave her a long hug and a kiss on the cheek and whispered, "Thank you for doing this for me." She walked over to Vincent, smiled at him, and gave him a kiss. "Let's go, honey," she said, and they left.

Arietta and James were alone.

"How do you feel?" asked James.

"I feel many different things," she said and thought about it for a moment, "but mostly I feel happy, excited, free, and alive." She put her arm through his and walked out the door, leaving that disgruntled part of her, her old life, in that room forever.

Chapter 27

"Two stops," said Arietta, "and that will be it for today."

"Where are we going?" asked James.

"First to the front lobby," replied Arietta.

James sat in an armchair and watched her talk to Janice then disappear with her into her office and come out again on her own.

"Now, to the Island Waves Bar to see my contractors, well, at least I hope so," she said with a cheeky grin.

They went into the bar, and she spotted them. "Hello, Gio, Rocco, Joey."

"Hi, Arietta, James," they replied.

"We just been going over what you want changed," said Gio, looking down at the floor plans and pointing as he talked. "Looks like here on the third floor just needs a wall added to split the room into two and another door, and on the fourth floor more walls added here, here, and here, to make smaller boardrooms, and this wall here and here taken down to make an open office space environment. Sound about right?" he asked, looking at her.

"That's it exactly!" she replied. "When do you think you can start?"

"Tuesday on the third floor," said Gio. "Rocco is going to see to it personally."

"Be done by two o'clock," said Rocco confidently. "In and out."

"And Joey will oversee the fourth floor on Wednesday," said Gio, looking over at Joey.

"That's a bigger job but we'll be finished by Saturday. That way you can start to use it as early as Monday," he said beaming. "And don't worry, you won't hear us on the third."

"That's great news," said Arietta.

"We'll keep hold of these," said Gio, rolling up the plans, "and once we are done, I'll get them updated for you."

"Wow, I don't know what to say, besides thank you!"

"Let's have a drink on it and seal the deal," said Gio, heading for the bar.

"Do you two always oversee these jobs?" asked James.

Rocco and Joey looked at each other and laughed. "No," said Rocco, "never."

"We have several guys who can do this with their eyes closed," said Joey.

"And one hand tied behind their back," added Rocco, and they both laughed. "Usually, we wouldn't even start this job for a month or so. We're pulling guys off another job."

"Papa is giving you the special treatment," said Joey, "and so he should."

"What you did for him, and Mamma was amazing! They haven't stopped talking about it since, and I don't think they ever will," said Rocco. "I have never seen my mother smile so much since that day; that was her fairy-tale brought to life, all because of you."

"If you would have asked Papa, he would have constructed a building for you by the end of the week!" said Joey, and they both laughed again; this time James and Arietta joined in.

"Here we go," said Gio, placing a tray of shots on the table, "take one." He waited until they did. "To good friends and long life! Salute!"

"Salute!" they replied and drank the shot.

"My dear, we have to go and meet the rest of the family for lunch," said Gio. "We'll see you at five thirty on the dock."

They hugged Arietta, kissed her on the cheek, and then did the same to James.

"How big of a boat did you charter?" asked James.

"Big enough," she grinned.

They went to their room and changed into their swimsuits, then pulled two chaises together on Arietta's porch and laid down on them, dozing off. Fifteen minutes before three, her alarm went off on her cell phone. Yawning, she reached over and turned it off.

"Time for Cheryl's signing bonuses," she said.

At three o'clock there was a knock-on Cheryl's door. "Just a minute, Arietta," called Cheryl from the bathroom.

"Mom, want me to get it?" asked Caleigh.

"If you wouldn't mind," she replied.

Caleigh opened the door and let out a shriek. Cheryl rushed out of the bathroom to see what was wrong. She couldn't believe her eyes and slowly said, "Mom…Dad…" She rushed over and threw her arms around them. "What are you doing here? I mean, I'm so happy you are, I just don't understand," said Cheryl excitedly and confused. "Come in, come in and sit down." Cheryl pulled the armchair close to the beds for her mom to sit in, and her dad sat on the edge of one bed opposite Caleigh and Cheryl on the other.

"I'm so happy you're here," said Cheryl. "What made you just decide to come?"

"Well, we received a call late yesterday afternoon from a lovely lady named Arietta," said her mom. "She told us that there were two tickets waiting for us at the airport, and to pack for a week and to get on a flight this morning to come here. I asked her why, and she told me that you had some good news for us and that you would tell us in person when we got here. She said you two were good friends and to please trust her. It sounded very urgent and important, and we already had the week off to spend with Caleigh, so here we are."

"We arrived at our room about ninety minutes ago, and before we put our bags down, there was a knock on the door, and we were given a note to knock on your door at three and were given some envelopes," said her father.

"Envelopes?" asked Cheryl.

Her father gave her one. "Says your name and to open first."

Cheryl opened it and read it out loud. "I thought you might want to tell your parents the news about the fund and new partnership and see their reaction, Arietta."

"What is she talking about?" asked her dad.

Cheryl told them all about Caleigh's fund and her parents' role; they were speechless.

"Lawrence, if I am dreaming, please don't wake me," said Cheryl's mom.

"Margaret, this is no dream, this is our dream coming true," he replied in disbelief.

"There is more," she said and told them about the partnership. Her parents jumped up and gave her a hug as her mother wept. Cheryl's smile couldn't be any wider.

"There is another envelope," said her father as they sat back down. "This one is for Caleigh, and says open second," he said, passing it to her.

Caleigh took it, ripped it open, and read the note to them. "That day we spent together you told me about a wish you had, Arietta."

Cheryl looked at Caleigh. "What wish, honey?"

Caleigh smiled a little. "I told her that after I got back home, Grandma and Grandpa were going to take me to Disney World for my birthday, but because they…" She stopped.

"Because they what, honey?" asked Cheryl.

"Because they spent a lot of money making me better, they couldn't afford it this year, and it made me sad because we couldn't go, and I know they really wanted to go and dress up like pirates and take me on the Pirates of the Caribbean ride, so I told Arietta that I wished they could have taken me, not for me, but for them."

"Oh, baby," said Cheryl with tears welling up in her eyes. "Grandma and Grandpa wanted you to get better first; that was most important."

"I know," she said. "I was sad for them because they were so happy when they talked about taking me." She started to cry.

Lawrence glanced down at the last envelope and read the note to himself, "Keep this to you and your wife, this is from you both, don't let Caleigh know any different and let her believe it's one of the reasons you're here today, enjoy the ride."

"Caleigh, come over here," said her grandpa, "and sit next to me. Grandma, come sit on the other side." He waited until she did and gave his wife a wink. "This envelope is the one that Grandma and Grandpa brought with us; it's another one of the reasons we are here today. You want to help me open it?" he asked.

"Okay," she said and wiped away her tears.

She opened it up, and inside were three airplane tickets to Orlando, leaving Monday, and a note that her grandpa read, "Transportation on the Disney coach to Disney World, a suite at the Animal Kingdom Resort, three six-day ticket passes to all the parks, front of the line passes for all rides, a dining plan for all your meals including one daily Character meal where you get to meet different Disney characters, and a Disney gift card with a two-thousand-dollar spending limit."

Caleigh screamed. "I don't believe it! I don't believe it! We are going to Disney! This is so amazing!"

"Happy birthday, Caleigh," said her grandma.

"Happy birthday," said her grandpa, and they did a group hug. "This last envelope is for you," said her dad, handing it to Cheryl.

She opened it and read it aloud. "We will see you all for dinner at the Terrace Restaurant at five and bring your singing voices for tonight. Caleigh, wait for a knock on the door, Arietta."

Shortly after there was a knock and Caleigh jumped up. She came back holding a big box and placed it on the bed. They all stood around as she opened it up.

"It's the dress I saw with Arietta. She said she would get it for me for a special night; isn't it beautiful? It's even got a matching bag and shoes," she said excitedly.

Cheryl was wondering what Arietta was thinking. How could Caleigh go tonight? Maybe it was just for her to wear to dinner.

"Here, Mom, there's a card inside with your name on it," said Caleigh, passing it to her.

She opened it and read it to herself. "By the way don't worry about a babysitter. I booked the top floor for the party tonight, which makes it a private function, so children are allowed. See you at five. Oh, sorry I tricked you with the signing bonus thing, I wanted to surprise you, Arietta." Cheryl smiled happily and looked at her family. After she left the meeting this morning, she had accepted the sad fact that she would be going on her own tonight, but that had all changed, because now she would be celebrating one of the best days of her life with her daughter, her mom and dad.

Chapter 28

"That was really nice what you did for her," said James.

"I could tell that Cheryl really wanted to see her parents' reactions to the fund, and with what was happening this morning, I figured why not bring them here, and she could tell them everything," she explained. "And it broke my heart hearing Caleigh talk about her grandparents and Disney," she said, pulling a pretend sad face.

They walked into the restaurant and sat down to wait for their guests. Cheryl, Caleigh, and her parents showed up a few minutes later and were introduced.

"How do you like my dress, Arietta?" asked Caleigh.

"It looks beautiful," she said, "and so do you."

"Thank you," she replied. "I love it."

During dinner James explained to Cheryl's parents the details of Caleigh's Fund. "So I'm really hoping you two will consider taking over the accounting and releasing of the funds portion, as well as attend the meetings with Sophie and Karen to review and approve the individuals who have applied."

"Consider it?" asked Lawrence, glancing over at his wife and back at James. "When do we start?"

Relieved, James smiled at them and sat back in his chair. "Why don't we meet the week after you get back? I will arrange to have Sophie, Karen, and Joanne there, and we can figure it all out then. We can talk about your salaries, which will be very competitive," he said reassuringly, "as well as your office location."

"I'm sure everything will be fine," said Margaret. "You have a very honest face."

Cheryl told them about the school Sara's children attended and how Sara grew up close to where she did. "We have so much in common, and she is so nice. She even offered to help me with Caleigh if I ever need her to get picked up or watched."

Arietta talked to Cheryl about her meeting with Gio and the renovations for the office then asked her about next week. "Caleigh had said that you were taking next week off to relax and take it easy, but I was wondering if you wanted to fly back with us on Monday afternoon to Manhattan. I could show you the office, the condo, and maybe Sara can show you the school, you know, get a feel for the place. We can also talk about the next steps for the business, and in between we can relax and pamper ourselves at the spa and do some shopping. What do you think?"

"I think that would be wonderful!" she replied, squeezing Arietta's hand. "I'm so excited I can't wait."

After dinner they made their way to the dock, meeting up with her brother and his group.

"Sure it's big enough?" asked Graham jokingly, pointing to the large boat.

No sooner had he said that when Gio and his group showed up. "Let's get this party started!" shouted Gio to gales of laughter.

During the forty-five-minute ride, everyone took advantage of the open bar and mingled. They disembarked, crossed over Veteran's Drive to the Haven Bar and Restaurant, and went upstairs to sit with James's family and their friends. D-Mon played music for a while to let everyone get comfortable and down a few drinks of courage, but as soon as the birthday girl finished singing the first karaoke song of the night, there was a list of people waiting their turn, and the party began.

Violet walked over to Arietta and Cheryl. "Can we talk outside for a moment?" she asked, and they followed her onto the balcony. "As you know the meeting for the merger is this week, and myself, Graham, and Vincent talked about having a social gathering to celebrate the merger publicly, and I wanted to ask, on behalf of the three of us..." She stopped and looked at them. "Who am I kidding? They're not interested in the details, they just want to show up and party," she said, and they all laughed. "I would like you to plan the event for me, for us. Maybe this week we can meet for dinner, go over the details, and pick a suitable date and location for the event," she suggested.

"Of course," replied Arietta. "Give us a call, and we can arrange a meeting."

"I will." She looked at them both. "I guess I should at least give you a feel for what I want…" She stopped and started to think.

"Vibrant," said Cheryl. "Attitude."

"Youthful, but mature," added Arietta.

"Colorful, wild and fun," said Cheryl.

"But sophisticated and charming," threw in Arietta.

"With the color violet sprinkled around," finished Cheryl.

Violet stood back. "You took the words right out of my mouth. That's exactly what I want, and I can see why you two are partners." She gave them each a hug. "I believe that your business will do extremely well, and by the end of the year, Manhattan will be yours. I'll be in touch," she said over her shoulder as she returned to the party.

"Our first event," said Cheryl, "for our new company."

"I know," replied Arietta. "Isn't it thrilling?"

Cheryl's face went serious.

"What's wrong?"

"What are we going to call our company?" she asked as she looked at Arietta's blank face.

"I don't know," replied Arietta. "But we're going to have to come up with one soon."

Cheryl quickly looked around. "While we have this moment alone, I just wanted to thank you and let you know how much I appreciate what you did for me this afternoon; my parents showing up, Caleigh's dress and arranging it so she could come, and their trip, all of it. I want you to know that having Caleigh and my parents here has made my night incredibly special, thank you."

"It just seemed right that your parents, your family, should be here to celebrate with you, and with us, and our families," replied Arietta. "I'm so happy it made your night."

Inside, James introduced Sophie and Karen to Lawrence and Margaret. Leaving them to talk, he joined Sara and Vincent. "How are things going?" he asked.

"Going great," said Vincent. "This is a great party. I'm just waiting for my name to be called."

"Oh no," said Sara. "Thanks for the warning."

"You said I sing great," said Vincent.

"Honey, I said I like watching you sing," she replied. "Let's leave it at that."

"Guess I should get another drink," he said, pretending to pout.

"Love you," she said, kissing him on the cheek and watching him make his way to the bar. "He isn't too bad, not too good either," she said as she turned to James. "Are you going to sing?"

"Maybe after a couple more of these," he replied, lifting his beer.

"Same here," she said in agreement. "I was wondering what your availability was like for tomorrow?"

"I would say any time after twelve, until whenever," he replied. "When were you thinking?"

"I was going to suggest early afternoon when the sun is brightest. I thought we could do the interview at three or four distinct locations around the resort, if that's okay?"

"That's fine," he said. "I'm leaving it all in your capable hands; just tell me what to do."

She went silent. She was uncomfortable but realized she needed to ask. "Are there any questions that you don't want me to ask you?"

"No," said James without hesitation. "I want you to ask anything and everything."

"Okay," she said. "Now this is just a high-level overview, but I was thinking of starting from the beginning, prior to your first three novels, then talking about each of them in some detail, then prior to your next three novels and talking about each of them in some detail. And as we talk about each of your novels, we can speak about any personal stories you would like to share or inspirations you had and so on, and then end the interview with what is next for you."

"That's perfect," he said. "I think you have a really good handle on it."

"How does one thirty sound?" she asked.

"One thirty is fine."

"Good, we will meet you at the front lobby."

"Okay," he replied and looked over at Vincent at the bar. "How is your photographer, slash videographer doing?"

"He is over the moon. He has all his equipment ready to go, and he's talking about background, lighting, sound, you name it, he's got it covered. He is very confident and exceptionally good," she replied. "Me, I'm nervous-excited; I have never done anything like this before, well, at least not on this scale, so I'm a little nervous, and also extremely excited to be doing my very first big interview, and it's slowly sinking in that I'm breaking a story on this huge literary secret." She looked at him and gave him a smile. "You know, two days ago I would have been content with just a picture of you, bragging to my friends, and a free dinner, but right now, at the very least, I'm going to rock Manhattan."

He smiled at her. "I like that 'I'm going to rock Manhattan.'"

"So do I," she replied. "I'm going to have to keep hold of that thought and see if I can work it in somewhere."

Vincent's name was called up to sing.

"You're going to have to excuse me. I need to go up to the front and hear my honey try his luck at rocking this place," she said, and they both laughed.

"Uncle James," said Elizabeth. "Me, Caitlin and Caleigh are singing next."

James looked at the three of them. "Could be bad timing," said James, teasing them. "The guy up next is supposed to be pretty good, means you guys have to do better than him."

"Really," Elizabeth replied, and they all looked at each other nervously.

"I need to go tell my mom and Arietta that we are singing. I think they're outside," said Caleigh. They all took off and came back moments later with the women in tow. Vincent had started singing, and Sara was right, he wasn't bad, but he wasn't good.

Vincent finished, and Elizabeth came over and gave James a smack on the arm. "Really, Uncle James, him…Very funny joke," she said, strutting away with her nose in the air.

This was followed by another smack on the arm from Caleigh. "Really, Uncle James, him…Very funny joke," she said and copied Elizabeth's exit.

Caitlin followed suit.

Arietta and Cheryl tried to smother their laughter. "Oh baby, don't you know not to mess with an all-girl band," Arietta managed to get out.

"I do now," he replied. "Divas and one of them is only twelve!" he replied, rubbing his arm.

Sophie and Ken came over and stood next to Cheryl to listen to the girls sing, which they did extremely well, ending in shouts and applause. Grinning, the three girls waved to the adoring crowd and sauntered off the stage.

D-Mon took a break in between the singing to play music so people could dance. James danced with Stephanie, and after the song finished, they went outside, and he gave Stephanie her present in private: an expensive set of diamond earrings and a matching necklace. He helped her with the necklace, and she kissed him before running off to show her friends.

"Need to cool off," said Graham.

"It's warm in there," replied James.

"Thankfully we have this breeze," added Violet.

Graham looked in the room at his sister. "I'm glad to see Arie smile and laugh again, it's been too long. I never noticed how unhappy she was." He looked over at James. "I feel guilty about not realizing it before and talking with her about it. I think I've been too selfishly wrapped up in my own world not to notice my sister was falling apart."

"I wouldn't beat yourself up over it; people have an effective way of hiding it. Sometimes they don't know it themselves until it hits them. One day they look at their reflection in the mirror and start questioning their unhappiness, themselves, and their life." He looked over at Arietta. "All she knew is that she needed to escape and ended up here."

"I'm happy she did," replied Graham, "or she wouldn't have met you."

James smiled at Graham. "Or me her."

Graham didn't say any more about it, and it went quiet.

Violet used the opportunity to change the subject. "I hear Sara is interviewing you tomorrow."

"She is."

"That's a really big step for her, but I think she will do fantastic."

"I think she will, too," replied James.

"Yeah, and Vincent is also getting in there. He tells me he will be credited with the photographs and the video. He is always trying to get that edge on me," said Graham humorously. "Cheeky guy told me tonight that the ball's in my court."

"You know it was by chance that he got asked?" said James.

"I know, I know," replied Graham. "Trust me, it's all in good fun with him and I, but it doesn't stop him from bragging about it."

"You know," said James, "I was thinking about something, and I believe you can help me; actually, both of you can."

Graham and Violet moved closer to him.

"We're listening," said Graham.

"At the end of next week, I was considering doing a press conference or maybe a book reading and was thinking of something to wear and—"

"We could put together an outfit for you," said Graham.

"Something calm, cool, summery, but bold, mysterious and hot," said Violet.

"We can say that we dress the most mysterious man in Manhattan," replied Graham, looking at Violet.

"And if Sara's interview takes hold of Manhattan like I believe it will," said Violet, "the publicity would be incredible."

Graham and Violet realized they were getting caught up in the moment. "Sorry about that," said Graham.

"Nothing to apologize about," replied James. "I understand now what Arietta means when she talks about the passion you two have; it's very captivating, and I believe it just sold me an outfit."

"Seriously?" asked Violet.

"Yeah, I'm serious," he replied. "You figure out something for me to wear and take whatever spin you want on it."

"Can we keep this between us three?" asked Graham. "Well, you can tell Arietta and Cheryl, but no one else."

"Deal," he said and shook Graham's hand.

"Oh, Vincent, how sweet this will be," said Graham in a sinister voice that made Violet and James laugh. "I'm guessing there will be a Q and A at your press conference or book reading?"

"There will be," he confirmed.

"Plant," said Violet.

"Plant?" asked James.

"A plant, it's an old trick but quite effective if used correctly," said Graham. "We plant someone in the audience to ask you a question about your book, you answer, and then they comment on your clothing and ask who you're wearing."

James shook his head, laughing. "You want to write my answer on a card?"

Graham grinned. "Can we?"

"Give it to me when I pick up the outfit," replied James.

Graham shook his hand. "Thanks, James, you're a real good sport for going along with this."

"I can't wait to design something one of kind for you," said Violet ecstatically. "Can we drop by your room to take your measurements tomorrow? Say around twelve?"

"Twelve is good," he replied.

"I promise you, you won't be disappointed," she said and gave him a smile. "Thank you."

Graham shook his hand and thanked him again and put his arm around Violet, and as they walked away, James could hear them talking about his design and their plan.

"Hi, stranger," said Arietta.

"Hi, there," said James. "Did I tell you how stunning you look tonight?"

"I don't believe so," she replied, looking away in dismay.

James moved close to her and whispered in her ear, "I think you are beautiful…funny…smart…and sexy." He could feel her breath on his neck, and he thought about moving his mouth to hers and kissing her.

She loved the way his voice sounded, and she could feel his breath on her ear. She closed her eyes and thought about moving her lips to his and kissing him.

"Uncle James, Arietta, it's your turn to sing," said Elizabeth.

"They're calling your names," said Caleigh.

The spell was broken, and they separated.

"Did you pick a song for us?" asked Arietta in a quiet voice.

"No, did you?" James whispered.

"No," she replied.

"Let's go," said the girls as they grabbed their hands, leading them to the stage. Dumbfounded, they stood on the stage and looked at each other.

"Maybe a shot," said Ricky, holding a tray with four shots. The culprit had revealed himself.

Arietta reached over and grabbed two shots. James waited for her to pass one to him and suddenly realized she was going to drink both. He picked up the other two, and they drank one. Ricky turned around to the crowd and waved his arms up and down to make them cheer loudly.

"Chug, chug," said Ricky as the crowd joined in.

Arietta and James tapped their glasses and downed the other shot.

D-Mon came over to them. "Are you ready?" he asked.

"Ready as we'll ever be," replied Arietta. "What song are we doing?"

"Rick Astley, 'Together Forever,'" he replied, handing them a microphone each.

"I know that song," said Arietta to James.

"Me too," replied James.

The song began, and they started to sing to the crowd. When the chorus came on, they looked at each other and sang, then turned back to the crowd. Feeling more comfortable, they started dancing to the beat and playing to the crowd. The crowd clapped and yelled enthusiastically. On the last chorus, they moved close to one another and gazed into each other's eyes and sang the words. The song finished, and the crowd cheered. They stood still and silent, lost in each other's eyes. There was no one else in that room, only them. He moved closer to her and her to him, and they softly, gently kissed. The crowd cheered loudly, and they suddenly realized they were not alone and quickly pulled away.

"Thank you, James," said Arietta into the microphone.

"Thank you," replied James to Arietta. "Thank you," he said to the audience.

They handed the microphones to D-Mon and quickly made their way off the stage.

"Now that's how we party here in Charlotte Amalie," said D-Mon. "Let's give it up one more time for Arietta and James."

The crowd applauded again, and family and friends came by and congratulated them on an impressive performance. When they were alone, Arietta excused herself and went to the bathroom while James headed outside. From there he saw her exit the bathroom and make a beeline to the bar. James made his way over to her and ordered a drink as well.

"That was fun," he said, trying to get past the kiss.

"Yeah, it was. My parents used to sing that song all the time," she said. "I really love it."

"It's a great song," he replied. "That brother of mine is a troublemaker."

"Yeah, we are going to have to get him back for that one day," she said. Or thank him, she thought.

"Or thank him," said James.

She laughed at him and touched his arm. "I was just thinking the exact same thing."

"Ladies and gentlemen, I am going to play a few dance songs before I start the last and final set of karaoke songs. This is my special gift to one of my favorite couples here tonight and a song I know they love."

Dean Martin's 'Amore' came on, and Rio and Gio were on the dance floor in a flash; other couples got up and joined them.

"Want to dance?" asked James.

"I would love to," she said.

They went onto the dance floor, and he held her close in his arms. As they danced, he softly sang the words in her ear. She closed her eyes and felt like she was in heaven. They danced the next couple of songs and then stood by the bar, close to one another.

Gio was called up to sing.

"Rio, where are you?" he asked. "Rio?"

"I'm here, Gio," she said, stopping in front of the stage.

"Don't move…well, you can dance, but don't go. This is a song we danced to when we were younger," he said and nodded to D-Mon to begin.

'Rio' by Duran Duran came on, and Gio started singing it to her. To everyone's surprise, he was really good. Rio started dancing, and she could move. She spotted Arietta and pulled her up to dance with her. One by one, they started pulling people up to dance as Gio sang. Arietta waved for James to join her, and they danced together. Everyone helped Gio sing the chorus.

The evening came to an end, and D-Mon spoke. "I want to thank you all. You guys have been great. I have one more song to play. I know many of you are going back home tomorrow or the next day, so it seems only fitting that we close this party down with this final song, the late, great Frank Sinatra's, 'New York, New York.'" The song came on, and everyone was arm in arm, singing and kicking their legs in the air; it was the perfect end to a perfect party.

Outside, everyone said their goodbyes with heartfelt hugs and kisses, and the group that came on the charter boarded and sailed back to the resort. Arietta and James sat with Cheryl and her parents. Within five minutes, Caleigh was asleep on Cheryl's lap and Grandpa lifted her off and held her in his arms. They talked about the party until the boat docked, then everyone got off and said goodnight.

Arietta opened the door to her room, and James followed her in. "I'm exhausted," she said as she flopped on her bed.

"So am I," James replied as he lay down next to her. "That was fun."

"It was," she said and looked over at him. "You have a busy day tomorrow, measured for clothes, an interview."

"I do," he said, sitting up. "I should probably get some sleep." He looked down at her. "Will you be there tomorrow?"

She grabbed his hand and smiled reassuringly. "You know I will."

"I know," he replied. "I just like hearing you say it." He jumped off the bed. "I have to go to bed and get some sleep. I'll meet you for breakfast," he said and started singing 'Together Forever' as he left.

"James," she said as he turned around. "Thank you for tonight, for everything."

He came back onto the bed and carefully pushed her hair away from her face and whispered, "Thank you," as he softly kissed her on the lips. He admired her as he gently caressed her arm, her shoulder, her hair, and her face.

Arietta loved the way he touched her, the way he made her feel. She closed her eyes and enjoyed every soothing, tender caress. Lulled into sleep, she quietly whispered, "Please don't fool my virgin heart."

Chapter 29

Arietta woke up the next morning with her clothes on and the duvet covering her. She quickly thought back, remembering his kiss, his touch, and smiled as she lay there thinking about them. She eventually got out of bed and opened the drapes to let the sunshine in. The phone rang, and she picked it up. "Okay," she replied, "be there in ten minutes." She went into the bathroom, took off her clothes, put her hair in a ponytail, got a wash, put on her pajamas and robe, and went over to James's patio. "Good morning," she said.

"Good morning. Did you sleep well?"

"I did, I must have been tired," she replied. "This looks good," she said, looking at the breakfast on the table.

"Got a little bit of everything," he explained. "Thought we could share."

Arietta sat down and was handed a plate that she quickly filled up; James did the same.

"Sorry I fell asleep on you, again."

"Don't worry, I came in here and collapsed on the bed. I was asleep before my head touched the pillow."

As they ate, she asked him about his plans.

"I have Violet, and I think Graham coming here at twelve, then I have to meet Sara at one thirty in the lobby."

"Do you know what you are going to wear?" she asked.

"Not really, any suggestions?"

"Middle of the afternoon, Caribbean, lots of colors and it will be hot…I would say something casual, comfortable, and plain."

"Plain?"

"For example, if you wear a multicolored shirt and you have floral colors behind you in the background, it will look chaotic so you're best to wear something like a blue polo or buttoned shirt, with grey or tan shorts or pants…plain colors, symmetric."

"Maybe you can help me pick out what will look best?"

"Okay," she replied.

They talked about Graham and his plan to upstage Vincent.

"I tell you, those two have been doing this for years," she said, grinning at the memories. "It will be fun to see it all unfold next week, and the good thing is we are just observers." She thought for a moment. "It's going to be really interesting to see what Violet designs for you. You know, this will be her first piece under the merger."

"I never realized that."

"I think it's a smart move for her and Graham what they are doing with you; in fact, I say it is brilliant," she said approvingly. Then she talked about Violet and the merger event and how much fun that will be. "You know, I just remembered something that Cheryl said last night: we don't have a name for our company."

"That's right, you don't. Won't you need to come up with one soon?"

"Within the next few days," she said, "at the latest." She finished her coffee and put her empty cup down. "Okay, let's have a look at what you can wear."

They went inside, and James laid out all the possibilities on the bed. She quickly picked out pants and a buttoned shirt. "This shirt will bring out your eyes," she said. "Now I'm going to go get ready, and I will be back here before twelve."

Arietta returned and sat with James on the patio when there was a knock on the door. James opened it, and Violet and Graham walked in.

"Hello," they both said.

"Hi, Arie," said Graham as he noticed her walking through the doorway. "Great party last night. You guys sang great; Gio, too."

"I loved the three girls. They were so cute and adorable," said Violet affectionately.

"I thought Vincent was the best," baited James. They all stopped and looked at him and laughed.

"Poor guy is tone deaf," said Graham, "but kudos to him; he gets up there."

"Poor us, you mean," said Violet. "We have to listen and suffer through it." She turned to James. "Okay, let's get started."

Like an artist with a paintbrush, she gingerly moved around James's body with her measuring tape, stopping intermittently to record the numbers on her pad.

"All finished," she confirmed. "Graham or I will call you in two or three days."

"Sorry that we have to rush out of here, but our plane leaves this afternoon," said Graham. "See you back in Manhattan."

They said goodbye and left.

At one fifteen James changed, and they walked to the lobby to meet Sara. She was wearing a pretty dress, hair styled, and makeup done.

"Wow! You look great, Sara," Arietta said.

"Thank you," she replied. "Vincent is setting up at the first shoot, so we will meet him there." They followed her past the spa and into the garden.

"This is where Cheryl and I had lunch after our spa day," said Arietta. "This is a beautiful spot."

"It is," replied Sara. "We have the gazebo, and inside, two chairs and a table set up, so we can capture the colorful flora in the background. I think it would be perfect for the first part of the interview," she added, looking at James.

James nodded.

"Hello, Vincent," they said.

"Hi, James, Arietta," he replied. "I have three video cameras set up. One diagonally focused on you, James, and the other one on this side focused on Sara. The third one will be in the middle, which will have both of you in frame; I will operate that one. The ones on the side will be running on their own, so try not to move your head too far to either side or we will lose you from the frame…think that is it. If you want to sit down in your chairs and give me a minute so I can get you set up for your personal cameras, then we can begin," said Vincent as he started adjusting the cameras.

"So, James, I'm going to hide a microphone here to record our interview, and this is what I will be using for the print version, then Vincent will edit the videos and put together the taped interview."

"Sounds great," replied James, impressed.

"As I said last night, I will start from the beginning, your background, how you got into writing, what inspired you and how you got your first break, then we will discuss each of the books, and when we finish the third, we will break and move to the next location, okay?"

James shook his head and smiled.

"Ready when you are," said Vincent.

"I will introduce myself first and then you as author James Davenport and then will start the questions," explained Sara.

"Good friend and author," said James.

"Okay," said Sara, smiling, then turned to Vincent and waited for his signal. "Hello, I am Sara Williams, and I am here with my good friend and author James Davenport on the beautiful island of St. John at the St. John's Resort." She turned to James. "Good afternoon, James."

"Good afternoon, Sara. Good to see you again," replied James.

Sara's questions covered the beginning of his career and the short articles he wrote. She spoke about his wife Clair and what an inspiration she had been to him and the support she offered him in his writing, all the way up to his big break; then she introduced his first published novel 'Hold Me In Your Arms.' She picked up the book and showed the cover, then started asking specific questions about the novel; she did this for all three. After James answered the last question, she turned and looked at Vincent's camera. "Each novel was written as beautiful as the flora behind me, but a very sad tragedy would befall on James Davenport; that story next."

"And done," said Vincent.

Arietta and Vincent clapped, and James joined in.

"That was incredible, Sara," praised Vincent.

"Unbelievable," complimented James. "You're a natural."

"Sara, I couldn't take my eyes off you. I was spellbound," declared Arietta. "And you're so sincere, sensitive, caring, funny…amazing."

"That's very kind of you all," said Sara, blushing. "I was a little nervous."

"It didn't show," said James. "You were very professional, articulate and the questions were spot on."

"And the way you weaved his personal life in and out was fantastic," said Arietta.

"I'm all packed up," said Vincent. "Next location." They moved to a secluded part of the resort and sat on chairs positioned on the lawn with hills and valleys in the background. Once Vincent had set up, they began the second part of the interview.

"Hello and welcome back. I am Sara Williams, and I am here with my good friend and author James Davenport on the beautiful island of St. John at the St. John's Resort." She turned to James and asked him questions about Clair, her battle with cancer and her death. About the troubles and struggles James went through, the support he had from his family, and the eventual help he received from a professional therapist and her advice to put down what he was feeling and going through on paper. James became teary-eyed at times but kept his composure and only faltered once; Arietta wasn't sure what was keeping him together. Arietta had tears rolling down her face; she was crying, and she realized that when people watch this, they will have the same reaction. He answered her last question, and she turned to the camera. "The road of life is unpredictable and full of hills and valleys but somehow we are able to get through them. You won't want to miss how James Davenport managed to forge on, and his biggest secret; all to be revealed, next."

"And done," said Vincent.

James stood up and walked off to one side towards the edge of the beach, visibly upset. Arietta wiped her eyes and went over to see him, and Sara went to follow but Vincent held her back.

Arietta walked up behind him and put her arm around him. "Are you okay?" She realized he was crying and stepped in front of him and held him close. He put his arms around her, and they stood there for a while.

He pulled away and looked at her. "I'm okay."

"Did you know she was going to ask those questions?" she asked.

"I did, I told her anything and everything, I wanted her to," he said.

"Why?" she asked.

"I'm tired of hiding, of the secrets. I just want everyone else to know, and I think it will be good for me, my mind, my heart, and my soul, to talk about everything once and for all." He gave her a smile and looked at her. "This is my confessional, and you were here, just like you promised. Thank you." He kissed her softly on the cheek. "It's time for me to move on with my life."

"I know," she replied and held him in her arms a few minutes longer. She let go, and they walked back to Sara and Vincent.

"I'm so sorry. Are you, all right?" asked Sara.

He smiled and looked into her eyes. "You are doing an extraordinary interview, and it's exactly what I wanted and expected. Don't change a thing. I said you had carte blanche with the questions, and you have risen to the occasion magnificently…Now," he said with a smile, "shall we let the cat out of the bag?"

She was speechless.

"Next location," said Vincent.

They moved to a secluded area on the beach and set up their chairs in the sand. In the background there were big boulders in the water and waves crashing against them, sending up magnificent sprays of water. Vincent set up and they began.

"Welcome back, for the third part of our four-part interview. Hello, I am Sara Williams, and I am here with my good friend and author James Davenport on the beautiful island of St. John at the St. John's Resort." She looked at him. "Or should I say…" It was James's cue to reveal his other name.

"Sara," he said, grinning. "Please do me the honor and look into the camera and tell them."

Sara's face lit up with excitement as she suddenly realized she was going to be the one to reveal one of the biggest literary secrets of the last several years. "Ladies and gentlemen, I am now sitting with my good friend and author James Brian…Yes, James Brian and James Davenport is one and the same." She turned to him and asked him about his name and how he chose it and why the secrecy, then several other questions leading up to the first book of his second trilogy, 'Genesis,' which she picked up and proceeded to ask questions about, then the second 'Paradise,' but on the third book, 'Demise,' she held it up and looked into the camera. "No spoilers in this interview," she said, smiling at James then back at the camera. "'Demise' will be on bookshelves Thursday." She turned to James. "Maybe in a month or so we can meet and talk about this final book in detail."

"It's a date," said James.

Sara turned back to the camera. "This trilogy is as beautiful and chaotic as the scenery behind me, but what does the future hold for James Davenport and James Brian? You are about to find out, coming up next."

"And done," said Vincent.

Sara jumped out of her chair and threw her arms around James. "I can't believe you let me tell them your name. I can't believe you let me be the person who announced to Manhattan that you are James Brian…Thank you, thank you."

"Sara, this is your interview, and you're doing an exceptional job. It is only fitting that you cap it off by revealing the secret," said James. "I should be thanking you. Thank you."

"This last location is the best one," said Vincent. "Well, maybe not for the scenery."

They walked into the Island Waves Bar and found as secluded a spot as they could. "I'm just going to use one camera for this last shoot and move around with it to make it look more natural and fun," said Vincent.

Arietta walked up to the bar and ordered four Rum Punches and put two on the table and one close to Vincent. "You need a drink if you're at a bar," she said, grinning.

"Welcome back, for the fourth and final part of our interview. Hello, I am Sara Williams, and I am here with my good friend and author James Davenport slash James Brian on the beautiful island of St. John at the St. John's Resort." She looked over at James. "James, we are winding down our interview here at the Island Waves Bar and enjoying a nice refreshing Rum Punch, and I'm sure your fans want to know what's next. First, let's talk about James Brian."

"Well, Sara, James Brian is going to be going into retirement at this time," he replied.

"Forever?" asked Sara.

"Well, I would never say forever," he teased.

"Let's talk about James Davenport. What's next for him?" she asked.

"You and your friends in your book club will be happy to know that I will be starting to write my new romantic novel as soon as I get back to Manhattan," revealed James.

"That is exciting and most welcome news for me and all your fans. James, any hints?" she asked. "Something to whet our appetite?"

"For you, Sara," he said with a smile. "The title is going to be 'The Virgin Heart.'"

"Intriguing and interesting," she replied. "Is there anything else you want to share?"

"The setting will be very similar to this location, and the main character will probably be female," he concluded.

Sara looked at the camera. "Well, there you have it. You heard it here first…James Davenport's next novel is 'The Virgin Heart.'"

She turned to James. "I know that your latest novel 'Demise' will be a tremendous success for you, and we look forward to your next novel 'The Virgin Heart' hitting the shelves in the very near future."

"Thank you," said James.

"Thank you for taking the time today to sit down with me." She looked into the camera. "This is Sara Williams saying, so long." She raised her glass to James, and they "cheered." Vincent faded out. "And done."

"Aaahhh!" Sara jumped up and screamed with excitement. "Are you kidding me? You revealed the title of your next book, too." She reached for her drink and took a big gulp. "I never felt so…so…"

"Alive," said Arietta.

"Yes, alive, that's it." She was euphoric.

James stood up next to Arietta and Vincent and applauded her; the other two joined in.

"Thank you," she said, bowing her head. Then everything hit her, and tears of joy rolled down her cheeks. "I did it."

Vincent went over and held her. "You not only did it! You nailed it! It was perfect! I'm so proud of you." He gave her a kiss and dried her tears. "Let's have a seat and celebrate."

They all sat down except Vincent who picked up his glass. "To Sara," he proudly announced.

"To Sara," replied Arietta and James. They all touched glasses and drank.

"James, I just thought about something. Would you mind if I got some footage of you walking up toward me from the beach and passing by? Just in case I want to add some solitary footage, you know, show you on your own, thinking?" asked Vincent.

"Not at all, do you want to do it now?"

"I think we should, before we finish this drink," said Vincent. He grabbed his camera, and they excused themselves.

"I want to thank you," said Sara. "You helped me get this opportunity."

"Well," said Arietta, "I may have mentioned it to James, but you have proven yourself more than worthy."

"I did, didn't I? I feel so good. I know they will both be great, the written piece and the interview." She was thrilled at what she had accomplished today and chatted for a while about what the reaction will be when it all goes public.

James and Vincent returned.

"Vincent, I just remembered; I need to get some still shots with James," said Sara.

"I took a few at each location," replied Vincent.

Sara looked at Arietta, and they both shook their heads. "I need a different outfit for the pictures," said Sara. "Want to come with me, Arietta?"

"Sure," she replied.

They left and were back in fifteen minutes. Arietta gave James another shirt to put on, and he changed at the bar. They went to a lovely spot on the beach where couples go to get their wedding pictures taken; except in this instance, Sara wasn't showing off her wedding ring, she was showing off her books. She had a picture taken with James with each of his books, then one for each of the trilogies, then one with all six. They went back to their table, ordered another drink, and looked on as James signed each book for Sara.

"I was talking with Arietta and wondering what to do next, with the print and video?" asked Sara.

"With the print, call the New York Times, and the video, CNN, Fox, Today Show," said James in a matter-of-fact way.

"You're joking," said Sara, laughing.

"No, I think you should," replied James affirmatively.

"You wouldn't mind?" asked Sara.

"Why would I? It's your work. They're your pieces," he said, looking at her. "Aim as high as you can. The worst they can say is…" He waited to let her answer.

"No," she replied. She looked around at them and stopped at Vincent. "I'm going to do it."

"Go for it!" said Vincent. "I think you should."

"Let's go. I can't wait to get back to New York," said Sara and stood.

"Sara," said James, "before you go. I was thinking about doing some sort of press conference or book reading with a Q&A for 'Demise,' maybe the end of next week, and I don't know a thing on how to set one up, and I don't have a publicist. Well, I have never had the need for one before, but I have the feeling I am going to. I heard you had some background as one."

"Some," she said. "You want me to help you out?"

"Well," he replied. "I'm not sure how much time is involved in doing that sort of stuff. I'm guessing part-time which means you can still do your journalism, so I was wondering, actually I was hoping you would be my publicist, and if it gets to be too much with the journalism and you want to stop, there would be no hard feelings."

She walked over to him. "Are you asking me to be your publicist?"

"I am."

"Oh my, Vincent, I don't believe it! I don't believe it!" said Sara.

"Give him an answer before he changes his mind," Vincent urged her.

"Yes, yes, yes," she said. "When are you back in Manhattan?"

"Monday evening," he replied.

"Let's meet Tuesday afternoon, and we can decide on what kind of 'thing' we need to set up," she said.

"How about two o'clock Tuesday? I will call you Monday night, and we can decide on a place," suggested James.

"Definitely," replied Sara and looked over at Arietta.

"That's nothing to do with me; it's all you," replied Arietta. "Congratulations!" She stood up and gave her a hug.

James also got up and hugged her. "Thank you for everything and welcome aboard."

Vincent shook James's hand and gave him a smile. "Thank you. You've made more than her day." He walked around and gave Arietta a hug, which surprised her. "Thank you."

"See you back in Manhattan," said Sara, and they both left.

As they watched them leave, Cheryl and Caleigh walked by them to their table.

"How did the interview go?" asked Cheryl.

"Amazing," said James. "Sara was excellent."

"That's great. You can tell me all about it on our flight home," she said, looking around. "We're having an early dinner inside and meeting my parents here. They have to leave in the morning, and I want missy here to get a good night's sleep."

"Are you excited about your trip to Disney?" asked Arietta.

"I am. I don't know if I will be able to sleep, I'm so excited," replied Caleigh. She looked at her mom. "Can I ask?"

"Sure," said Cheryl. "Go on."

"Uncle, I mean, James, I was wondering if I could call you Uncle James. You see, my mom has no brothers or sisters, and I have no uncles, and Mom says since you're like a brother to her…so I thought I could call you Uncle James?" she asked.

"Of course, you can," he replied. "It would be an honor."

"Arietta, you are like a sister to her, so I was wondering…"

Arietta reached for her hand and pulled her close. "Of course, you can." She gave her a big hug and a kiss.

"Okay, Caleigh, let's go," said Cheryl.

"Bye, Aunty Arietta and Uncle James," said Caleigh as she went to her mom.

"Bye," they said in unison.

Cheryl shook her head and glanced up to the sky at her daughter's antics. "See you tomorrow in the lobby," she said. Holding her daughter's hand, she led her inside the restaurant.

Moments later, Lawrence and Margaret stopped by.

"They just went inside," said James.

"Actually, we wanted to come over and talk to you privately and thank you personally for the Disney trip. And rest assured, we will pay you back," said Margaret to Arietta.

"No, don't be silly," said Arietta. "It's a gift."

"Are you sure?" asked Margaret.

"I'm positive," replied Arietta. "I know Cheryl loves Caleigh and would do anything for her, but I think you taking Caleigh away gives Cheryl some much-needed downtime. It's also giving her the opportunity to come with us to Manhattan and look around; I think it will do her the world of good."

"We also thought Cheryl could do with a well-deserved break," said Margaret. "We were glad to hear she is going back with you; she needs to let her hair down and have some fun with people her own age, and I think this move to Manhattan is just what she needs."

"So, it works out for everyone in the end," said Arietta. "What was Cheryl's face like when she saw you both at the door?"

"She lit up like Times Square," said Lawrence.

"Mom, Dad, there you are," said Cheryl from behind.

"We have to go," said Margaret. "Nice meeting you, and thanks again."

"See you next week," said Lawrence.

They watched them walk away and into the restaurant.

"Are you thinking what I'm thinking?" asked James.

"Let's get out of here before someone else drops by," replied Arietta.

"Grab my hand, and let's make a run for it."

She did, and they quickly left the bar. They decided to get changed and go for a swim in the sea.

"What should we do tonight?" she asked as she swam up to him.

"How about you join me on my patio for cocktails at six, then dinner," he suggested.

"Cocktails," she repeated. "I guess I should dress up."

"Think that would be a very good idea," he said as he pulled her close to him.

She wrapped her legs around his waist, and he put his arms around her. "You going to tell me what we are going to do?" she asked.

"No, you will have to wait and see."

Chapter 30

At six, Arietta walked over to James's patio, wearing a tight, black, knee-length dress, a little makeup, red lipstick, and her hair curled down around her shoulders.

"You look stunning," said James as he admired her. "Absolutely stunning."

She smiled at him. "You look extremely handsome," she complimented as she took the glass of wine from him. "What a beautiful evening."

"To our last evening here," said James as he touched her glass and drank. They talked about the day, the last two weeks, and going back to Manhattan.

A waiter appeared from around the corner. "Sir, when you are ready."

James looked at Arietta. "Shall we?" he said.

She put her arm through his, and they followed the waiter off to a secluded part of the resort. On the lawn was a round table with white linen and two place settings. In the middle of the table was a vase containing a bouquet of red ginger flowers. Next to the table was a covered dinner cart and next to that, a bottle of champagne chilling in an ice bucket.

"Wait, wait," said Arietta in a panic. "Don't move, stand right there! You too…Simon!" she said, reading his nametag, and ran off.

James looked over at Simon, shrugged his shoulders, and gave him a look as if to say, "Not sure what's going on."

She quickly returned with something in her hand. "Okay, Simon."

"Please follow me," said Simon, and he sat them at the table.

"Simon, can you take these glasses away?" she asked as she pointed to them. Arietta watched him remove them, then placed a champagne glass in front of James and one in front of herself.

James looked at her in wonderment. "You took the glasses."

"I did," she replied shyly.

"I went looking for them and thought you had put them in the hallway," admitted James.

"I thought you might," she said. "You have got to be quicker than that," she advised and looked at Simon. "Fill them up, please."

Simon opened the champagne, filled up their glasses, then proceeded to the dinner cart and removed the first course: garden greens with raspberry vinaigrette dressing. He placed one in front of Arietta, the other in front of James. "Will you need my help any further?" he asked.

"No, thank you, Simon," replied James. "I'll take it from here."

"Enjoy your meal," he said and left them alone.

Arietta lifted her glass. "To James."

"To Arietta…"

Arietta sipped her champagne and looked out at the sea. "This is a beautiful spot, and we will see the sunset perfectly from here, and it's so quiet; it's like there is no one else on the resort…It's very romantic."

James smiled at her. "I'm glad you like it."

"I love it," she replied and began to eat.

James took the empty plates and replaced them with the main course: lobster tail, filet mignon, and asparagus, followed by a chocolate truffle mousse dessert. He poured the last glass of champagne, and they drank and admired the setting sun.

"Looks like we're going to have to hunt down Simon for another bottle," said Arietta, emptying her glass.

No sooner had she said that; Simon turned up with another bottle of champagne in a new ice bucket, uncorked the bottle, and took the old bucket and bottle away.

She looked over at James. "Wow, either he's a really good waiter or maybe he's psychic?" said Arietta and took a sip of her drink.

James made a weird sci-fi sound to emphasize Simon's psychic ability, then stopped suddenly and said, "Or maybe I just told him to bring us another bottle in thirty minutes," he said, chuckling.

Arietta laughed out loud, and as she did, champagne sprayed from her mouth. James grabbed a napkin and gave it to her. "You did that on purpose. You waited for me to have a drink," she said, as she playfully hit him with the napkin.

James made the weird sound again.

"Oh, you think you're funny, do you?" she stated and laughed with him. She loved the way he made her laugh and feel just right.

The sun had set and the distant lights from the harbor and the resort created a soft, romantic ambiance. They watched the stars appear one by one.

"Would you like to dance?" asked James.

"There is no music."

"It's okay," he replied. He grabbed her hand, and they moved around the table and closer to the beach. The tender glow of the moon shone upon them as they started to slow dance. James quietly sang Van Morrison's 'Moondance' in her ear, and she melted in his arms. He finished the song, and they stopped dancing. She held him close for a while; she had never been so content in all her life.

"You want to go for a walk along the beach?" she whispered.

"That would be nice."

They kicked off their shoes, leaving them by the table. He filled up Arietta's glass and handed it to her, then filled up his and picked it up, along with the bottle of champagne.

"Let's go," she said and put her arm through his. They went to the water's edge and very slowly walked along the beach, away from the resort toward a very secluded area.

She looked over at him. "There was something I wanted to ask you."

"Yes," he said, turning to face her.

"'The Virgin Heart' how did you come up with that?"

He looked at her a little puzzled and then understood; she had forgotten she had said it to him before she fell asleep last night. "Just something that came to me last night before I went to sleep," he replied teasingly. He noticed she looked perplexed. "Why? Does that mean something to you?"

"Well," she said, thinking of how to word her answer. "It does, it's just so odd that you came right out and said it today."

"I know, I saw your reaction, it looked like you had seen a ghost."

"It definitely caught me off guard," she confessed. "You could have pushed me over with a feather." She looked at him curiously.

"Before you fell asleep last night, you whispered it to me," he revealed.

"Hmm, I thought I may have said something to you in my tired, drunken state," she said and laughed a little. She was glad she had because now it gave her the opportunity to talk about it. "Why did you decide that for your title?"

"I thought those few words stirred up so many feelings, emotions and thoughts, and it was a powerful image, and being in the Virgin Islands, I thought it was perfect." He looked at her. "Why? What does it mean to you?"

"I will tell you, but first let me say something." She smiled to herself as she looked ahead and said, "I envy you." She looked at him. "I envy you…Don't get me wrong, not in a jealous or resentful way, quite the opposite."

"Why would you envy me?" he asked, puzzled.

"Because you have experienced real love, true love with Clair, someone who you loved and loved you," she revealed. "I never have." She stopped and sadly looked at him. "That is why I believe I have a virgin heart; because it has never loved or felt true love."

"Never?" he asked.

She shook her head and looked down at the sand.

James looked at her for a moment. "What about Vincent?" he asked.

"I think we cared about one another, but we were never in love. I believe we were in love with our work, our socializing and compatibility. We fell in love with an idea, but not with each other."

James looked at the moon and thought for a moment. "The divorce was a while back. Was there no one else?" he asked, looking at her again.

"Not really, after the marriage failed, I felt like I was to blame, and I didn't want to make that mistake again, so I was very careful. I dated people on and off but nothing serious…I let work occupy a lot of my time, and what free time I had I kept to myself, mostly. I did date once in a while, just enough for people not to notice that I was really on my own, alone, and lonely." She paused for a moment. "After a few years went by, I started to look back and realized that people were moving on with their lives, and I wasn't. I looked at my job and where I was in my life and became very unhappy, so I hid where it was safe, in here," she said, pointing to herself, her heart.

James put the bottle in the sand, reached over and took the hand that was pointing and held it.

She didn't let go as she sat in the sand, and as he sat next to her, they put their glasses down, and she continued. "When I was younger, before work became my life, I was so happy. My dream was to have a career I really enjoyed, share my life with someone I loved, eventually get married and one day have children, but somewhere along the way, everything got distorted and complicated, and worst of all, I suddenly realized I had stopped being me." She thought for a moment. "After looking in my mirror at home and my reflection in my office window for the hundredth time and asking myself the same questions over and over again. Who am I? What am I doing? Is this the life I want? I realized I need to get away, to run away, to escape; so I did, and landed here." As she said this, she played with the sand and looked at the water behind James and the starry sky in the distance, then focused back on him. "These past two weeks, my mind has become so clear, and I have come to realize what I want to do in my life, with my life, and how to accomplish it…I feel extremely happy and excited…I feel alive…and I feel like the person I once was and wanted to be." She looked at the sand in her hands and let it slip between her fingers and looked at James. "And with all my heart I know that it was you that helped me get there." She looked deeply into his eyes. "That is why I know I had a virgin heart; because it had never loved, until now." She looked at James and gently caressed his face. "I'm in love with you."

James smiled at her. "When you are away from me and I am on my own, it feels like a piece of me is missing, and when I'm with you it's like I found it, and I'm complete." He reached over and gently caressed her auburn hair. "You are as beautiful as the red ginger flower," he said and gently kissed her on the lips, "and perfect in every way." He kissed her again. "I'm in love with you."

She responded by kissing him passionately and pulling him down on the sand next to her. He kissed her softly on her neck, her cheek, and then he stopped and looked into her eyes.

"What?" she asked.

He anxiously smiled at her. "It's been a very long time for me, and I'm a little nervous."

She put her hand through his hair and caressed his face. "That's okay, it's been a long time for me, and I'm very nervous."

He kissed her fingers as they touched his lips. "What would you like me to do?"

She looked at him for a moment and thought, then whispered, "We both said these last two weeks have been full of surprises, surprise me."

She moved her hand away from his face, and he kissed her gently on the lips, then her cheek, then her neck. She felt the soft touch of his lips and his breath on her skin, and her heart started to beat faster, her breath quickened, and she waited anxiously for his lips to touch her again and again. He lightly licked her ear, and her body trembled. Sensing her reaction, he did it again and again. She smiled at the sensation she was feeling. He gently sucked on her lobe, causing her to shiver, and she tried to regain her composure as he sucked and nibbled, but her senses owned her now, and all she could do was surrender to his touch.

He placed small, delicate kisses down her neck and along her shoulder, and when he reached the end, he gave it a gentle bite, which made her jump and catch her breath; she was helpless. He kissed her down her arm, past her elbow, to her fingers, and then put his hand under and moved her onto her side to face him, and as he kissed and nibbled on her shoulder, he slowly unzipped her dress and unhooked her bra. He moved his hand and laid her back down and continued kissing up her arm to her shoulder, and with his hand moved her dress and bra strap down her arm. He kissed her where they used to be, before moving to her neck, then her ear, her cheek; her body reacting to every kiss. He continued to explore the other side of her body and removed her dress and bra strap off of that shoulder and down her arm. At the same time, he reached over and pulled the other side of her dress and bra down as she moved her arms through. He kissed her neck, her chest, and pulled her dress to her waist, leaving her bra covering her breasts. He went to her unexposed nipple and with his tongue gently flicked it through the lace and playfully teased; he then placed his teeth on it and gently pulled, causing her to moan. He moved back and forth from one nipple to the other. Her breasts aching for his tongue on her skin, she gripped the sand with her hands to try and regain some control, but it was too late. She was already losing the battle; and he had only just started.

She helplessly looked down, as his seductive eyes looked up, and his mouth pulled on her nipple. "Please, please, take it off, please take my bra off," she begged. Or did she? She wasn't sure; did she say it or just think it? He saw the pleading look in her eyes and removed her bra. She gave him a smile as she put her head down and arched her back, waiting for his wanting mouth. At first, she felt nothing and was tempted to look down, but then she felt it, his breath on her nipple, then nothing, then his breath, then nothing; then suddenly his wet tongue darted across it. He blew lightly, and his warm breath dried up his wetness, making her nipple harden and tingle; he did this several times, and each time he did, her body arched higher and higher toward his mouth. He breathed once again, and she waited patiently for his lick. Instead, he took her whole areola in his mouth and sucked it; it surprised her, and she let out a moan and eased her back slowly to the ground. As he sucked, his tongue darted back and forth, and around and around. He moved his mouth to her other nipple, leaving his fingers to play and pull on the nipple he had just vacated. She looked at the stars and closed her eyes and succumbed to his touch.

James kissed his way down to her stomach and lifted her bum and moved her dress down to her thighs. He kissed her waist and then her thigh, and as he moved down her leg, he pulled down her dress, then went back and forth from one leg to the other, kissing the areas the dress once occupied, and did this all the way to her feet, and until her dress was removed. He grabbed each foot and started to move them apart, knowing what he wanted, she accommodated him by spreading her legs. He started at her ankle and slowly and purposefully kissed his way up her leg, past her knee, her inner thigh, and towards her mound. She was trying her best not to squirm and thought, one more kiss and he would be there. James deliberately skimmed over her mound and as he did, could smell the sweetness of her juices and feel her wetness as his nose and lips brushed over her lace, and as he did, he breathed on it; his breath penetrating through the lace and hitting her labia. She felt his breath on her and squirmed and tried her best not to lose control; she wanted his tongue on her, in her, now. He went to her other ankle and slowly kissed his way up her leg. This time he stopped over her mound, and she felt his breath again. All of a sudden, his tongue licked up and down her panties, up and down, up and down, right over her folds, and she felt the pressure against her labia and her juices flowed freely, drenching her panties. James moved away and kneeled, grabbing her legs, he rested them on his chest. She lifted her bum and little by little he pulled down her panties and flung them aside. This time she didn't wait for him, and moved her legs back to the position they were in. No more teasing, she thought. I can't take it. He moved his face between her thighs and licked around her shaven vulva. She felt his tongue dance around her and spread her legs as far as she could, then nothing. She looked down to see why he had stopped; he was looking up at her and gave her a smile, then stuck out his tongue and looked into her eyes as he placed his tongue deep inside her, licking from bottom to top. She wrapped her legs around his shoulders, not only to give him easier access, but to give her the benefit of watching him. James applied a little more pressure with his tongue, and she started to moan steadily. She moved her hips rhythmically with his tongue; she was close. James moved to her clit and rolled his tongue around and over it, keeping the same steady pressure; her moans started to get louder. Then she felt his fingers rubbing the folds of her labia. He slowly placed a finger deep inside her; she let out a long moan. His tongue darted over her clit and his finger went deep, in and out, in and out, and she moved her hips faster and moaned louder. James felt her juices on his hand and her vagina quiver. "James! James! James! James!" she said and let out a large moan. He continued with the same motion as she slowly stopped and looked down at him; she had this look of passion and despair as she pulled him up to her.

"I want you to make love to me. I want you inside me," she begged and kissed him passionately on the lips.

She helped him remove his top, and he lay next to her as he took off his pants and boxers. Her labium was swollen and aching, and he was so hard in her hand; she wanted him inside her. James lay on top of her. She could feel his shaft up against her folds and the tip of his penis rub against her clitoris; she moaned. He moved it in between her labia and slowly slid it deep inside her. Arietta loved the way he felt and let out a loud moan.

As James moved in and out, she responded by moving her hips in unison with his, and the quicker they moved, the louder she moaned. James adjusted his position slightly higher so that the top of his shaft was rubbing against her clit. She was breathing heavily as she kissed his neck, ears and full on the mouth. Over several minutes, their pace quickened, and they went faster, faster, faster. Her juices flowed, and James's penis and testicles were soaking from her waves.

"Oh! Oh…I'm cumming! I'm cumming!" she moaned, looking into his eyes. "Cum with me! Cum with me!" She let out a loud orgasmic scream as she came, and James let out a moan as he came deep inside her.

She held him tightly and after catching her breath whispered slowly, "I love you so much."

"I love you," he said, out of breath and kissed her.

He continued to slowly slide his manhood inside her as they held each other, and after a while, he rolled on his back, and she put her head on his chest, holding him tightly.

"That was amazing," she whispered. "You are incredible."

"You are," he replied.

She smiled as her hand wandered over his chest; she never imagined it could be like this.

They stood up, held hands, and walked over to the sea. The moon glistened off the water as they waded in, and the gentle waves caressed their calves, their thighs, and their stomachs, before they dove in. James stood up, and Arietta swam to him and put her arms around his shoulders and her legs around his waist, and they kissed for an exceptionally long time. She let go of him and laid back and let the warm water soak her hair. He held her waist until she motioned with her arms for him to pull her up, and she held him again.

Arietta kissed him and whispered, "When did you first notice me?"

"The day you arrived; I saw you walking from the minibus towards the ferry."

"You did?"

"You were wearing a mint-green dress, and your hair was blowing in the breeze. You were a striking scene; you looked like a movie star."

She smiled at his compliment. "I didn't see you. Where were you?"

"I was on the balcony at the Haven Bar, having a drink. The second time was when I got on the ferry, and I was searching for a seat, and you had your eyes closed and your face up towards the sky. I thought you were meditating or something, I wasn't quite sure."

"Oh, how embarrassing!" she said as she put her head on his shoulder. "I was enjoying the sun and the wind on my face."

"Sure," replied James and made the Om sound that people sometimes make when they meditate.

"You think you are so funny," she said, trying to hold back her laughter, but unsuccessfully.

"When did you first notice me?" he asked.

"I actually heard your voice first. You were talking to Caleigh and Cheryl. I could overhear you guys talking, and your voice, it just sounded so calming and so…"

"So…?"

"Sexy," she answered. "Very sexy." She moved in front of him. "So I wanted to see whose face that voice belonged to and was going to get up and go to the bar, until Caleigh sat next to me and foiled my plan. But luckily Cheryl came over, and when she walked away, I watched her leave, and I saw you for the first time. I thought you were extremely handsome." She moved closer to him and kissed him on the lips.

"Then I caught you looking at me," said James.

"What? When?" she said and pulled away, so she could look at him.

"Just before the ferry landed. You smiled at Cheryl and Caleigh, then looked at me, busted."

"You are something else, mister. I was smiling at them, and I caught you looking at me and quickly looked away to save you any further shame and embarrassment."

"That's your story?" he asked. "And you're sticking with that?"

"No, that's not my story, that's the truth."

She pretended to pout, and he tickled her stomach which made her jump and laugh. He kissed her and whispered, "You are so beautiful, that everything else in this world pales in comparison."

She loved the way he made her feel. She kissed him and held him for a long time.

They left the water, and she put on his shirt, and he put on his boxers. They carried the rest of the clothes, the glasses, and the bottle of champagne back to her patio. They removed their damp clothes and went inside and got a shower. They washed each other's hair and bodies and talked, laughed, and kissed. They put on bathrobes, and he sat on the bathroom counter and talked as he watched her dry her hair. They went outside and filled up their glasses and lay together on the chaise and held one another and stared at the stars.

"Out of all the nights I have looked at the stars this will always be my favorite," said James.

She snuggled on his chest. "Mine too," she replied and thought for a while. "What has been your favorite moment?"

"I have so many with you, but I would have to say tonight."

"Definitely tonight, it has been so special." She looked up at him, "thank you," and kissed him on the lips. "And I loved dancing with you as you sang to me." She kissed him again. "You know 'Moondance' is always going to be our song."

"Without a doubt," he replied.

"If I hear it and I'm on my own, I'm going to text you and let you know it's playing, no matter where I am or what I am doing."

"Same here," he said and gently squeezed her close to him. "That song will always remind me of you."

"'Together Forever' that's definitely our karaoke and dance song, especially after a couple of wines at home." She smiled at the thought of her home and him being there and them dancing around her living room.

They drank their champagne, and far out on the horizon they could see an electrical storm and watched it for a while until it disappeared. She stood up and offered him her hand, and he took it, and they went inside. She kissed him and removed his robe, and then he removed hers.

"Lie in the middle of the bed," she said softly, which he did. "Now, it's time for me to surprise you." She went to the end of the bed and with each hand grabbed his feet and slowly began to rub them, then moved to his calves and his thighs, and as she reached over, he could feel her breasts and nipples brush against his legs. She opened up his legs, moved onto the bed, and kneeled in between them and leaned down and slowly began to lick his inner thigh, stopping just before his scrotum; she then went to the other thigh and did the same. She did this several times, and James's body tingled with excitement. Arietta noticed he had become extremely hard and blew her warm breath down the length of his shaft, and then leaned over and slowly let her hair sway back and forth over it. He looked down at her auburn hair swaying back and lifted up his hips and moved himself closer to her mouth. She glanced up and gave him a naughty smile and kept her eyes fixed on him. She could see the torment on his face and licked her lips, and then moved her tongue to his stomach and licked it, allowing her breasts and nipples to swing and play over his hardness. Arietta licked and flicked his nipples with her tongue, then lightly sucked and pulled on them, making him shudder with excitement. She kissed his chest, his neck, and playfully licked his earlobe, before sucking and nibbling it. The sensation of her breath in his ear and her tongue was too much for James, and he felt like he was going to explode. She looked at James, kissed him on the lips, and told him she loved him. She licked her way down his chest, past his stomach to his erection, and gently licked the shaft and around the head, but she was in no rush and made him wait. She slid her tongue along his shaft and teasingly licked around and underneath his mushroom head as he moaned. Arietta suddenly stopped and pulled away; he looked down at her and she looked up at him, smiling, then opened her mouth wide and motioned towards him and pulled away at the last second, then ever so slowly licked his head; she was teasing, taunting him, and he was at her mercy. She moved away and licked her lips sensually and opened her mouth. She went toward him, and this time took it as deep as she could. She sucked it in and then let it out, in and out, and in and out. He ran his fingers through her hair and moved his hips to her rhythm. Her mouth released him, and she eagerly licked and rubbed him, then continued to suck and lick his shaft, his head, and his balls, making him extremely hard.

She could feel the wetness between her thighs and stopped. She rubbed him as she kneeled over his waist and placed it deep inside her folds. James squeezed her breasts and pulled on her nipples as she moaned, then moved his lips to them and gently sucked and pulled on them. She moaned louder and started to move quicker. His hands moved hungrily over her body as her hands wandered over his chest and through his hair. He smiled at her, and she smiled back, and she leaned over and kissed him full on the mouth, and as she did, James gently squeezed her firm bum and moved his hips up and down off the bed, sliding his penis deep inside her. He felt so good inside her, and she uncontrollably moaned. She moved away from James's mouth and sat back on him and excitedly moved her hips back and forth as James's hands caressed her breasts. Sensing she was close, he grabbed her hips and helped her move over him, quicker, quicker, quicker. She looked down at him. "James! James! Oohh, Jaaammess," she screamed and came. James continued to move her hips back and forth, and let out a load moan and called out, "Arietta," and came.

Exhausted, she collapsed on him and put her face in the curve of his neck. He kissed the top of her head and held her; she loved being in his arms. She lay there for an exceedingly long time before kissing him and rolling on her side. She lay with her back into him, and James put his arm around her, and she took hold of his hand and held it tightly against her heart. He whispered he loved her. She kissed his hand, said she loved him, smiled, and drifted off to sleep.

Arietta woke up on her side, facing the open patio door. The drapes were open, and the sheer white curtains were gently swaying with the wind. She could feel the warm sun shining on her face, and in the distance, she could hear the waves softly kissing the beach. She panicked for a moment, wondering if it was all a dream; then she realized she was still holding his hand tightly against her heart and smiled.

"Good morning, beautiful," he whispered.

She turned around, kissed him on the lips, and made love to him. She then got out of bed and walked over to the window and looked out at the beach at the sea and felt the warmth of the radiant sunshine through the window. "What a gorgeous day," she said.

James lay in bed and admired her lovely legs, her shapely bum, and her lovely auburn hair. "Arietta," he said, and she turned around. He looked at her gorgeous face, her firm breasts, and her sexy body. He stood up and walked over to her and kissed her on the lips and put his hand through her hair.

She put her arms around him and held him for what seemed like an eternity. She took his hand and walked him into the shower. They held each other closely and kissed as the warm water fell on their bodies. They washed each other as they talked and laughed. They dried off and put on robes, ordered room service, and ate it on the bed, then held each other for a while.

"I need to go and pack," he said. "I will be back soon." He kissed her on the lips and headed for the patio door.

"James," said Arietta as she ran into his arm. "I love you so much." She put her head on his chest.

He held her tightly and kissed the top of her head. "I love you," he whispered.

She let go. "Be quick," she said and watched him leave. She went into the bathroom and looked at her reflection in the mirror, and for the first time in a very long time, she smiled at herself and said, "I love you." She washed her face and looked up at her reflection again and said, "and James loves you." She got ready and was packing when James returned.

He placed the empty champagne bottle and the two champagne glasses on the desk, handed Arietta her dress and her panties and held up her shoes. "I guess Simon dropped these off, mine too," said James. "Both pairs were on the patio next to our clothes." They looked at each other and both laughed.

She smiled as she packed her shoes and thought about them making love on the beach. She rinsed the glasses, dried them, and wrapped them in her clothes. "I don't want these to break," she said.

"Looks like we will be carrying on a family tradition," he said as he watched her wrap them up.

She liked the sound of that. "I believe we will," she replied. She zipped up her suitcase, and James picked it up off the bed and placed it on the floor. She held his hand. "One last time," she said and led him to the patio. As they looked out at the beach, the sea, and boats in the harbor, he put his arm around her, and she rested her head on his shoulder. She turned toward him, and they held each other. She looked at him and kissed him on the lips. "Let's go home," she whispered.

They grabbed their luggage, went to the front desk, and met Cheryl. The three of them walked to the dock and boarded the ferry. Cheryl talked about her dinner last night and about Caleigh and her parents leaving this morning and how excited and eager Caleigh was to get there, and then they talked about Manhattan.

The ferry docked, and they disembarked, and something caught James's eye, and he excused himself and crossed the road. He went up the stairs and onto the balcony. "I thought it was you," he said and walked over and gave her a hug. "I was hoping I would see you before I left." He pulled out a picture and gave it to her. "This is Clair. It was taken on our first date. I just wanted you to know her name and what she looked like."

"She is just how I imagined her to be," said Lily, looking at the photograph.

"We went to Medieval Times, and they had this knight's armor set up, and you could stand behind it and put your arms through and your face in the helmet. She took a picture of me and called me her knight in shining armor; then she changed it and said my James in shining armor, and it stuck." He smiled at Lily. "I just wanted to let you know that."

"It's closure for us all," she said. "Clair is at peace now, and so are you, James." She handed him back the photograph.

"I know," he said and kissed her on the cheek. "Thank you."

She blushed. "You take care of yourself and Arietta," said Lily. "I see good things for you two."

"I will," he promised. He looked around. "Where is D-Mon?"

"He's in the back," she said and shouted out his name.

He came out. "James," he said. "You're leaving today."

"Yeah, I wanted to say goodbye. Arietta and Cheryl are outside. Come out and say bye."

They followed him out, and they said their goodbyes. James told them anytime they were in Manhattan to drop in, and then they jumped into a taxi and left for the airport.

They walked outside and onto the tarmac. Cheryl climbed the stairs and boarded the airplane. James and Arietta stopped at the bottom.

James looked at Arietta. "There is something I need to tell you," he said.

"Okay," she replied.

"I want you to know that my heart will always belong to you, forever."

"I know," she said, caressing his face. "And in the Virgin Islands I fell in love with you and lost my virgin heart."

"I love you, Arietta."

"I love you, James."

They kissed passionately for a while, and then walked off the tarmac, onto the stairs, and onto the airplane, and as they did, everyone applauded. They smiled and politely nodded their heads. James took the window seat, and Arietta sat in the middle.

"I would like to thank our final two passengers for boarding the airplane and showing the crew and passengers what it is like to be in love," said the captain. "Please fasten your seat belts, crew prepare for takeoff."

As the airplane taxied, Cheryl explained to them. "They were waiting for you two to board, and the captain saw you at the bottom of the stairs and came over the speakers and told everyone on the left side of the airplane to look outside their windows at the couple who was holding us up and to give you a clap when you came on. The people on the left side told the people on the right that you were making out."

"Oh no," said Arietta as she sunk down into her chair.

James just grinned and took hold of her hand.

"I'm so happy for you two," said Cheryl. "Tell me, what happened last night?"

Arietta quickly sat up and turned to her. "It was so romantic," she said ecstatically and proceeded to tell Cheryl the story from start to finish, leaving out the explicit details.

"That is so romantic," said Cheryl.

During the flight, they talked about all the things that were happening this week. From the office makeover to the event meeting with Violet, going through the Gmails, meeting with the lawyer, the merger meeting, and setting up their new business. And about James's latest book hitting the shelves and speculating what was going to happen with his print and video interviews, and about Sara being his publicist. They discussed Violet's suit design for James, Graham's plan, the condo, the school for Caleigh, and her charity fund.

"There is so much going on," said Arietta. "I can't wait to see how it all turns out."

"Me too," said Cheryl and James at the same time, and they all laughed.

The airplane started to make its descent into New York City, and Arietta looked out the window and caught her reflection. She was an attractive forty-year-old woman with long auburn hair, stunning emerald-green eyes, a beautiful smile, and a flawless, creamy complexion. She thought back about how many times she had looked in a mirror and asked herself, "Is this my destiny? Is this me? Is this all there is?" She looked over at James and smiled and then back at her reflection and said to herself, "Yes, this is my destiny! This is who I am! And there is a whole lot more of me to come!"

Chapter 31

When do you say enough is enough? Leave everything you own, think, and know behind? When do you sacrifice it all, take that chance, and find the strength and courage to find you? Arietta had struggled with these questions far too long. She knew what she had to do, but deep down she knew the truth; she was scared, scared of taking that step into the unknown…But not anymore.

About the Author

Kevin McGann lives in
the small, beautiful town of Aurora,
Ontario, Canada.

You can contact him on his website:
www.kevinmcgannauthor.com
Or on Facebook:
Kevin McGann – Author